A

RAZOR'S EDGE OF

REVENGE

Taboo

Also by the Author;

A Victims of Justice

A Razor's Edge of Revenge

A Struggling Soul

"A Razor's Edge of Revenge"
- Taboo
"Free Taboo Publishing LLC."
Copyright © 2023

ISBN: 979-8-9865779-2-0

Preface

In no way does this author or Free Taboo Publishing, LLC. wish to glorify or promote gangs, drugs, or violence. Kids should take it as a warning, of what could happen, as well as what those consequences can be, and adults should teach the kids to avoid drugs, and gang activity, and to know the value of life. Do not throw your life away. All life is precious.

That being said, this book is a work of art, fiction, and meant to be entertainment. None of the people or names are real, nor are they intended to resemble anyone in real life. It does include real places to make it more real, as well as some real situations. It is FACTS that Congress has passed the First Step Act bill that takes the stacking out of the 924(c) stacking law, yet they consciously made the decision to allow all of those sentenced under this draconian law to stay imprisoned under this outdated and unfair sentencing enhancement. There are tens of thousands of people sentenced to hundreds of years, just like this author is currently sentenced to 91 years for non-violent, victimless drug and gun possession charges.

The current average federal sentence for murder is 22 years. This author was sentenced to over four times the national average federal murder sentence. Just for possession of things. Not for anything violent. Not for any victims. Not for using the guns. He could have committed four murders and gotten less time.

Our sitting congress this year, 2022, has the SAFE Justice Act, the First Step Implementation Act, and many more bills for criminal justice reform just on hold in front of them. We need Congress to act NOW! Stop these unfair and ridiculous sentences! I encourage all of you who believe that the 851 and 924(c) laws are unfair to call or write to your Congressman and ask them to pass these bills! Ask for a change in this Criminal INjustice System!

TABOO

Dedicated to...

To my son Anselmo, "Sammy".

Only 16, but already a better man than I could ever be.

I love you.

Acknowledgement

All thanks to my Lord Jesus Christ above all else. Also, to my readers and fans who are in love with my work and support my dreams. To MoneyRed for all the help with this book. A special thanks to Ruth Okocha for all her efforts towards editing this and 'A Victim of Justice' and putting them together gracefully. Also to the graphic designer who does an amazing job! My mom Kathy and stepdad Dave Evans, for raising my son to be a good person. To Lindsey for raising my daughter, you've always had my heart, and always will. My sister Laurie, for always being there for me. Mike Lee for ridin' this bid with me. Shane and Travis Stubblefield, my brothers from another mother.

Thanks to Vini for pushing me to achieve my goals and her artistic influences on me, and for being a great friend. My family Big Eric, Lil' Eric, and Mikey. Kira and Bella, Nichole Criss, Desiree Locke, and Chad Lobsinger. Dina for always making me smile.

To Carmen and Melissa Bezares, Bladimir, and Roger. Alyssa McCown for all your support on this bid! Fransisco and Jessica Alejandro, Kristi and Michelle "Momsdukes" Warner, Breanna Klein, Momo, Niki Hill, Craig Williams, Janel, Heather Campbell, Tiffany, Tammy, Cassie Cabrera, Tasha Diaz, Zack, Fallon, Laura

Mathis, Ivy, Rico, Lori & Athena Bailey, Ena Weeks, Brandi Carter, Randy Abott, Budda, Miss Cheryl Yeary-Eisen, Jamie & Debbie Barrow, Natalie, Brat, Stephanie & Nicole Lewis, Stephan & Livi Smith, Paulie, Samantha, and all of the homies in the Penitentiary: To my friend and colleague D.C. Redz, and MoneyRed. To Kic-Doe, Kojac, Dizzy, Chance, Bankroll, Money Mark, Gutta, Al, Revenue, Fat, Tay, Fruit, Checkmate, AP, Bogie, Zoe, Tank, Iceman, Run-Run, D, Truly, O, Herb, Nard, Cheeks.

To all the dead homies, gone but not forgotten: Savannah Balcom, (who saved my life when I got shot 3 times), My father Mike Yeary, Jovan 'Wolf' Gomez, Chris 'Chuck' Waters, Leighton Peale, Todd Reynalds, Christian '561' Scott, Eugene 'Chico' Simon, Manuel 'Slim' Valbueno, Jaime Medina, Paul 'Big Daddy' Martinez, Charlie Kline, Dave Barrow, Charlie Shultz, Miss Debbie Yeary, Brandon Gilcher, Tenesha Faria, Rick Marsh, and Maria Castro.

To Congress: Thank you for passing the First Step Act, so my 91-year sentence for non-violent, victimless crimes has now been illegal for 4 years, we need for you to make it retroactive! Pass the SAFE Justice Act immediately!

To the best lawyer besides Mike Salnick, my guy Mike Smith who fought like hell to give back these 91 years, even though we lost I loved his fight! Good guy!

Prologue

Maniac

- Two Years Ago -

Maniac sits at the kitchen table bagging up weed in 8ths and coke in 8-Balls before setting them aside in their separate piles on the table. He checks his Trac-Phone briefly, seeing a text from Sin saying he's 20 minutes away. Sin and Maniac have been doing business for a couple of months and so far, things have gone smooth. Maniac is waiting for him to come buy 5 pounds of Lemon Kush and a quarter brick of cocaine.

He looks over and watches his son, Kian, who he has nicknamed "Kilo"- and his friend Quan, as they play Call of Duty on the X-Box 360 in the living room. He goes back to his task but after a couple of minutes, he realizes that he's out of baggies and calls Kian over.

"Key! Come over here real quick!" Maniac hollers through the opening from the dining room to the living room where the boys are chilling.

"I got you, Pops," replies Kian, as he and Quan pause the game and walk over. Both boys are staring at the table in front of them covered with drugs that Maniac is working at, 'getting to the bag', as the saying goes.

"I got some business coming over here and I need you to go and get the sandwich bags out of my room for me real quick," Maniac instructs, sending the boys to the back of the house to look for the requested items.

Maniac's phone chimes with a text from Sin, "I'm outside." He gets up from the chair and places a backpack on the table containing the merchandise that Sin is going to purchase before putting the bagged up coke and weed in a Folgers coffee can on the counter.

Maniac hears a knock at the front door and walks over to answer it, already knowing it's Sin out front. He opens the door and sees Sin texting on his phone, standing on the front porch. He looks up momentarily.

"Was' good, bruh?" greets Sin as he puts his phone away and gives Maniac a hand shake.

"I'm good, bruh," replies Maniac, leading Sin inside the house and over to the table to conduct their business.

Maniac opens the backpack and pulls out one of the pounds of Lemon Kush so Sin can check out the Smell and potency of it, as usual.

"Like always, I'ma do you a sweet deal on the P's, bruh, just give me twelve hunnid a piece and eight bands for the QB, ya feel me?" says Maniac, noticing that Sin is texting on his phone more than usual while they're conducting their business transaction.

"Yea, that's cool," says Sin distractedly, as he continues to type on his phone keyboard.

"Ok, cool," says Maniac cautiously, starting to feel the awkwardness settling over him and thinking to himself that this will be the last time he deals with Sin. Sin looks up and smiles, before placing his phone in his pocket and walking over to put his hand on Maniac's shoulder. "Sorry about that bruh, I was just making sure I had these loose ends tied up real quick, while the opportunity was still available," Sin says, smirking again, causing Maniac to feel uncomfortable, but he brushes his suspicions away once again.

"You good, homie, I understand," Maniac agrees, as he puts the pound of weed back in the backpack and zips it up, looking at Sin and noticing that his eyes are roaming around the house like he is checking his surroundings suspiciously.

"So, whas'sup? You got the bread?" asks Maniac, trying to hurry up and finish this deal so he can take Kian and Quan to football practice across town at Lake Worth Middle School.

"Yeah, about those 14 bands, bruh, I'on got it," says Sin, with a wicked smile spreading across his face. "But I do got this," he says, pulling out a .44 Bulldog revolver from the small of his back and pointing it at Maniac menacingly.

All Maniac could think of are his kids, Jermaine, Kian, and Imani. Sweat breaks out on his forehead and he tries to think of how he can get out of this situation with his life. He realizes Kian and Quan are still in the back room, and prays to God for the protection of the two young boys, hoping they'll remain back there a little while longer.

While Sin pointed the revolver at Maniac, he takes the back pack off of the table and puts one of his arms through its straps as he backs up towards the front door, the gun still pointed at Maniac.

"You know this shit ain't gonna be sweet once you walk out of here, right?" asks Maniac, as he watches his rent money and re-up money being carried away by Sin on his back.

"Shit, why not, bruh? I ain't got shit to stress about," Sin replies, as he places his hand on the handle of the door, preparing to leave with the drugs in the backpack.

"You taking food out my mouth like I'm pussy or some shit," growls Maniac angrily, as he unconsciously takes a step towards Sin, his pride swelling in his chest.

"Yeah, I sure the fuck am," mocks Sin, "but you don't need this shit where you're goin', homie."

He says this knowing Maniac has a reputation in the streets for violence, which means that if he leaves him alive, Maniac will definitely cut him down for his revenge. Maniac sees the cold creep into Sin's eyes and it's like time slows down, as he watches Sin's finger start to tighten on the trigger. His family's faces flash through his mind, as the gun jumps in Sin's hand, the bullet flying through the air faster than the speed of sound, welcoming Maniac into the darkness. His body slumps over and falls to the ground. Blood starts pooling around his head on the wood floor next to the kitchen table.

Sin spins quickly and races out of the front door of the house, not even bothering to close the front door behind himself before jumping into his Impala and speeding off down the street. Excitement and adrenaline went coursing through his veins at the ease of the robbery he just pulled off, not realizing that he had made a fatal mistake; not checking the house for any witnesses that could identify him.

Chapter One

Kian

Kian and Quan hear the men arguing in the kitchen part of the house while they search for the baggies Maniac had asked for.

A gunshot could be heard, loud and misplaced in the silence of the rest of the house. But the sound of the gunshot makes the boys jump in surprise and look around the room for a place to hide.

"Get under the bed, Quan!" whispers Kian, as he rushes over to the dresser and rips out the drawers looking for the black gun he had seen his dad stash there before. His hand lands on the handle of it and he races out of the bedroom door and stealthily creeps down the hallway towards the kitchen. He rounds the corner of the living room and sees Maniac lying on the floor with blood pooling around his head through the entryway from the dining room to the living room. He immediately runs over to kneel at his father's side, tears streaming down his face.

"Pops? Pops! Wake up! Please get up!" sobs Kian, as he shakes Maniac's lifeless body while he cries. He hears an engine revving up and burning rubber, which draws his attention towards the front where he watches through the still opened front doors as a purple bowling ball painted 1996 SS Impala on '28s speeds off.

"That's Sin's whip..." Kian thinks to himself in surprise as he places the gun on the floor beside Maniac's body and runs over to the house phone on the wall, dialing 911 desperately and screaming for an ambulance when the operator asks what his emergency is.

"My dad is not breathing! He been shot! Please help me!" Kian cries into the phone, his body shaking uncontrollably as he looks around the house in despair, trying to figure out what else he could do to help. "What's your location?" asks the operator before Kian tells them his address and hears the operator tell him that emergency vehicles are on the way. He puts the phone on the ground by Maniac's head without hanging up.

"I'm so sorry, Pops," cries Kian, putting his head on his father's cold chest, as tears fall from his eyes. "I swear on my life that someday I'll catch Sin," Kian promises, as he hears sirens approaching in the distance and he lays down next to his father's lifeless body and cries his young broken heart out for the murder of his father, his hero, his bestfriend. He hears boots thumping around him inside of the house and looks around in shock and confusion at the EMS personnel and the police that swarm into the house to secure the scene and try to pull him away from Maniac, which causes Kian to fight and scream trying to return to his dad's side in desperation.

Kian's mind is in a fog, as he is led away from Maniac's body and placed in the back of a squad car once the police secure the house and found the gun lying next to Maniac with Kian's fingerprints all over it. At first they think that he is the suspect that shot and killed Maniac, but once Quan is discovered and the boys were taken down to the Sheriff's office at Gun Club County Jail for questioning, the detectives confirmed that they were telling the truth; their stories matched.

After about 5 hours at Gun Club Road Sheriff's Office, Kian's mother, Skyla, comes to pick them up with Kian's brother and sister, Jermaine and Imani in the car with her.

"Baby!" cries Skyla, as she runs over to where Kian is sitting at the table with Quan silently, still in shock over his father getting killed. Skyla places her hands on both sides of his face and presses on the top of his head, making him squirm beneath her.

"Thank you God for my baby's safety," she sobs, looking up towards the ceiling as if she can see through it all the way into heaven. "Are you ok?" she asks, as she begins to run her hands all over Kian's body, checking for marks or bruises.

"Yeah, I'm straight," says Kian coldly, brushing her hands off of him, as he rises out of his chair and heads towards the door of the Sheriff's Office lobby to go outside to the car with Quan trailing behind him sullenly.

"Just a minute please, Mrs. Hayworth," calls one of the two detectives, walking up to her before she could follow after the boys.

"Do you know if your husband had any enemies or people that would want to hurt or harm him?" asks the black detective, whose name tag says 'Jones'. As they stand in front of Skyla, their eyes roaming all over her face, searching for a hint of knowledge or guilt.

"None that I know of officer, he was a hardworking husband and a good father," Skyla says emotionally, her eyes tearing up.

"Well, if there's anything that you can remember, will you please not hesitate to give us a call," says Detective Jones, handing her a card. "This situation could have been worse Mrs. Hayworth since there were kids in the house," Detective Jones adds, once again running his eyes over Skyla's distraught face, her emotions breaking over her like a storm.

"I will definitely give you a call sir," Skyla says, taking the card from Detective Jones and walking towards the door to head outside before getting into the silent, emotionally stuffy atmosphere inside the Honda Civic with the kids and pulling off, heading home. The loss of a beloved father weighing heavily in each of their hearts.

Chapter Two

Kian

- Two Weeks Later -

Kian stands beside his wailing mother in front of the coffin containing his father's body. Maniac is dressed in a suit he had picked out from Burlington Coat Factory a few years before for a daddy/daughter dance he had taken Kian's little sister, Imani to. Jermaine stands on Kian's left side with Imani leaning against him sniffling softly inside of the church, where a small gathering of family and friends are gathered to pay their last respect to the deceased and his widow and kids, left without a father.

A short balding black man, Kian recognizes vaguely as Pastor Collins, climbs the steps to the pulpit and clears his throat before beginning to speak.

"Family and friends, we gather here today to not only mourn the passing of a humble man, but to celebrate the life of Marcus Hayworth, who was tragically gunned down in his own house in another act of black on black violence," Pastor Collins says before pausing, letting his eyes scan the scarcely populated room of the church.

"He was loved by many and hated by few, which makes his death extremely sad, as he leaves his beautiful wife and their three children without a husband and father, a mentor, and a comforter," continues Pastor Collins, as he gives the eulogy.

Hearing it started causing Kian to scowl, as his face darkened in anger of the memory. "He obviously don't know my pops at all," Kian thinks to himself, as Pastor Collins finishes the eulogy and leads them all in a prayer before disappearing from the stage as

8

the pall bearers came forward, closed the casket, and began the process of carrying it outside to the plot, which will be Maniac's eternal resting place.

Kian stands with the remains of his broken family and watches his father's coffin being lowered into the ground as the pouring rain begins to fall, soaking up everyone gathered around the hole in the ground. Kian doesn't even feel the icy rain sliding down the back of his black button-up shirt as he watches the dirt begin to hastily be thrown on top of the coffin to cover up the grave before the rain turns it into a Florida sink hole.

Kian turns away, leading his mother, brother, and sister, back inside the little church as he vows to hunt down his father's killer someday. He is the man of the house, he has to be strong for them all now, everything falls on him.

Chapter Three

Skyla

- Funeral Day -

Skyla pulls up to the house and parks in the driveway before turning her car off and sitting quietly in her seat, listening to the engine tink and click softly, as it cools down. She watches her oldest son, Kian, open his door and storm out of the car and into the house, his emotions swirling openly across his face, igniting her own inner yearn for the ability to comfort him and ease his suffering, if only she knew how. She steps out of the car as Jermaine and Imani follow her inside the house and drift off their own way.

She walks into the kitchen and leans against the counter as she breaks down crying, once again the feeling of loneliness has settled into her soul and she realizes Maniac is not coming back, that he's really gone. Memories of their time together flashes through her mind as she remembers how they first met.

Back when he was a young hustler selling weed at the park on Gun Club Road, where all the teenagers and young adults would hang out playing basketball or chilling with friends, drinking and smoking, they had met. He had just finished playing basketball and sweat made the dark ebony skin of his chest gleam, emphasizing the muscles of his chest and stomach as she watched him approach the water fountain that she and her friend, Elise, were standing in front of.

She watched as his eyes scan her first, then briefly turn towards Elise before returning on her. He smiled a beautiful white smile that lit up his eyes with friendliness.

"How you doin', ma?" asked the fine, dark skinned brother standing in front of them.

"We're good," replies Skyla, as she shyly smiles back, hiding her eyes from his penetrating gaze.

"You mind if I get right there for a second?" he asked, gesturing to the water fountain that she and Elise were standing in front of, obviously blocking his way.

"Oh, shit, I'm sorry, go ahead," Skyla says, embarrassed, forgetting all about the water fountain while she stared at his physique, watching him as he leans over to take a drink from the fountain. He stands back up and scoops some of the cold water into his hands before rubbing it into the back of his head and neck, to cool down.

"So, what's your name, shawty?" he asks Skyla, looking her over once again, his eyes lingering on her breasts and hips momentarily before returning back to her eyes.

"My name's Skyla, and she's Elise," Skyla says, waving her hand at her friend standing next to her, practically drooling over the boy in front of them.

"I'm Maniac," he says, placing a hand on his chest in way of introduction.

"Oh, great, another crazy nigga," says Skyla, sighing and rolling her eyes at the mention of his name.

"Nawl, baby girl, I got plenty of sense," Maniac says with a grin. "So, whassup? Y'all smoke?" he asks, pulling a pack of Dutch Masters out of his gym shorts and holding it up.

"Of course we smoke, nigga, but how do I know you won't be on some weirdo shit like the rest of these niggas out here?" asks Skyla suspiciously, as she crosses her arms over her chest and cocks her hips slightly, yet very cutely.

"Because I'm one of a kind, shawty, and I like to build a foundation first when I meet someone, ya feel me?" Maniac shoots back smiling, and turns, beginning to walk off towards a picnic bench, leaving the girls a choice of whether to follow or not.

As the day progressed, Skyla remembers that Maniac had kept her laughing all day, and then before she even realized it, he had captured her heart as the weeks turned into months and they finally ended up having sex for the first time, which led up to her giving birth to their first child, Kian.

Skyla snaps back from the past, as she wipes the tears falling uncontrollably from her eyes. She stands up and angrily slaps the closest thing to her, a Folgers Coffee tin, off the counter, in her frustration to vent her rage. She watches the contents spill out onto the floor. She is frozen for a moment as she looks at all the bags of weed and coke lying in front of her, and only when she started to pick them up off the ground, she realized Kian was standing in the entryway, watching her.

"You okay, ma?" he asks, as his eyes take in the scene before him, "I heard a loud crash and wanted to make sure that you are alright," he added, as he bent down to help her pick up the items strewn across the floor.

"I got it, Kian, thank you," Skyla says quickly, as she tries to collect all the bags off the floor and put them back into the coffee can, not realizing that Kian already knows exactly what was inside.

"Okay, I'll be in my room," Kian says, as he stands up and helps her to her feet before returning to his room and shutting the door.

Skyla takes a glance behind her to make sure that he was gone before grabbing a bag of weed and a bag of coke out of the tin and heading towards her own room for privacy. 'I just want to numb the pain for a while', she thinks to herself as she locks the door behind her and dumps the coke onto a magazine that is lying on the nightstand by the bed.

She rolls up a dollar bill that she took from her purse and snorts two lines of the fish-scale-looking powder. A feeling of euphoria started to spread through out her whole body, as she lays back on the bed and replays in her mind, all of the memories of her and Maniac together. Her personal movie of happy memories playing, she drifts from consciousness finally, as exhaustion took a hold of her, helping her loss and take the backseat of her emotions. If only for a moment.

Chapter Four

Sin

Sin sits in one of his trap houses off of Lake Worth Road and 57th in Greenacres, and counts through the money that he had raked in within just the last 2 weeks since he had robbed and killed Maniac. The day he had pulled up to Maniac's house, Sin was taking care of a buyer who was willing to pay 15 hundred an ounce for the cocaine and 2 racks a piece for pounds of kush, as long as both were top grade, of course.

Sin ended up selling him 5 ounces of coke after he had dropped some super mannitol in it, and 2 of the pounds of Lemon Kush, making an easy $11,500, which he then used in buying himself some new Salvatore Ferragamo boots, some Gucci pants and shirts, and a new Cuban link chain with a pinky ring, before picking up some TVs and music for his Impala.

He took the rest of the drugs over to his other trap house and had a bitch he fucks with named, Mercy, drop the powder for him to maximize his profits with the crack.

"Eighteen, nineteen, twenty, twenty-one," counts Sin silently to himself as he thumbs through the $100 bills from the crack slabs he has been pumping through the hood, which caused all of the hustlers to slide his way for the prices that he was offering.

He picks up a rubber band and secures the stack of bills with it, before placing the bundle on the table with the rest of the money that has been pouring in hand over fist. He picks up the blunt that is laying in the ashtray and lights it, taking a deep pull off of it, letting the potent weed smoke fill his lungs as he leans back in his chair. He watches as the smoke spirals lazily towards the ceiling from the red tip of the blunt as his mind drifts towards the easy money he made with Maniac in prior business deals, before Sin's greed took a hold of him, making him feel stagnant on the block.

'The whole reason I took the shit is so I could fill *my* own plate!' Sin grumbles to himself, feeling annoyance for the guilt that settles over him. "It doesn't matter anymore, he can't hold me back now," Sin says out loud before grinning as his phone chimes with a call from a new plug who is willing to consign him a brick for every brick he pays for upfront.

"Yo! What's goodie, Big Bruh?" Sin greets enthusiastically, when he answers the phone for 'Cien Fuegos', the Cuban plug that his brother Rey put him down with that owns the body shop that he works at.

"How are you my friend? Are you still prepared to meet with me today for lunch as planned?" asks Cien Fuegos, with a heavy accent, speaking in code about Sin coming to buy a brick from him today.

"Yeah, man, I'm about to be on my way to the restaurant now, I just had to cash my check," replies Sin, getting up from his chair and putting the stacks of money into a duffle bag he had close by.

"Okay, I will see you soon 'Chacho," says Cien Fuegos, before hanging up, as Sin gets ready to go pick up his 2 bricks, which he knows will open the door for him to takeover the hood. As he walks out the door of the trap house, he smiles, putting on his Versace sunglasses and says to himself, 'Now, nobody can stop me! I'm on top of the world, Manolo', quoting Scarface, his favorite movie.

Chapter Five

Kian

- One Year Later -

Kian walks into the gym at John I. Leonard High School for the orientation of the 9th grade students just entering high school, looks around at all the students sitting on the bleachers, before spotting Quan and walking over.

"What's good, bruh?" greets Quan, excited about being able to go to school together again with his best friend, Kian.

"Not shit, bruh, just goin' through the motions, ya feel me?" replies Kian, as he watches the groups of girls giggle and chat amongst themselves around the bleachers.

"Look at this shit Key, it's like America's Next Top Model in here!" Quan says, referring to all of the girls with their hair, makeup, and clothes meticulously put together.

"Looks like a 'THOT' convention," says Kian, with a smirk on his face before his eyes set upon a slim, light skinned girl in Tommy Girl Jeans and a Bebe top with Chinese bangs, walking into the gymnasium and looking around shyly.

"Bruh, who the fuck is *that*?" asks Kian suddenly, grabbing onto Quan's shoulder to get his attention and pointing at the girl still standing in the doorway, looking for a seat in the crowded bleachers.

"Shit, I don't know Key, but we'll find out eventually, ya feel me?" says Quan, staring at the beauty in front of them as well before she is lost from their view amongst the crowd of rowdy teen students towards the front. Kian was still looking towards the doors when he notices a white boy saunter into the gym, look around with obvious disdain, before walking all the way to the end of the gym, where a group of upperclass-looking white kids are seated at and joining them.

A white overweight man walks to the microphone and clears his throat to gain the attention of the students before speaking.

"I am Principal Saunders, and I'm glad to welcome all of you to John I. Leonard High today," he said, greeting the students seated before him in the crowded bleachers. "Today, we will go over the rules here at school, before we move on to discuss classes and after school activities that are open to take, as long as you keep your grades up," Principal Saunders says with a smile, while looking around at the teenagers. "Afterwards, you will be released for lunch and handed your schedules in the front office since today will be filled with getting acquainted with the ebb and flow, here at John I. Leonard," Principal Saunders went on, before glancing behind him at a line of seated teachers.

"Next, I would like to introduce each one of these amazing teachers, one by one, so you can get to know them, in case you ever need to talk, so you'll know where to find them," Saunders added, causing Kian to groan and slump down in his seat in boredom, as the next two hours slowly crawled by, before the lunch bell rings and the students pour out through the gym doors.

They head to the cafeteria for a much needed break to chill and mingle. Kian stands in line with Quan behind him, as they grab trays of Pizza and tater tots, before heading to an open table to sit down.

"So, I been thinking about trying out for the football team again this year, you down?" Quan asks, once they both started to eat their pizza.

"Shit, I don't know if I'll have time, Q, I been taking care of shit at the crib, cause it's like moms been on a decline lately," Kian says sadly, looking up at Quan from his tray.

"Damn, that's fucked up man, but you can't let yourself get sucked into the depression, Key, it's fucked up what happened to your pops, but you need to live for yourself instead of everybody else," Quan states empathetically, upset about not being able to chill with Kian as much as they used to. Kian just nods distractedly as he pops some tater tots into his mouth, thinking about how he should've done more to help his dad the day he died.

"If I would've done *anything* different...anything...He would still be alive," Kian thinks in self pity.

"Bruh, check shawty out," whispers Quan, interrupting, as he nudges Kian's arm, shaking him out of his regret and pointing to the girl they saw earlier in the gym, walking pass their table to the snack stand.

"I'ma be back, Q," says Kian quickly, as he races out of his seat and heads in the direction the girl, so he can see what's up with her.

As he approaches the waiting students standing in the line to buy snacks, he purposely bumps into the girl, causing her to gasp in surprise and spin around to face him.

"Oh, shit! My fault shawty," apologizes Kian, raising his hands to show he didn't mean to cause any harm.

"You're fine," says the girl quietly, causing Kian to have to lean forward slightly to hear her.

"It's my first day, so I'm just getting used to finding my way around, ya feel me?" Kian explains apologetically, as he maneuvers slightly to get a better look at her eyes, hidden behind her bangs.

He realizes that she has light hazel colored eyes. Beautiful. At that moment, he decides to eventually make her a part of his team.

"Yeah, well, it's my first day here too," says Pretty Eyes, snapping Kian out of his thoughts, as he stares into her face as if in a trance.

"My name is Kian," he says, offering her his hand politely, as the snack line moves forward around them because they are standing there blocking the way.

"Isabella," she says shyly, taking ahold of Kian's hand and shaking it, as she smiles faintly and lets her bangs fall back over her pretty eyes, hiding them from him.

"So, what classes are you taking?" asks Kian, as they walk up to the counter of the concession stand. Isabella picks up some cookies, a Powerade, and a pretzel, before responding.

"I still have to go to the front office to get my schedule after lunch," she replies, looking in a small clutch for some money to pay for her snacks.

"You good shawty, I got you," Kian says, pulling a $20 dollar bill from his pocket and placing it on the counter, before asking for some Cool Ranch Doritos and a Minute Maid Apple Juice.

"Thank you, Kian," says Isabella, as she grabs her items off of the counter and turns to walk away.

She turns back around and after taking a couple of steps, smiles at him, before asking, "You going to the front office after lunch to get your schedules?"

"Yeah, me and my homie Quan got to head up there," Kian replies.

"Okay, I'll see you later, then," Isabella says, as she walks away, leaving Kian standing in his place, staring after her.

Chapter Six

James

James stands by a black kid and a light-skinned girl with hazel eyes and bangs. He is listening, as the kid is trying so hard to hold the girl's attention with his stupid conversation.

'These blacks think they are so smart,' James thinks to himself, a smug smirk permanently plastered on his face from a comfortable life of wealth.

James' father is a well respected business man who owns his own used car dealership, Reliable Rides, and they've just recently relocated to Lake Worth, downtown to expand the family business from West Virginia. After the boy and girl left, James heads back to the table he is sitting at with a few other white kids whose families are also well off.

"So, James, tell us about living out in 'Hicktown'," teases a kid named Matthew whose parents invested in Apple years ago, which he just loves to brag about in every conversation.

"Well, first off, Matt, we didn't live in Hicktown, as you so eloquently call it, but in Bridgeport, and my dad's dealership was in Morgantown, where the West Virginia University is," replies James, looking at Matthew, seated across the table confidently.

"That's a respectable area," says a sophomore named Aaron, who is volunteering to show the group around a little bit after lunch, when they head to the front office for their schedules.

"How do you know?" sneers Matthew, turning his gaze on Aaron, as if to challenge his knowledge about the authenticity of the affluence in West Virginia. Aaron looks around cautiously, before leaning in towards the center of the crowded table, motioning for the rest of them to do the same, which everyone does.

"My dad has some business associates he deals with that gather out there every couple of months and he brought me with him last time since I'll be a junior next year," says Aaron quietly, as his eyes scan each of the faces seated at the table before continuing. "So, when we got there they had us staying in a big ass log cabin in the mountains and I thought I'd be bored as fuck, but then later that night, he brought me with him to this huge bonfire. There were a bunch of people dressed in white robes with red crosses on their chests," Aaron says seriously, as the group gasps in amazement.

"You went to a Klan ritual?" asks Matthew doubtfully, suspicion evident in his voice, as he looks at Aaron.

"Yeah, that's what it was," Aaron replies. "They stood around a huge burning cross and were...like, chanting and shit."

"I know what you're talking about, dude, my dad goes to the same retreat every two or three months for a week or so, and won't ever tell me what it is," says James jealously, while he stares at Aaron in amazement.

"What do they do after the ritual?" asks a pretty blonde girl named Emily, whose mom owns a chain of beauty salons, as she looks back and forth between James and Aaron with interest.

"After the ceremony, everyone gets something to drink and heads to a big room with chairs and a fireplace. They call it the 'business lounge', and it's where all of the business deals are made," replied Aaron with a smirk appearing on his face at all the looks of wonder and amazement his story is generating.

"Every time my dad comes back from one of his trips, he's always excited about a new business venture he's come up with for the dealership," says James, as he thinks about all the trips his dad has taken, and returned from, excited about working with a new business partner he just seems to have met out of the blue.

"My dad told me that it's better we keep our money in our own circles, so the darkies can't get none of it," Aaron says, laughing as the lunch bell rings and everyone starts to get up to dump their trays before heading to the front office to get their schedules. "The only kind of darkie I want to be around is one that works himself to death for my business," says Aaron, making everyone laugh as they walk out of the cafeteria.

Chapter Seven

Quan

Quan and Kian walked through the courtyard of the school towards the front office to get their schedules and take their time at it, admiring all of the pretty girls that are sitting outside for lunch.

"Look, Q," says Kian, pointing at a group of beautiful and thick girls that are laughing together in their own secluded circle, obviously the popular clique, as it looks like they're all wearing designer clothes and have long natural hair and athletic bodies.

Quan sighs in resignation, coming to grips with the fact that he will probably never be able to get any closer to those beauties than he is right now, admiring them from 50 feet away.

The two of them walked into the front office and took a moment to look at the trophies in the display case at the front of the school from all the years that the various teams won. The boys noticed that the last football trophy was won in 2020, two years ago, and looked at each other, realizing that their school's football program might not be up to par with their skills.

"You still trying to decide if you wanna try out for the team, key?" Quan asks, staring at his best friend, trying to read his reaction.

Ever since Maniac got killed, Kian has been distant and has been taking care of his family as best he can. Quan's mom told him to be careful going over to Kian's house because she heard from one of her best friends that his mom, Skyla, has been doing drugs and she doesn't want him exposed to that kind of lifestyle, especially since he's been showing some real promising signs playing football. Quan shakes his head trying to clear his thoughts as he feels the anger creeping back up on him again at the thought of cutting off his best friend over something that was never his fault to begin with.

'He needs me right now, more than ever with the deck stacked against him like it is,' Quan thinks to himself silently, resolving to push Kian as hard as he needs to, so he can get through this rough patch in his life.

"I don't know bruh, there's a lot of shit goin' on at the crib right now with mom and shit, and money's kinda tight," Kian says, avoiding Quan's eyes, as he turns away from the glass case and heads toward the counter where a matronly looking woman in a flowery blouse and thick glasses is sitting, shuffling through a big stack of papers and putting them in a grey bin.

"How can I help you young men?" she asks, after taking a second to put down the stack of papers she was sorting through.

"Yes, Ma'am, we came to get our schedules," Quan says politely, as the woman cleans her glasses with the corner of her blouse before replying.

"I'll just need both of your names, and I'm sure I'll be able to accommodate you fine young gentlemen since you've been so polite and respectful," she says with a smile, as a group of nicely dressed white kids walk up to the counter and stand behind them, led by an older looking boy with light brown hair.

"How are you doing today, Mrs. Snyder?" the kid asks, causing Mrs. Snyder to beam at him.

"I'm doing splendid today Aaron, thank you for asking," she replies, before turning back to the bins where the piles of papers are stacked.

"I'm assuming that you are all here for your schedules as well?" Mrs. Snyder asks, looking at Aaron for confirmation.

"Yes Ma'am," Aaron replies politely, before turning his eyes to Kian and Quan, mugging them briefly, before turning back to the conversation taking place behind him with the rest of the white kids, and listening, casually dismissing Quan and Kian.

"What are your names?" asked Mrs. Snyder, as she steps up to the counter with a stack of papers clutched in her hands, where they are standing.

"Joquan Adams and Kian Hayworth," replies Quan, as he watches the woman begin to shuffle through the schedules before pulling out two of them and handing them to Quan.

"Y'all got some good teachers on there," she says with a smile, before turning towards the white boy, Aaron and asking for his friends' names.

"Matthew Gilcrest, James Deckard, Emily Scott, Ryan Davis, Rebecca Taylor, and Justin Wilshire," he recites from his list, as each of the white kids step up to take their schedule from Mrs. Snyder. Quan and Kian were still comparing their schedules, when the light skinned girl from the gym, walks into the office and joins them, after spotting them standing to the side.

"Hey, Kian," says Isabella shyly, surprising Quan and making Kian look up from his schedule quickly, the surprise evident on his face.

"Was'sup, Isabella?" he greets, before adding, "This is my homie, Quan," clapping Quan on the shoulder and shaking him slightly.

"How you doin'?" Quan asks, nodding his head at the girl standing before them.

"Came up here to get my schedule," Isabella says, before heading to the desk, while Mrs. Snyder is still standing behind it with schedules in her hands.

"You came up here for your schedule too, sweetheart?" Mrs. Snyder asks sweetly, looking at Isabella, who nods her head in acknowledgement.

"What's your name, dear?" Mrs. Snyder asks, shuffling through the papers.

"Isabella Perelli," she answers faintly, as she shuffles her feet and waits while Mrs. Snyder looks through the stack and pulls out a sheet of paper, which she hands over the counter to her.

"Have a good day!" Mrs. Snyder calls after Isabella, who retreats from the counter and walks back over towards the trophy case before pausing in front of Kian and asking who his teacher for math is.

"I got Mr. Stubblefield," Kian says, glancing down at his schedule and looking back up at Isabella, who hides her eyes after a second of Kian looking at her.

"I do too," she says, her bangs falling in front of her eyes as she lowers her head, pretending to study her class schedule intensely.

"I'ma see you there tomorrow then," says Kian with a grin, which Isabella returns, before nodding her head and turning away, walking out of the front office back to the courtyard.

Quan looks over at Kian and shakes his head as he sees his best friend staring after Isabella with a stupid grin plastered on his face.

"C'mon loverboy," Quan says, laughing as they head back out to the courtyard to walk around some more before they have to go to homeroom.

Chapter Eight

Isabella

As Isabella walked out of the office, she could hear Kian's friend call him 'loverboy', as she hurries her pace and walks into the courtyard. She looks around at all the kids and their groups of friends before noticing the popular girls off to one side of the courtyard. She lowers her head before they can spot her gawking at them and scurries away.

"I'll never be that pretty in my whole life," Isabella thinks sadly to herself, as she walks to the hallway that her homeroom class is in with Ms. Reaves. Isabella's mind drifts to faded memories on her mother Leti, who is still in Baltimore somewhere, doing God knows what. Her father and mother split years ago when Isabella was only 5 years old, because her mother would disappear for weeks at a time, and when she would pop back up she would always be dirty and on drugs. It got to the point that her dad gave Leti an ultimatum: Her family, or drugs. Her mom left the next day and after 2 months, her dad moved her all the way to West Palm Beach, Florida to a house with a swing in the back yard, where they stayed, up until 2 years ago before moving to Downtown Lake Worth.

Isabella remembers the last time she asked her dad where her mom was, he had sat her down and looked into her eyes before telling her that nobody would ever love her like he did. Isabella is her father's princess, and he has always done everything he could to provide her with a sense of security and wellbeing. He could deny her nothing.

Isabella walks into the classroom and is greeted by Ms. Reaves, before taking a seat at the front of the room and settling in. The final bell rings as the rest of the class trickles into the room and find seats while the teacher stands up from behind her desk to address the class.

"Good afternoon to all of you today, and welcome to my class," Ms. Reaves says, smiling at the students staring back at her. "Homeroom in my class is just for catching up on any assignments that you need a relaxed environment to work in," Ms. Reaves states, looking around at individuals and making eye contact, before moving on to another set of eyes.

"Today, you obviously don't have any work to do, so for the remainder of the class you may talk quietly amongst yourselves to get to know one another," she says before sitting back down behind her desk, taking a thick book from a drawer, and leaning back in her chair to read.

Isabella looks around at all the students in the rows behind her, whispering with each other and decides to pull her sketch pad and pencil out of her tote bag, starting to draw a bouquet of blossoming roses, as she daydreams. Her mind wanders for a while before settling on thoughts of that cute boy Kian, whom she had met earlier that day. Her father had always told her that boys ain't shit, but Isabella wonders what it would be like to hang out with him, if she wasn't cursed with a habit of being shy. As she doodles, she tunes out the conversations that are going on around her and almost jumps out of her seat when a girl next to her nudges her elbow.

"What are you drawing?" she asks, looking over Isabella's shoulder at the roses on the paper.

"Just some flowers," replies Isabella, as she scoots over in her chair slightly and lays her pencil down on the desk.

"You're really good," the girl says with admiration. "I'm Jenna ," she adds, looking at Isabella with a smile.

"Isabella," she replies, returning the greeting before picking up her pencil, adding a little bit of shading around one of the delicate petals on the paper.

"I just moved down here from Orlando, so I don't really fuck with nobody down here," Jenna says, as she looks at Isabella, watching her draw.

"It's cool, I don't really hang out with too many people either, I'm kind of a homebody," Isabella replies, as she turns the page and proceeded to work on the completion of a bird sitting on a tree branch that she had spotted that morning.

Jenna continues to watch Isabella draw and the girls continue to talk during class, until the bell rings and they end up walking out together to their next classes. "What class do you have next?" asks Jenna, looking at her schedule and seeing P.E. on it, which causes her to grimace.

"I have English with Mr. Faulkner," Isabella says, handing Jenna her schedule, so they might compare classes.

"At least we have homeroom together," sighs Jenna, as she hands the schedule back and waves goodbye as they split ways and both head to their respective classes, anticipating the end of the first day of school already.

Chapter Nine

Detective Jones

Detective Jones sits at his desk, going over the accumulated evidence and recent reports about an influx of drugs in the City of Lake Worth and Town of Greenacres from the reports of multiple sources. From his reviewed witness testimony from snitches trying to make a deal, to local business and traffic cameras, and he has even employed undercover buyers who managed to snag a few low level dealers, hence, the rats, but otherwise hasn't come across anything ground breaking yet. Something Detective Jones is hell bent on rectifying.

"Yo, Jones! Captain wants you in his office," says an old cop by the name of Tomas, who used to be a street cop until he got shot in the leg with a .40 caliber that put him behind a desk permanently, until he gets his three quarters pension.

Jones gets up and walks through the cubicles and knocks on Captain Reider's door, before hearing the wheezing bellow off, "Come on in," followed by a fit of coughing, as he sits in one of the chairs in front of the desk.

"You wanted to see me, Cap?" asks Detective Jones, looking at his superior with an inquiring gaze.

"Have you made any headway with the drugs in Greenacres at all?" asks Captain Reider, as he takes a bottle of pills from his desk drawer and throws a few of them back, chasing them with a healthy swallow of Pepto Bismal from a bottle on his desk.

"I'm still working on that, Cap, we're getting real close, it's just that nobody knows much because there are too many levels of insulation from this motherfucker in place," replies Detective

Jones, feeling slightly angry at the thought of an individual who would flood his community with drugs, poisoning their own neighborhoods.

"Well, get back out there and bring that scumbag in, detective, that's an order," wheezes Captain Reider, covering his mouth with a fist.

"Yes sir," replies Jones, rising out of the chair and leaving the room, a renewed sense of duty trailing in his wake.

Chapter Ten

Sin

Sin sits in the soft plush leather interior of his Mercedes Benz S550, as he weaves through the slow traffic crawling through the streets off of Lake Worth Road. He turns up the heated seat as his eyes scan the street corners where some of his workers are posted while slanging crack. His phone rings and he picks it up, seeing it's his plug, Cien Fuegos, making his smile get really big as he answers the phone enthusiastically.

"Fuegos! What can I do for you, my friend?" asks Sin, as he bends the corner and pulls onto the street that his main traphouse is located, over on 12th Avenue South.

"Sin, I am doing well, but I am not calling to exchange pleasantries. We have a problem," says Cien Fuegos, causing Sin to frown, as he enters the door of his trap and is greeted by the sight of many naked women, walking around and cooking and bagging up crack.

"And what is this problem?" asks Sin, as he walks past a beautiful high yellow girl, he vaguely remembers her name as Latoya, and he smacks her on the ass, causing the girl to jump as he passes by and heads to the bedroom he stays in sometimes when he works here late, and doesn't feel like leaving.

"I will not say too much until we have met, but there is somebody poaching in our lake," Fuegos says vehemently.

Thoughts run through Sin's mind as to who would dare have enough balls or resources to try a covert takeover of his turf. They have been fruitful years for both Sin, and Cien Fuegos, ever since they started doing business together, and Sin has occasionally taken care of problems for Fuegos, which he had been greatly compensated for. After Sin had killed Maniac and met up with Cien Fuegos to buy a brick, receiving another brick on consignment, they had structured a deal where Sin would pay $20,000 per brick if he returned and purchased five at a time. Sin cut back on his lavish spending and extravagant purchases, so he could focus on running up a check and getting to the bag, as he built an empire cloaked in the shadows.

As time went on, he carefully cultivated a team around him from corner boys, to crack cooks, to distributors, who never saw his face so they couldn't ever reveal his identity to the police if they ever got caught. They only knew an alias he uses as SC, which stands for Sin's City, and he goes by that when he has something delivered to a customer he has never dealt with before.

"Do you have anything more to tell me that could be helpful?" Sin inquires further, as he opens a carved wooden cigar box containing some hand rolled Cuban Cohiba cigars. Gifts from Cien Fuegos. He carefully selects one and rolled it between his fingers then cut the tip off, before lighting it, savoring the rich flavor of the smoke rolling around in the inside of his mouth, then expelling a thick cloud.

"Yes, but as I said before, I do not wish to speak on this matter any further until we meet," Cien Fuegos reiterates, always very careful about what he says on the phone.

"I'll be over there in 20 minutes," says Sin, before hanging up, putting the cigar out, and rushing out of the house. He jumps back into his Benz, pulling off into traffic, thoughts of murder swirling around in his mind as he whips through traffic, heading to Cien Fuegos' autobody shop, Grove Custom Auto in Delray Beach.

Within 10 minutes, Sin pulls up in front of Cien Fuegos' garage. The garage door is quickly rolled open for him to enter, before it is lowered again after he pulls in, by Chavez, Fuegos' right hand man.

Sin has never once heard Chavez so much as utter a single word since he had been dealing with Cien Fuegos. Chavez then led him into the back office, where he is greeted warmly by the man himself, who is sitting in a huge leather chair behind the desk. "Welcome, mi amigo, come in, come in," says Cien Fuegos, leader of the Y-Los and the Cuban plug from the small ciudad of Cien Fuegos. He stands up to shake Sin's hand, before he lowers himself back into the chair and leans back, getting comfortable for this hard piece of business he had to handle.

"Would you like something to drink?" offers Cien Fuegos, holding up a bottle of Patron Silver to Sin, who nods his head and receives a glass with two fingers full. He immediately gulps it down, before receiving a refill, after which they settle in to discuss the matter at hand of great importance to them both.

"So, what's this shit you told me about somebody stepping on our toes?" growls Sin, angered by the thought of some bitch ass upstart taking food out of his mouth after he has struggled for all of these years to get to where he is at now.

"Calm yourself, mi amigo, calm yourself so that we may prepare," says Cien Fuegos, as he takes another slow sip of the good tequila, his eyes locking onto Sin's face.

Sin scowls as Cien Fuegos laughs, clearly reading his emotions, and able to see the eagerness in his features, wanting to take care of this problem and get back to making money.

"So, from what I have heard, there is a crew called the ZMA, or Zoe Mafia Affiliates that has been moving in from West Palm Beach and Riviera, made up of some Haitian Sensations that broke away but mostly from Zoe Mafia Family and most aren't even Haitian but Americans. They have already started putting heroin, fentanyl, flaka, and cocaine into the streets at competitive prices," Cien Fuegos explained, pouring more Patron into his glass and offering the bottle to Sin, who accepts it and adds some more to his own glass.

"What else do we know about them?" asks Sin, as he takes a swallow of the strong Tequila and feels it burn a path down his throat to his stomach.

"Not much, but we'll find out more with time and I'll let you know," says Cien Fuegos, as they settle in and the conversation turns to how they can set a trap for their new rivals.

Chapter Eleven

Skyla

Skyla sits on the couch, chilling with her friend Nikki, while they drink wine coolers and smoke a couple blunts of loud that Nikki managed to talk her new man out of before she came over for some girl time to catch up, while the kids are at school.

"I swear bitch, he might not be the best at puttin' in work, but he makes up for it where it counts," says Nikki, as she shakes her head and takes a sip of her wine cooler.

"What you mean, Nikki?" asks Skyla, looking at her friend quizzically, before adding, "What could be better than a nigga knowin' how to put it down in the bed?" as she looks at Nikki like she's crazy.

"Shit, a man with a big wallet is better than a broke nigga with a big dick any day," Nikki says seriously, shaking her finger at Skyla.

"Preach girl!" laughs Skyla, as she takes a toke of the weed and coughs, before passing it back to her friend and shaking her head sadly, saying, "It's been a while since I know what either of those blessings from a man really felt like," as her eyes start to tear up.

"Oh, honey, don't do that, come here," says Nikki softly, scooting over on the couch and hugging Skyla, as tears start to drip from her eyes.

"I'm fine," Skyla says softly, dabbing at her eyes, as she sniffles and rubs her nose, suddenly craving some powder.

She gets up from the couch and heads to her bedroom before opening a drawer on her night table, pulling out two grams of cocaine, and returning to a puzzled looking Nikki.

"Where the hell did you rush off to like that?" she asks as Skyla sits down on the couch again, before grabbing a magazine off an end table and placing it on her lap.

"I had to go get this," Skyla says, holding up the little baggie in front of Nikki's eyes, before dumping it onto the magazine and proceeding to chop it up into lines.

"Ohh! Bitch, you didn't tell me you had some white girl!" says Nikki excitedly, as she watches her friend Skyla make two lines, before snorting hers, and passing the magazine over to Nikki to do hers.

Skyla tips her head back on the couch and pinches her nose closed, as a wave of warmth spreads throughout her body and the cocaine takes effect, transporting her to bliss. Her mind feels like it's replaying a movie on a projector screen, as she remembers Maniac laying her down on the bed and running his fingers across her breasts. He replaces his hand with his tongue, which he circles around her areola before sucking her hard, sensitive flesh into his mouth and lightly caressing her with his tongue.

The memories feel so real, and Skyla feels herself respond, as she moans lightly and arches her back, trying to draw Maniac's head tighter against her chest while she feels his hand travel down her stomach and pull the front of her shorts loose before rubbing her clit with experienced fingers, making her instantly wet. She rotates her hips slowly as he works his fingers in a circle before slowly sinking two of them into her tightness, causing her to gasp and open her eyes, realizing that it's Nikki making her feel this good. Nikki gazes back at her with lust on her face as she slowly flicks her tongue across Skyla's nipple, making her moan again.

"I know it feels good, Sky, just trust me," Nikki says sensually, as she lowers her head and kisses her way down Sky's stomach, bunching up her shirt before swirling her tongue in her belly button and working her shorts off.

Skyla raises her hips to speed up the process as her mind races, "Is this really happening with me and Nikki right now?" she asks herself.

Nikki's tongue swipes against her clit, causing an explosion of ecstacy to flow through her body as she presses her hand into Nikki's hair and proceeds to grind her pussy against her face, resulting in an amazing climax which leaves her face flushed as she gasps for air. Nikki crawls back onto the couch with a grin on her face and engages her in a deep, passionate kiss, giving Skyla a taste of her own sweetness.

"What the fuck was that, Nikki?" pants Skyla, as she looks at her friend in astonishment, still seeing a glaze of her juices on Nikki's chin, as a smile spreads across her face, remembering the amazing climax she just experienced after so long of using a toy.

"I just needed you to know that there's still fun out here in the world. I hate seeing you so down and cooped up in this house," Nikki gushes, as she leans forward and kisses Skyla again, using her tongue as they explore each other's mouths.

After a couple of minutes, they separated as Skyla came to her senses and looked at the clock, realizing with alarm that it's now 3:30pm, which means the kids will be getting off of the bus soon and heading home. "Oh, shit girl, the kids will be here soon!"

She stands up, getting off of the couch and fixes her clothes quickly, before snorting another line of coke and passing the magazine over to Nikki to do the same, as she hurries to clean up the multiple wine cooler bottles that were laying around the living room. She dumps them in the trash bag in the kitchen and returns to the livingroom, where Nikki is picking up her purse and preparing to leave, "Where you going, girl?" asks Skyla, looking at her friend.

"I got some errands to run, girl, but let me know when you free so we can link back up," Nikki says, with a smirk, as she straightens her shirt and does a quick check in her compact mirror before hugging Skyla.

"We absolutely need to link back up bitch after that shit you just pulled today," Skyla says, with her own smirk, as they hug and she walks Nikki to the door.

"It ain't no problem Sky, I knew it'd been a while and I just wanted you to relax, but I got you," Nikki says, walking out of the door before getting into her car and pulling off.

Skyla heads back into the house and spreads out one more line of coke before the kids get home, afterwards she sits on the couch, waiting for them to walk through the door.

Chapter Twelve

Jermaine

Jermaine walks with his little sister, Imani, down the center isle of the bus, after it pulls up to their stop. As they walk down the street heading home, Jermaine looks around at his surroundings. He passes by dopeboys standing on the corners, serving junkies who keep popping up out of nowhere, as they shuffle their way over to buy their choice of poison. Jermaine wishes he was old enough to have the freedom to make his own decisions, but being only 12 years old, he knows that he'll have to continue to feel like a slave to his mother's rules in the house and rules at school. He wishes that his dad was still alive so he could take him to basketball and football games like he used to, and wrestle with him and Kian.

Ever since his father died, Jermaine has noticed that his mom has been acting weird and is always having mood swings now. She sniffs and pulls at her nose a lot, like she's sick or something. He hopes that she is not sick, because he doesn't want her to die and leave them orphaned, because he doesn't know if he will be able to stay together with Kian and Imani, who he doesn't ever want to be separated from. They walk up the driveway of their house, and he puts his key into the door, then walked into the living room where Skyla comes over to greet them, a dopey smile on her flushed face.

"Hey babies! How was your first day at school?" she asks, bending down to kiss him on the cheek first, then Imani, who hugs and kisses their mother back.

"It was fine," Jermaine replies, as he dumps his backpack off of his shoulders and onto the floor, heading off to his room, sulking.

"What's wrong with him?" asks Skyla, as she looks at Imani for an answer. Imani shrugs her shoulders and follows her mother over to the couch, before sitting down next to her and turning on the TV.

"Have you seen Kian, yet?" Skyla asks Imani, who stares transfixed at the television in front of her and gives a negative head shake in response.

Jermaine hears his mom ask Imani if she has seen Kian yet, as he walks down the hallway to his room. He closes the door behind himself, before sprawling onto his bed and throwing darts at a dartboard across the room. He watches as most of the darts he throws, bounce off of the board and fall to the floor as he thinks about how he would get his own money if he was old enough to do what he wanted and didn't have to listen to the bullshit the teachers or his mom were always telling him he had to play by because he was a kid.

"If I still had a dad, he'd show me how to be a man," Jermaine grumbles to himself, as he waits on his big brother Kian to get home, animosity festering in his young heart at the injustices he has had to deal with at such a young age.

Chapter Thirteen

Kian

Kian waits for Quan at the bus loop when the final bell rings, signaling the end of the first day of school. Kian leans against the wall and watches the girls walk past as he sees Quan turn the corner, walking quickly in his direction.

"Whats good, bruh?" greets Kian, as they dap hands and head towards the line of buses, looking for number 32, which is their ride home.

"Not shit, just glad to have this day over and done with," replies Quan, as they walk down the sidewalk, following after a group of girls laughing and talking in front of them.

As they approach their bus, Kian spots Isabella walking next to a pretty red haired girl with freckles, and waves at her, causing her to blush and wave back shyly, as Quan and him climb up the stairs to find their seats. The bus pulls off and the boys talk about what they plan on doing about joining the football team this year.

"So, you going to get on the squad with me, Key? Or nah?" asks Quan, looking at Kian pleadingly, trying to coax him into agreeing.

"I already told you, Q, that shit ain't right at the house right now!" says Kian, frustrated that Quan keeps pestering him about getting on the football team.

Their bus finally pulls up to their stop and they prepare to walk a mile or so to their street. They walk through the hood and begin to cross an intersection off of 12th Avenue South, near Dixie Highway, but they hear a crash and a short yell that abruptly gets cut off. Kian pauses and looks towards the alley and starts to head in that direction but Quan grabs his arm, stopping him. Kian turns to look at Quan silently, wondering why he stopped him.

"C'mon man, you don't know what's goin' on over there," Quan says, but another loud scream hardens Kian's resolve and he turns away from Quan, yanking his arm free as he runs towards the alleyway behind the old Lake Worth Flea Market plaza.

He rounds the corner and discovers three mangy looking smokers beating the shit out of a skinny hustler in a torn and bloody Nike shirt, as he tried to fight back against the uneven odds. Kian stands in the alleyway momentarily frozen in one place as he takes in the scene in front of him and he tries to make up his mind as to what to do. Time runs out as two of the basers turned as they get the guy onto the ground and suddenly catch sight of Kian standing there watching.

"Hey! What the fuck you got for me, muthafucka?" yells one of the raggedy dressed fiends, as they yell and charge straight at Kian, scaring him into a quick decision.

He grabs a rotted wooden crate from behind the fish store off to one side of the alleyway and smashes it over the head of the first junkie to get close enough to him, causing him to scream and clutch his face with hands so dirty and covered in scabs from picking at them. The second junkie freezes up at the sight of his homeboy yelling and bleeding on the ground in front of him, and this gave Kian an opportunity to slam him against the grimy brick wall and punch him repeatedly in the face. A crunch could be heard.

Kian feels the man's nose break against his fist even if he didn't hear it, and drops him to the ground at his feet as he slumps over, the fight beaten out of him. Kian turns around after dropping the second baser and picks up a chunk of brick and throws it at the last remaining baser, catching him on the side of the head. The junkie yelps, clutching his head as he stops digging through the guy's pockets that they had jumped and takes off down the end of the alleyway, vanishing from sight.

Kian rushes over to the man lying on the ground moaning with blood dripping from his nose and kneels down on the side of him. "Yo, homie, you straight?" asks Kian, placing a hand on the guy's shoulder, which makes him crack open his eyes and stare at Kian in confusion.

"You good, homie?" Kian asks again, shaking the man slightly, as he groans and attempts to sit up with Kian's help.

"I'm straight bruh, I appreciate you," says the man, as he stands up on wobbling legs and leans against the wall for support.

"What's your name, bruh?" Kian asks, looking at the discombobulated man try to work the blood back into his legs as he takes a moment to collect himself.

"Niggas call me 'Glizzy'," he says, holding out his hand to Kian, they dap hands and Kian motions for Glizzy to follow him back out of the alleyway.

"So, what the fuck happened, bruh? 'Fuck they jump on you fo'?" asks Kian, as they walk out of the alleyway and discover Quan standing out at the curb nervously, waiting on Kian to reappear.

Quan looks at Glizzy in surprise at seeing his bruised and swollen face, and looks at Kian in alarm, asking, "What the fuck, bruh? What was that?"

Kian looks at Glizzy momentarily and introduces them, "Glizzy, this is my day one nigga, Quan, he good people," as Glizzy inclines his head in a 'what's up' motion, causing Quan to do the same.

"Shit, so anyways, them crackhead fuck niggas got the drop on me when I was catching a play back there and jumped me," says Glizzy angrily, shaking his head in frustration.

"Damn, that's fucked up, man," says Quan in surprise, since he doesn't really have any idea what some people have to do to survive the streets.

"Yea, tell me about it dawg, they got my whole lil' pack!" growls Glizzy as he runs a hand through his short dreads in frustration.

"I got to shoot off and head back to the crib before moms dukes starts tripping bruh, but stay up and stay safe," says Kian, as he daps up Glizzy and starts to head off in the direction of home.

"A'ight bruh," says Quan, chucking up a duces at Glizzy, who responds in kind, and following after Kian, as Glizzy heads off in the other direction limping slightly.

Kian and Quan walk a little far off, before Quan looks at Kian and asks, "What kinda shit you tryna do, Key? Just runnin' off and savin' niggas 'n shit?" as he shakes his head at Kian in amazement at his audacity.

"Man, if it woulda been you back there, wouldn't you want a muthafucka to help you if they was around?" replies Kian, as he stares at Quan with a smirk on his face.

"Of course bruh, what kind of question is that?" retorts Quan quizzically, looking at Kian as if he bumped his head.

"Then shut yo scarey ass up!" says Kian, grinning and shoving Quan's shoulder, as they walk up the street to their houses.

He stopped, pausing in the middle of the street, "You comin' over?" asks Kian, as he turns to walk up the driveway to his front door.

"I got some shit I gotta take care of, bruh, but just hit me up on Facebook or call the house, and I'll let you know," says Quan, as the boys dap each other up and head in their different directions, Quan feeling guilty for lying to his friend.

Chapter Fourteen

Glizzy

Glizzy limps in the direction of his uncle's traphouse as thoughts of revenge and frustration swirl around in his head. "Pussy ass basers got the drop on a nigga!" he thinks to himself angrily, as he speeds up his pace, approaching the plain yellow colored house at the end of the street with an Infinity QX37 and a Kia Sorento SUV sitting in the driveway, both on "26 inch chrome floats.

He shuffles up the driveway and knocks on the door, as he waits for Dice to open the reinforced steel door. He hears someone's heavy tread on the other side of the door and when it swings open, he looks into his uncle's shocked face at seeing his appearance.

"Yo, what the fuck happened to you, Z?" asks Dice, moving aside to allow Glizzy to enter the cloud filled room, shutting the door behind them. He follows his nephew into the living room in near shock. Glizzy lowers himself down onto the couch with a grimace on his face as a low groan slips out against his will and Dice begins to pace the floor.

"Yo, Glizzy, what the fuck happened to you, my nigga?" asks Dice, more forcefully as anger creeps into his voice, ready to set the score straight for a hit against his own nephew.

"It ain't as bad as it seems, Unk," says Glizzy, as he picks up a half smoked blunt sitting in the ashtray on the table in front of him, and fired it up.

"What you mean, bruh?" asks Dice in confusion, as he ignores the ringtone on one of the various cellphones laying scattered around the coffee table between them.

"Shit, I was serving one of the juggs in da cut, and three more buddies ran down and stole off on me. They took the pack I had on me, Unk," says Glizzy, getting mad all over again at the setup.

"How the fuck you get away with that minor shit then?" asks Dice, pointing at his face, asking about the various scrapes and bruises spread out across his nephew's face.

"Ohh, some young boy jumped into the mix and helped a nigga out from a rock and a hard place, ya feel me?" says Glizzy, as he hands the blunt to Dice, who takes a puff of the potent weed and growls at the continued ringing of the phones.

He passes the blunt back, grabbing one of the phones before pressing the answer button and barking a terse, "what you need?" into the mic.

Glizzy sits stoically on the couch, puffing on the blunt as he watches his uncle take care of business. Dice hangs up and looks at Glizzy with a serious expression on his face, causing Glizzy to pause in anticipation with the blunt halfway to his mouth.

"Wha's good, Unc?" asks Glizzy, already on point to his uncle Dice's mood swings when it's time to put shit into action.

"That was Haze, he said them Cubans from around the way in Greenacres actin' up again," snarls Dice, as he heads over to the kitchen, grabs his FN SCAR 16s, essentially FN's answer for an AR-15, off of the counter, and prepares to leave with it cradled in his right arm.

"Say less," says Glizzy, as he heads to a sectional couch in the corner and pulls a Glock .40 from between the armrest and the cushions. He lifts his shirt and slides it along his right side before letting the shirt cover the weapon. Dice tosses him an ounce of Fruity Pebbles Kush, and they head out the door to see what's going on with their people, as they jump into the Infinity QX37 and swerve off into traffic.

Chapter Fifteen

Sin and Cien Fuegos sit inside Fuegos' candy apple red Range Rover with YFN Lucci pumping out of Bose speakers, as YFN drops jewels while they wait, watching the activities on the corners of the 12th Avenue South intersections with the alphabet streets. Sin splits open a Optimo blunt and fills it with Gorilla Glue #3, before rolling it back up, applying the flame to the tip, and taking a deep pull. Cien Fuegos scans the block once again in front of the store, digging his pinkie nail into a bag of cocaine powder and snorting some into both nostrils.

A tall, yellow skin dude is pulled off the sidewalk by two Cuban Y-Lo's in tank tops and fitted jeans. They led him into an alleyway behind the wig store before robbing him at gun point and making him leave the area in his boxers. Sin snickers at the man running for his life in a pair of cheap, dollar store boxers, as he hurriedly makes his way out of the area now swarming with Cubans.

"That was the fifth one," laughs Sin, as he rolls down his window at the approach of a short Cuban man called Jorge.

"Oye, que vola acere?" asks Cien Fuegos, looking at Jorge, waiting on an update to the terror they're putting into the ZMA hustlers. The Zoe Mafia Affiliates. Who had been running this side of town and this intersection until about an hour ago.

"Nada, Jefe, we just found out they workin' for someone they call Dice," informs Jorge, in a heavily accented spanglish, as his eyes sweep the area slowly.

"Who the fuck is that?" asks Sin, eager to move against his opponents so he can cut the head off of the snake and get back to the money.

"He just a middle man of sorts," replies Cien Fuegos, as he turns to look at Sin, "He controls the street soldiers and corner boys, but to get to the top and wipe them out we need to watch first for what his response to this is," Fuegos finishes saying, before the screeching of tires can be heard from around the corner, instantly putting the men on alert as they grip the weapons holstered on their waists.

A gunmetal grey Infinity QX37 whips around the corner and pulls into an open parking spot in front of the store. "I'd put money on it that a ZMA nigga is in that truck," says Sin quietly, as he keeps his eyes glued to the car sitting across the street from them with its occupants still inside. They watch as a dark skinned man, probably a Haitian, run across the street with his phone pressed against his ear, climbs into the backseat of the truck, before its brake lights turn on, and it backs out of the parking space, pulling off slowly.

"They came to figure out what was going on for future preparations," says Cien Fuegos ominously, as the men ponder the events that just took place, trying to gage their rivals so they can checkmate them early in the game for dominance.

"What you want us to do, Jefe?" asks Jorge, as he turns his attention back to Fuegos, waiting for instructions on how to proceed with their newly acquired block.

"Post some men around the stores and have them watch out for our workers so they won't be retaliated against right now," says Cien Fuegos, as he dismisses Jorge and turns to look at Sin, "Now, we set the stage mi amigo, and it's chess, not checkers," Fuegos finishes, as he puts the whip in drive and they head to the auto body shop to strategize back in Greenacres.

Chapter Sixteen

OG Dice, Zoe Mafia Affiliates

Dice and Glizzy pass a blunt back and forth between themselves, as one of their hustlers, Nicklez, sits nervously in the backseat of the Infinity truck, the tension thick inside the truck. Dice's phone rings and he answers it on the first ring with a curt, "speak". Listening to the caller for a couple minutes before hanging up, he switches lanes, heading toward one of his big homie's spots to figure out what was going on.

After a ten minute ride in tense silence, they pulled up in a residential neighborhood in Lake Worth city off of Federal Highway and 18th Avenue North and pull into a driveway of a two story tan and white stucco house. They all jump out of the truck and head towards the front door where an older looking bald headed Haitian nigga waits. Dice daps him up waiting in the doorway before introducing his nephew, Glizzy, and the nigga, Nicklez, they had just picked up.

"Glizzy, Nicklez, this right here is the Big Homie, Gunz of Zoe Mafia Affiliates," Dice states, looking at his nephew and Nicklez with a stern look on his face, as they dap up the big homie and head inside.

They walk down a short hallway and Gunz opens a door that leads up to the second flight of stairs going to the attic, which is decorated like a mancave with a pool table, two big TVs attached to a PS4, and an XBOX 360, a double-sided glass refrigerator with multiple selections of drinks, including beer, liquor, and sodas, a weight bag and a bench press off in the corner. Red, purple, and green neon lights shining on the walls with posters of exotic looking naked women posted everywhere.

They sit down at a sectional couch in front of the televisions and Gunz looks at Dice silently. Dice interprets the look and turns his attention to Nicklez, who sits up a little bit straighter, as he nervously looks around the attic.

"Nick, tell us what the fuck happened while you were out there," says Dice, as he leans back on the couch, watching the young hustler fiddle with his hands nervously.

"So, we was out there grinding for a while and everything was cool and running smooth as usual, but I started to notice a lot of chicos coming around to cop work one after the other, you feel me and then niggas started getting robbed and told to stay away from the block," says Nicklez, in a rush, as his wide eyes sweep across the stoic faces seated around him.

"That's it?" asks Glizzy in exclamation, looking at his Uncle Dice with anger on his face, at Nicklez weak explanation to what happened on the block earlier with all of their ZMA hustlers.

Dice ignores the outburst and waves his hand towards Nicklez to get him to continue.

"They started stripping niggas and kicking them off the block at gun point, talking about 'fuck ZMA' and 'this is our block now' and shit like that," Nicklez adds, trying to remember anything else that could prove to be important information to help him or ZMA.

"Started stripping niggas of what?" asked Gunz, speaking up for the first time, the deep baritone of his voice echoing around the attic.

"They was taking our drugs, money, and our clothes, OG," says Nicklez seriously, as he looks at the surprise on Gunz's face at this revelation.

"Taking y'all clothes?" asks Dice, as he shakes his head before continuing, "What the fuck they do that for?"

Nicklez squirms in his seat for a moment, taking a second to collect his thoughts before responding to Dice's question. "I think they just doing it to humiliate a nigga, you feel me? Ain't nothing more humiliating than making a dude run away in his boxers," Nicklez states, as the other three men take a second to reflect on the young hustler's statement.

"Did they pull up together, or was it like one by one, until you realized something was up?" asks Dice, as he tried to put the pieces together in his mind's eye.

"There wasn't any of them around 'til a red Range Rover pulled up, and then it was like a steady flow of 'em, 'til we was overrun," replies Nicklez, as he relays the facts to the Big Homies.

"There was a red Range there when we picked him up," interjects Glizzy, remembering the whip sitting in its parking spot with a chico looking dude standing outside of it, when they had pulled up to get Nicklez, after Haze had called Dice's phone at the trap.

"Yea, it never left bruh," says Nicklez, as they come to realization of what's beginning to transpire.

"So, what you wanna do, Big Homie?" Dice asks Gunz, as the men wait for the order to retaliate or not.

"Just keep the other blocks running like they are for now, and if they try this shit again, light their ass up. From now on, nobody goes anywhere without a strap, it's on sight if they cross the line, we can't allow this to happen again," says Gunz, pausing briefly before adding, "we know they tryin' to push us out, so we dig in deeper, and everyone stay on point 'til we find out what this pressure's bout and who we dealing with."

Dice nods in agreement, as he dials Haze, his second in command, to relay the orders from up top and once he hangs up, he looks around at Nicklez and Glizzy, and they follow Gunz back down the stairs to the front door and climb into the Infinity, while Dice and Gunz talk privately for a second.

"I'ma go check out the other spots to make sure shit one K, Big Bruh, and I'll let you know what the move is," Dice says, as he daps up Gunz and climbs into the whip, before backing out of the driveway, and heading off to check the progress the other blocks are making, moving the product through the hood.

Chapter Seventeen

Kian

Kian walks into the house and is greeted with the sight of his mother sitting on the couch next to Imani, pulling on her nose, a clear sign of cocaine use or addiction. He can feel his heart constrict inside of his chest at this revelation, as he heads deeper into the house closing the door quietly behind himself and putting the backpack on the kitchen table. Imani hears his footsteps and turns with a huge smile on her face before hopping off the couch and running in his direction.

"KIAN!" she squeals with delight, as she jumps into his arms and he picks her up, receiving a fierce hug from his baby sister.

"I had a fun day at school, and I signed up for an art class, and I hate my new math teacher, 'cause he made us do decimals on the first day!" Imani fills him in, constantly jumping topics, typical of a 9 year old.

"Hey Key," greets Skyla, coming over to kiss him on the cheek, also eager to hear about his first day back to school.

"Hey ma," Kian replies, accepting her kiss stoically before carrying Imani back over to the couch and setting her down so he can go check on Jermaine in the back room they share. He walks down the hallway to the room and can hear the thunk of darts being thrown against the board as he enters and spots Jermaine sitting on the bed with a scowl on his face.

"Whas'sup, lil bruh?" greets Kian, as he shoves him playfully on the shoulder, causing Jermaine to miss his next throw, the dart falling harmlessly to the floor after bouncing off of the wall.

"Dick," grumbles Jermaine under his breath, as he turns to face Kian. "I hate my life," says Jermaine sullenly, not surprising Kian in the least with how he has noticed his little brother's moods lately.

Kian sighs, knowing where this was coming from, as he lowers himself onto Jermaine's bed, before putting his arm around his shoulder sympathetically. "Look, Jay, I know shit's been hard as fuck without Pops around, but trust me, it'll get better, I promise," Kian says, hoping that he isn't giving his brother any false hope, that everything really will work out.

"How do you know, Key?" asks Jermaine, in a little boy's voice, reminding Kian that he just turned 12 and doesn't have a lot of problem solving skills yet.

"I don't know, I just know that it will, okay?" says Kian, as he glances back over to Jermaine, who is sitting stone still, next to him, hanging his head in depressed anguish.

"Hey, have I ever lied to you?" asks Kian forcefully, shaking Jermaine by the shoulder to get his attention, causing Jermaine to shake his head 'no', in response.

"I found something in mommy's room yesterday when I was looking for one of dad's hats to wear to school..." says Jermaine ominously, before searching behind the headboard of his bed into one of his hiding spots, pulling out a baggie containing white powder.

Kian can feel his heart drop for a second as anger, then fear, grips him and questions fly through his head as to what it is doing in Skyla's room, to what the fuck Jermaine has done with it previously, before showing it to him, to sadness, as he remembers his mom pulling at her nose and sniffing when he had walked into the house earlier and observed her without her knowing it.

"Where the fuck did you get this?" Kian whispers angrily, remembering to keep his voice down, so it doesn't travel through the house as he snatches the baggie of cocaine from Jermaine's hand roughly.

"Out of mommy's nightstand," replies Jermaine, as he looks away from Kian, hiding his face from his big brother's angry inquiring gaze.

"You didn't fuck with this shit, did you?" asks Kian, receiving silence in response to his question, making his heart beat faster as he grabs Jermaine's shoulder and turns him towards his angry face, before spotting the tears silently running from his little brother's eyes.

"No," whispers Jermaine, as he leans against Kian's chest, already knowing what finding that stuff in his mom's room meant.

The two brothers sit silently in the room, both struggling with their emotions, as they think about their dad getting killed and wondering about the future, drawing strength from each other. "Everything is gonna be okay, little bruh, I promise you," says Kian emotionally, as he prepares himself to step up to the plate for his family.

Chapter Eighteen

James

James sits in the wingback chair in his father's office as he listens to him argue over the phone with somebody about the price of some mechanic work on a couple of the vehicles from the dealership his father owns that had been having problems.

"Okay, so what does that entail, if we bring the three SUVs over for work to be done?" asks his father angrily, before waiting for a response, and judging by his facial expressions, James figured he doesn't like what he is hearing.

"Okay, so I'll have to bring them over now while there's available space?" his father asks before pausing, listening to whatever is being said on the other end before agreeing and hanging up. "Fucking beaners couldn't find their own ass but expect me to pay outrageous prices for routine maintenance on our vehicles," his father puffs angrily, before taking a slug of the Wild Turkey whiskey sitting in his glass in his desk and smacking his lips in adoration of the taste.

"Get ready, Jimmy! I'm going to need your help bringing these cars down to the shop to be worked on," his father says briefly, before picking up the phone again and dialing one of his employees from the dealership named Buck, and telling him which SUVs to prepare to take to get worked on at the shop.

James gets out of his chair and heads to his room to get a T-shirt on over his wife beater and put on his Nike Airmax, before heading back downstairs and waiting in the foyer for his father, as he leaves his office and grabs his keys, briefcase, and coat from the closet. They head outside and climb into the family Subaru and take the 20 minute ride to the *Reliable Rides lot*.

"How much is it going to cost to get the work done on these cars, dad?" James asks his father, as they listen to some light country music playing on the radio.

"Well, to be honest, it isn't going to cost me anything. I'll just claim it as a tax write off, since under my LLC I have the business EIN number and I'll just say that it was work done on our company cars," his father explains, as they sit at a stop light and after changing the station, a song by Keith Sweat comes on the radio causing James to reach for the volume knob and turn it up, as he thinks about what his father just explained to him.

"So, why are we going to use this mechanic when we usually use your friend Mark's garage for repairs and stuff?" asks James, as the light changes to green and he waits for his father to reply.

"Because Mark has some shit to take care of back home and isn't available and we wouldn't be using those idiot Cubans and besides, Mark is well aware of our arrangement with work being written off for tax deductions, but if something unexpected happens, I can always blame those Cubans, or Mexican or whatever the hell they are," says his father with a smirk and a laugh, with James following suit, as they pull into the car lot his father owns, where all the cars for *Reliable Rides* are parked.

They parked in his father's designated parking spot and head into the office where they find Buck sitting at his desk, going over some paperwork from the auction where James' father buys most of the inventory for the dealership.

"Howdy y'all," greets Buck, standing up to shake James' hand after he finishes greeting his boss.

"Is everything ready?" asks James' father, clapping Buck on the shoulder and steering him back outside to the three SUVs that they are going to take to get serviced.

"Yes, sir, Mr. Deckard," replied Buck, before launching into a detailed explaination of what he thinks is wrong with the trucks, based on reading the auctioneer's reports and the notes from the last mechanics that had worked on them before they had arrived at *Reliable Rides* lot. James tunes them out as he leans against a silver Kia Sorento SUV and fires off a text to Emily, the blonde girl that he met on the first day of school, about his family taking their boat to the Bahamas a couple years ago, as he waits for Buck and his father to finish. Mr. Deckard walks around the side of the Kia and spots James texting Emily, and clears his throat to get his attention, causing James to look up in annoyance.

"We're ready to head over there now, Jimmy, just follow behind Buck so you don't get lost," says Mr. Deckard, before heading over to a bronze Toyota and starting the engine.

He rolls down the window before giving Buck one last directive, pulls the vehicle out onto the gravel, so Buck can start the white family van he'll be driving and he pulls out into the slow moving traffic. James climbs into the driver's seat of the Kia and follows Buck's white van as he programs the radio for some music and he awaits Emily's reply to his text. His eyes scan the buildings and landmarks of Lake Worth, as he heads to the mechanic shop his father had selected to get the cars serviced at, and he settles into a comfortable state of boredom during the drive over to the garage in Delray Beach.

Once they've all arrived, he pulls into the mechanic's parking lot at Grove Custom Auto and parks next to Buck's van, as he waits for his father to give him further instructions. He spots Mr. Deckard coming around the back of the SUV and opens the door, handing his father the keys, as he follows behind him into the front office of the small mechanic shop. There they waited for the receptionist behind the desk to finish her call. She finally sets the phone down and turns to them. His father begins to explain that he is there to get a couple of his SUVs worked on as quickly as possible, so that he can get them back on the lot. He asks for the supervisor.

"Yes sir, the manager is in the back right now, if you'll wait for a second, I'll go and get him," she replies, before scurrying down a hallway.

James hears her yell for somebody named Chavez. She returns after a couple of minutes, followed by a leathery skinned Mexican looking man who stares at them dispassionately before the woman speaks up. "This is Chavez, he'll lead you to the back to speak with the management."

As the man turns silently, James and Mr. Deckard follow after the man, around the front desk and down a hallway, stopping in front of a door with a caution sign and a handwritten note stating, "Serious Punishment for Unauthorized Entries."

The weathered Mexican--'Or maybe he is Cuban', James wonders to himself, 'though they are all the same'--knocks on the door and James hears a voice yell from the room telling them to come in. The trio walk into the office and Mr. Chavez closes the door behind James and his father, standing behind it. James watches his father approach the desk and extend his hand to the scarred spanish man sitting calmly at his desk smoking a cigarette.

"How ya doing? I'm William Deckard, CEO of *Reliable Rides*," says James' father, in pure business mode.

As James watched the men shake hands, the Spanish manager introduced himself as Enrique Mendoza, owner of Grove Custom Auto. His father sits down to discuss the problems going on with the cars he has brought to get worked on today.

"So, you see, I have one of my men outside who knows a little bit about the trucks and has gone over the reports and paperwork from the auction and the last mechanics and says the cylinder is misfiring on one of them..." Mr. Deckard starts to explain, as James feels his phone vibrate. He takes it out, seeing a text from Emily, and tunes his father and Mr. Mendoza's conversation out as he replies.

They come to an agreement and James follows his dad out of the office to the lobby to wait until they meet back up with Buck. Mr. Deckard informs him that the trucks most likely won't be done for a couple days and to arrange for a ride for them back to the house. Buck proceeds to dial a number on his cellphone and relays Mr. Deckard's request to someone briefly before hanging up and telling them that Tracy, another one of Mr. Deckard's employees, is currently finishing up a sale and will be out to pick them up in 20 minutes.

James settles in, texting Emily back and scrolling through Facebook, as the 20 minutes crawl by slowly as sand passing through in the minute counter.

Chapter Nineteen

Sin

Sin leans back in his seat as Nikki's mouth slides up and down the length of his manhood and he feels her tongue against the base of it as they sit enclosed in the plush interior of his Mercedes Benz. Sin groans and twists his fingers in Nikki's short *Halle Berry* styled hair, as she gently squeezes the base of his dick and cups his balls with her small, soft hands. He can feel his balls begin to tighten up as he grinds her head into his lap harder, causing her to choke a little bit, but she quickly adjusted her mouth around him like the pro she is.

As he shoots off into her mouth, trying to blast her dome off, Nikki slurps it all up and proceeds to milk him dry as the light turns green and Sin tries to focus on driving the German made luxury vehicle without crashing.

"Fuck! Shawty, where the hell you go to school at?" jokes Sin, complimenting her supernatural head skills.

"The school of the hard knocks, nigga," states Nikki giggling, as she wipes her mouth and leans back in her seat, putting her pretty pedicured feet up on the dashboard.

After Sin had got back from watching Cien Fuego's men take over the Zoe Mafia Affiliates' block earlier, he had hit up Nikki to get his freak on. They've been fucking with each other on and off for a couple years, and every time they link up, Nikki always leaves him drained of every drop of stress, with a memory full of dirty deeds that would make the devil blush.

Lately, Sin has been trying to convince her to bring in a girlfriend along, so they can have a threesome and record it together. The only thing keeping him from it is Nikki trying to get her claws into him to become exclusive, which he doesn't want at all. Just the thought of settling down with her is laughable. Sin knows that Nikki is a ghetto-fabulous, gold digging slut, and has no qualms about doing whatever it takes to get to a nigga's pockets, and he doesn't mind dropping a bag on her to get to experience some of his fantasies.

"So, Daddy, where we goin'?" asks Nikki, while Sin fires up a half smoked blunt that was sitting in the ashtray and takes a deep pull, contemplating the question.

"I was thinking about going out to the Cheesecake Factory to eat, then maybe go to a hotel or something for the night shawty, if you cool with that?" Sin says, with a grin on his face, knowing that it's unlikely that Nikki will turn his offer down.

"That sounds good," she replies, as she looks at him seductively, before pouting and asking for a hit of the blunt.

"You know I don't just smoke with anybody, baby girl, but look in the glovebox and lift the case in the back," says Sin, as Nikki complies with his instructions and unzips the black CD case before opening it and flipping through it to discover a vial with about four grams of coke lodged in the spine of the CD case.

She squeals happily, as she uncaps it and inserts her acrylic pinkie nail inside, scooping a little bit of the snow white powder out and snorting it up both nostrils then pinching her nose closed and leaning her head back against the headrest as a smile spreads across her face. Sin smiles inwardly to himself, as he steers the car to the restaurant for them to eat before he takes this bitch to a hotel to blow her back out.

They pull up to the restaurant about 15 minutes later, after listening to a couple Musiq Soulchild songs, and head inside after Sin parks close to the entrance. They're led straight to an intimate, privately secluded booth. The waiter appears after a couple minutes with menus, before taking their drink requests and vanishing into the back to fix their drink orders. After looking over the menu, Sin settles for a serloin steak with garlic butter, baked potatos, and mixed vegetables, while Nikki chooses a Greek salad with blue cheese crumbles. Their waiter reappears with their drinks and takes their orders, before collecting their menus and dissappearing again.

They joked and teased each other, as they wait for their food. Eventually, the conversation turns sexual as Nikki leans forward seductively putting her full breasts on display to Sin's eyes, as she whispers about what she plans to do to him once they get to their hotel. "I'ma make sure your hands are tied good before mama gets on top and rides that big black dick, so you can't leave no marks on me like last time when I put it down on you too hard," Nikki teases, as she licks her lips slowly trying to entice Sin.

"Shit, ma, you ain't sayin' anything scary to a nigga of my caliber, fuck you mean!" replies Sin, as he leans forward and rests his forearms on the table before continuing. "But I been thinking lately that I wanna watch you fuck a bitch first, before we tag team her together, and maybe record that shit, ya feel me?" Sin says with a wicked grin on on his face, as he watches Nikki's face for a reaction.

She ponders about his statement for a second, and Sin can see the gears turning in her head, to see how much this request of his is worth and how much she can get out of him before she paints a smile on her face and rakes her nails down his arms slowly, causing goosebumps to break out all over his skin in anticipation. She turns her eyes to his and replies cryptically, "We'll see, Daddy," as their food finally arrives and they begin to eat, Sin excited for the rest of the plans to fall in place.

Chapter Twenty

Skyla

Skyla digs through her night stand looking for the last gram of cocaine from her stash that she swore she put here earlier, after she had chilled with Nikki. She sniffs and wipes her runny nose, as frustration begins to set in and she starts to toss things around the bedroom in anger, searching for her coke.

She hears her cellphone chirp from the bed where it lays buried under clothes and random stuff from her night table, as she ceases her frantic digging and retrieves her phone, seeing that it is a text from Nikki. Skyla unlocks her phone and scrolls to the text as she sees that Nikki is asking her if she's down with coming out to a hotel to entertain a man with her tonight, which she made sure to include being rewarded for afterwards.

Skyla isn't sure she is comfortable with fucking a stranger with Nikki, and is about to reply to her friend to tell her 'no', but as she begins to type her response, Nikki sends her another text that changes Skyla's mind. She sees Nikki added that he also has 'party favors', which generally means that he has drugs. Skyla is pretty sure it's cocaine, because until earlier, Nikki didn't even know that Skyla fucked with the 'white girl'.

She texts Nikki back, asking her if she is sure it's safe and gets an immediate response, telling her not to worry about anything, that they are going to be together the whole time anyways, and to get ready. Skyla heads to her closet, picks out an outfit of some black leggings and a blouse to show off her breasts, before laying it down on her bed and walking down the hall to Kian and Jermaine's shared room. She knocked on the door before opening it, Kian was sitting on his bed with the laptop. He looks up at her briefly with a questioning look, folded the laptop down and set it to the side, before walking over to her standing in the doorway. "Whas'sup, ma?" Kian asks, towering over her in the hallway.

"I have to go out tonight, so can you do me a favor and watch your brother and sister, please?" Skyla asks, looking at her oldest son and trying to curb her urge to rub at her nose, as her addiction rides her back.

"Why, where you goin'?" Kian asks, narrowing his eyes in annoyance at the request, as he shifts his stance and leans against the door frame, crossing his arms over his chest.

"Boy, don't worry 'bout what the fuck I'm doin'!" snaps Skyla irritably, causing Kian to scowl and shake his head in response.

"So, you tryna tell me not to worry about where you goin', even in case your safety becomes an issue?" Kian asks, making Skyla instantly feel bad about snapping on him.

She reaches out for a hug, which he reluctantly steps into. She hugs her son and softly tells him that she is going to take a shower and then go meet up with Nikki for a little bit to look for a job bartending.

"OK, I gotcha, ma," concedes Kian, as she steps away from him with a smile on her face and turns to head to the bathroom to get ready to meet up with Nikki.

As Skyla closes the bathroom door, she lets her smile slip off of her face, not happy about the fact that she just lied to her son so she can go out and do some THOT shit for some excitement and coke. She turns on the water and proceeds to bathe herself thoroughly before stepping back out of the shower and starting to apply her makeup in the mirror.

Her phone rings with an incoming call from Nikki. "Hello?" answers Skyla, placing her phone on speaker as she leans forward in the mirror and puts on mascara.

"Hey, bitch, where you at?" Nikki asks excitedly, as she giggles at something on her side of the phone.

"I just got out of the shower now, Nikki and I'm putting on my makeup," Skyla replies, as she purses her lips and coats her lips with peach flavored lipgloss.

"Okay, well just text me and let me know when you're ready so I can come get you, or you can drive here if you want," Nikki slurs into the phone, letting Skyla know that she is already tipsy, and has probably started the party well before asking her if she was free.

"Alright girl, I gotchu, just give me a couple of minutes to finish getting ready and you can come get me," Skyla says, hurrying out of the bathroom with her towel wrapped around her body, as she tip-toes down the hallway, the cold air assaulting her sensitive skin.

She selects a sexy black and pink matching bra and panties set and begins to get dressed. She puts on her black leggings, aquamarine colored blouse, and some Michael Kors sandals before spraying Chanel No. 5 perfume on her wrist and rubbing them together and on her neck. She texted Nikki to let her know that she is ready and asking if there is anything else that she should bring. Nikki texts her back telling her just to bring her sexy self and lets her know she will be there in 20 minutes to pick her up.

Skyla settles in to wait and begins to clean up her mess from earlier when she had torn up her bedroom, searching for her missing bag of cocaine while the minutes tick by slowly. She thinks about her decision to hang out with Nikki and her "friend" for whatever Nikki has in mind. Just as Skyla finishes putting the drawer back in the nightstand neatly, she hears a horn honk from the driveway and gathers her purse and phone before pushing out of her room, and passing Kian standing in the hallway of the foyer, looking out of the open front door in confusion as Nikki climbs out of the passenger seat of a shiny black Mercedes-Benz and stumbles her way up the walkway to the front door.

"Hey, nephew," Nikki greets drunkenly, squeezing his cheek, as Skyla rushes out the door before Kian could assess Nikki's drunken state and be able to ask countless questions.

"Thank you Kian, I'll be back later tonight," says Skyla, as she lets Nikki lead her to the car and climbs inside, where she finds a good looking dark-skinned nigga with braids sitting in the driver's seat.

Skyla looks back as the car backs out of the driveway, and is momentarily confused by the pure rage and hatred that she thinks she sees spread across Kian's face before he disappears from view, as the Mercedes bends the corner and pulls off into the dark street, shuttling her closer than she could ever know to the devil's most addictive pleasures...

Chapter Twenty - One

Kian

Kian stands frozen in place inside the open doorway as he trembles in rage at once again seeing the face of his father's murderer close enough to see the smirk plastered across his features. "What the fuck is moms and Aunt Nikki doing with that fuck nigga?" Kian rages out loud, as he spins around on his heels and dashes into the house, headed for Skyla's bedroom. He flings the door open hard enough to cause it to slam against the wall and he begins to tear through the dresser drawers, searching for Maniac's old black Glock .40 that he knows is still hidden within.

After searching frantically through the dresser for 10 minutes, he flips the mattress, and when that produces no results, he starts searching through the closet. After climbing on some boxes, Kian finally stumbles upon Maniac's gun, wrapped inside of his old Florida Marlins baseball shirt. He reverently brings the gun down from the hiding spot his moms had chosen to keep it and checks the magazine to make sure it is loaded. Kian counts 12 bullets in the clip, and for what feels like the first time in a very long time, he can feel the muscles in his cheeks stretching uncomfortably. He realizes that he is actually smiling, and he hasn't done that in a very long time.

He heads out of Skyla's bedroom, leaving it looking like it was hit by a Category 5 hurricane. He heads into the room he shares with Jermaine, startling his little brother as he was watching something on the laptop, still sitting on Kian's bed.

"What the hell, Key?" gasps Jermaine, as he shifts away from Kian's bed. Kian storms past him, and starts pulling a black hoodie and black sweatpants out of his side of the closet and begins putting it on over his clothes, before grabbing his backpack and snatching up his phone charger and stuffing it inside as he slings it over his shoulder and prepares to leave the house.

"I thought Mommy asked you to watch us?" asks Jermaine innocently, as he watches his older brother scan the room, making sure he is not forgetting anything important.

"She did, but you're in charge until I get back, J," says Kian seriously, his tone of voice leaving no room for argument.

"Ohhh kaaaay..." Jermaine responds, as Kian comes over and hugs his brother quickly, before dashing out of the room to go hug his baby sister Imani, who is watching cartoons in the living room, then heading outside the house and walking down the street.

He posts up on one of the corners on 12th Avenue South, pulls his hoodie down over his face as he leans against the building and proceeds to wait for his enemy's return.

Chapter Twenty - Two

Sin

Sin reclines against the headboard of the California King sized bed in the hotel suite and watches as Nikki circles her friend's hard nipple with her tongue, as she slides her fingers between her own wet pussy lips. The other bitch throws her head back and moans. Sin strokes his manhood as he watches the two women perform before him and he grins to himself in anticipation.

"First I fuck Maniac out of his product, now I'm going to fuck his wife!" Sin thinks to himself proudly, fascinated with the turn of events that led him to pulling up to the house where he gunned Maniac down almost two years ago, before he began his rise to the top.

Sin never knew that Nikki would ever give him such a spectacular gift that would make him want to fuck with her more than he already was as convenient pussy. That all changed tonight, when she agreed to give him a threesome and it ends up being his old business associate's wife.

"Ohh shit, Nikki..." Skyla moans, as Nikki continues her assault on one of her breasts, before switching to the other one and flicking her tongue across Skyla's areola, causing her to shutter in pleasure.

When they had arrived at the hotel, Sin had ordered room service and had some wine and Grey Goose delivered for the women, while letting Nikki casually coax her friend into submission before he produced the cocaine he knew they were both low-key craving. As they sucked up the lines, he watched as they both began to relax and become sensual, before eventually the alcohol and drugs took effect and they started rubbing each other down and kissing.

After they started rubbing each other down, kissing and getting freaky, he let them have control, since he already knew that Nikki wouldn't disappoint, and since he has the added benefit of being on the verge of fucking Skyla, Maniac's wife. He's sure that tonight will go down in his memory as one of the most memorable nights of his life.

He watches Skyla gasp and arch her back, as Nikki begins licking on her pussy from the front, making her close her eyes in pleasure. Sin realizes that he's been speeding up as he continues to stroke himself while watching the women play, which forces him to slow down and relax, before he busts too early and ruins his fun before it even gets started. Skyla pushes Nikki away and pins her down onto the bed before diving, face first, into her pussy and slurping up the wetness seeping from between her legs, and her puffy lips.

"Ohh shit, bitch!" Nikki hollers, as she grinds her hips against her friend's face.

She turns to smile wickedly at Sin and watches him play with his dick for a minute before bending toward him and putting his small dick into her mouth and sucking greedily.

"Shh-shhh," Sin gasps, while Nikki expertly works her mouth around his shaft as her hand juggles his balls and he feels himself begin to tighten up, signaling climax.

"Hold up, shawty, hold up," Sin begins to beg, not wanting to nut too soon, but Nikki shows no mercy, as she performs one more deliberate lick, causing him to explode in her mouth and leaves him gasping.

Sin reaches for a blunt already pre-rolled on the nightstand and lights it, while he watches the girls continue to eat each other's pussies, as they now settle into a comfortable 69 position while laying on their sides. He spends the next 20 minutes alternating between smoking and trying to jack his dick back to life, before finally giving up and searching through his Gucci backpack. Pulling out two triple stack ecstasy pills and popping them, he starts praying that they will kick in soon, and help a nigga out.

After about 10 minutes of a frustrated Sin trying to revive his lil' soldier, he finally gets him to stand at attention, puts a condom on before laying Skyla down on her back on the bed, and positioning Nikki on her hands and knees between them. He lines his dick up with Nikki's pussy and slides in. Sin begins fucking her from the back as Nikki eats Skyla's pussy.

Sin works himself into a frenzy as he clutches onto Nikki's hip and thrusts himself inside of her wet walls. After a couple of minutes of this, Sin begins to feel his balls tighten up as Nikki throws her ass back against him. The room is full of watery sounds, moaning and slurping. He orders the girls to switch positions and he can feel Skyla's nervousness as he prepares to enter her.

"It's cool ma, just relax," Sin instructs, as he shoves his dick inside her tight walls and begins to fuck her. Skyla lowers her head and eats Nikki's pussy as Nikki shoves her head deeper into her coochie and moans at the top of her lungs, egging her friend on as she tells Skyla how great it feels and how sexy it looks watching Skyla eat her out. It finally becomes too much for Sin to keep from holding back and he begins twitching and groaning, as he tries to fight off his climax. Nikki realizes what is happening, jumps up, and pulls his condom off, before sucking him dry, making sure not to miss a single drop, as Sin slumps over on the bed and promptly fights off a yawn.

"Aww hell nah, nigga! You're not going to sleep, you got to take us back," scolds Nikki, as she slaps Sin's shoulder and begins to shake him.

"A'ight, a'ight, shawty, chill, just lem'me collect my thoughts right quick," Sin grumbles, as he sits up on the bed and looks around for the bottle of Grey Goose to take a swig of.

"We're going to go shower and freshen up, then we'll be ready to go," instructs Nikki, as she grabs Skyla's hand and leads her into the bathroom to shower, closing the bathroom door behind her, leaving Sin sprawled out on the bed thoroughly drained and satisfied, as he sips from the bottle and begins to drift off again.

Chapter Twenty - Three

Skyla

Skyla shivers as she and Nikki climbs into the shower together. The water takes a second to heat up, while the women cower against the tile wall trying to escape the cold. Once the water heats up enough, they begin to lather each other up tenderly, before Nikki finally speaks up. "Well, bitch, what do you think?" she asks carefully, as she scrubs her arms with a wash cloth, waiting for Skyla's reply.

"I didn't expect anything amazing to happen once I saw what he was working with," Skyla says, referring to Sin's small dick, causing Nikki to burst out laughing .

"No lie, girl, but trust me it's worth it in the lonnng run," Nikki says, putting extra emphasis on the word 'long', trying to coax a smile out of Skyla. "Anyways Sky, that's not what I meant..." adds Nikki cautiously, knowing that since Maniac died, Skyla hasn't been fucking anybody.

"I know what you meant, Nikki," Skyla starts to say, before pausing to carefully consider her choice of words. "I think that it's been almost two years now since he died, and I need to start to re-emerge," Skyla finishes, surprising Nikki and causing her to experience a wave of happiness at being able to help her friend heal from the traumatic events.

"That's my girl!" Nikki exclaims with glee, as they finish their shower and step out to dry off, grabbing the big white, fluffy hotel towels off of the rack and patting their bodies down before wrapping up their hair.

Nikki bends over the counter and starts to re-apply her makeup, as Skyla heads out of the bathroom to grab their clothes. She walks into the suite and sees Sin passed out on his back in the huge bed and an involuntary smile takes over her face as she collects her and Nikki's clothes quietly.

"Mama's still got it!" Skyla thinks to herself, proud of the way her pussy's been putting niggas to bed, even after pushing out three children. She scurries back into the bathroom and closes the door silently before she starts getting dressed.

"Bitch, why you ain't wait for that, it's cold as a motherfucker in here now!" whines Nikki, as she pouts at Skyla and rubs her hands up and down her arms to warm herself up.

"My bad," says Skyla, grinning at her friend, as she starts to gather up the sample size shampoo and conditioner hotel bottles and stashes them in her purse to bring home.

They finish getting ready and Nikki saunters into the suite's bedroom and sighs in disappointment once she realizes that Sin couldn't keep himself awake. She pounces on him and Sin jumps in the bed, surprised to be woken up with a heavy weight settling itself around his pelvis, but relaxes once he sees that it's Nikki straddling his waist.

"Wake up, tired ass nigga!" she purrs playfully, and leans forward to kiss Sin on his neck.

Skyla's heart skips a beat in her chest as she remembers how she and Maniac used to act toward each other in moments like this, quickly pushing the thoughts out of her mind, not wanting to disrespect his memory at a time like this. Especially not right after the sexual acts that she just committed with another man. Skyla's keen eye didn't miss Sin's hand creeping carefully back from underneath the pillow resting beside his head. "Ohh, so he's a street nigga," Skyla thinks to herself in amusement, as she carefully logs this information in the back of her mind for future recollection, as Nikki drags Sin out of the bed.

"C'mon, daddy, we got places to go, and people to see," she sings, as she leads him by the hand to the pile of clothes so he can get dressed to bring Skyla back to her house.

"Okay, bitch, I got it," grumbles Sin, tiredly, as he begins to dress himself slowly, causing Nikki to huff and puff impatiently.

Sin finally gets dressed and they leave the plush hotel suite and climb into the beautifully comfortable interior of Sin's Mercedes-Benz as he presses the push start button and the German engine purrs to life. The sleek black vehicle glides over the highway, as they leave behind the gorgeous downtown scenery of City Place and burgler bars start popping up on the windows of businesses and churches, going down Tamarind Avenue, signaling the change from comfortable living into poverty as they enter the hood.

Nikki gives Sin directions on where to turn, but Skyla strangely notes that Sin seems to have already memorized the way to her house, almost as if he's been there before other than tonight. Skyla dismisses it as Sin being from the hood, relaxes when her house comes into view, and realizes that tonight is the first time she's left her kids home alone since the day their father was murdered.

This sudden remembrance causes her to yearn to hold her children, as she urges Sin to pull into her driveway already. After what seems like forever, he finally parks the car in the small driveway and leaves the engine running, as Nikki turns around in her seat and the women hug over the center console.

"Tonight was fun, Sky, make sure you hit me up tomorrow so we can make plans, okay?" gushes Nikki, as she kisses Skyla on her forehead, making her blush.

"I got you girl," Skyla replies, as she watches Sin smile at her in the rear view mirror. She opens her door and steps out. She then stood watching, as the Mercedes backs out of the driveway and slowly drove back down the street.

Skyla is about to head inside to relax, but before she could take a step, the sound of gun fire explodes into the night. She watches as the sleek black Mercedes-with Nikki inside-side swipes parked cars parked along the side of the road, as it takes fire from a building buried deep in the shadows of Dixie Highway.

Chapter Twenty - Four

Kian

Thunder and revenge fly from the barrel of Maniac's old .40 caliber Glock, as his son keeps his finger tight against the trigger, squeezing repeatedly.

Boom! Boom! Boom! Boom!

The gunfire echoes in Kian's ear like a firefight in Afghanistan as he watches the Mercedes side swipe a couple of cars parked on the far side of the street. He starts to run forward into the road to finish the job, but had to duck down to take cover when suddenly, someone in the back seat starts to return fire, Sin having jumped into the back as the shots started and the car crashed.

Boc! Boc! Boc! Boc! Boc! Boc!

The flash of the muzzle from inside the pitch black interior of the car illuminates Sin's face as he fires in Kian's direction with a monstrous looking pistol.

Boom! Boom! Boom!

Kian shoots back at his father's murderer over the hood of a parked car and hears glass shatter, followed by a woman's piercing scream.

He lets off a couple more carefully grouped shots before retreating off into the night, his gun almost empty and knowing that the police will be arriving in the area soon. He weaves his way through the hood's landscape from memory as he emerges into the backyard of his house and enters through the backdoor into the kitchen stealthily. He begins to creep around the doorway of the kitchen as he prepares to sneak his way down the hall to his bedroom, trying to pretend that he never left, but as he steps around the corner, his gaze locks onto the terrified face of his mother cowering on the floor behind the couch with his little brother and sister clutched to her chest.

Kian watches his mother's face as her fearful eyes take in his appearance all at once, from the sweaty, dirt stained black hoodie and sweat pants he's wearing, to the big, black, gun still clutched in his hand. As her eyes roam over him, she realizes what he's just done.

Kian stands stone-still and watches as if in dream, as his mom pushes Jermaine and Imani behind her protectively, and she storms towards him with fury blazing in her eyes.

"What the fuck did you do, Kian?" she screams, as she approaches him from the living room, still making sure to shield her two youngest children with her body, as if Kian is a demon, that has come to steal their souls.

"I did what I had to do," Kian states calmly, puffing out his chest and putting the gun in the small of his back, as his mother angrily stalks towards him gathering force like a storm.

"What the fuck you mean you 'did what you had to do'?! You're a little boy!" rages Skyla, as she attempts to slap the fire out of Kian, but only grows more angry when he easily evades the blow.

"Your Auntie Nikki was in that fucking car, stupid ass nigga!" Skyla screams, as she swings at Kian's stone cold face, trying to claw the heartless expression off of his face.

She screams in rage when he weaves her blow again. She begins to sob uncontrollably as she attacks him with both fists, swinging wildly. Kian gets tired of her assault after deflecting a couple swings and taking a few licks on his cheek and chin, he pins her against the wall and grabs a hold of both of her hands. He manhandles her hands against the wall and stares coldly into her eyes for a second, before he drops the bomb.

"So, I'm a 'stupid ass nigga' for shooting at the nigga that killed my pops in cold blood, right?" Kian asks, staring into his frightened mother's eyes momentarily, before he continues laying it all out for her. "The same nigga who killed your husband, is the same nigga you was just fucking with 'Auntie Nikki', stupid ass bitch!" Kian roars, as Skyla's eyes explode wide open from the shock as Kian releases her and steps back, his chest rising and falling rapidly from the emotions surging through his veins.

Skyla slides along the wall and crumples to the floor in horror as her mind races, replaying conversations with Maniac as well as with Nikki, as she had introduced Maniac to a lot of his people. She just couldn't for the life of her, remember anyone named Sin except for when Nikki introduced him to her. She *had* been the one to introduce them, she thought to herself, remembering vividly the situation.

"You're lying!" she screams suddenly, jumping up from her position on the floor and running back into the living room to grab her phone out of her purse, just not able to accept what could've been a set up by Nikki from the gate. "Get the fuck out! Just get out of my house, before I call the police on your ass!" Skyla screams, trying to unlock her phone to dial 911.

"You're going to find out the truth eventually," Kian spits venomously, as he backs away from her towards the back door of the kitchen.

He takes one last look at Jermaine and Imani hiding behind their mother, with terrified looks on their little faces and Kian's heart breaks at what has to be done to settle the score.

"When you find out the truth, you'll hate yourself! You won't be able to live with yourself, then you *really* gonna be on that dope! You shouldn't be able to forgive yourself for the rest of your miserable fucking life! You fucked your husband's killer!" Kian adds forcefully, one last time, before vanishing out the back door into the night, leaving an already struggling broken family, even more shattered in his wake, as Skyla, Jermaine, and Imani, stare through the open back door after him.

Chapter Twenty - Five

Detective Jones

After receiving a personal call from Captain Reider about the shooting in the middle of the street and hearing reports from the radio chatter, Detective Jones jumps into his squad car and burns rubber, racing to the scene. As he roars down I-95 with his concealed emergency lights activated and flashing in the dark night, he wonders if the shooting has anything to do with the recent influx of drugs being distributed throughout the hoods of Greenacres, Lake Worth City, as well as all throughout Palm Beach County and Martin.

He shakes his head and mentally clears his mind as he turns onto the off ramp on the 6th Avenue South exit, not liking to get into the habit of speculation when handling a case.

As Detective Jones approaches the crime scene, he looks out his side window at the dark-skinned man with braids standing next to a beautiful chocolate complexioned sista with a short pixie hair style, favoring Halle Berry's back in the day. As he sweeps his eyes over the couple a second time, looking more thoroughly, he notices that the man seems nervous with all of the police activity and almost seems to disregard the woman standing right next to him looking like America's Next Top Model. Even being attended to by the EMS medics, she *still* looked beautiful to him.

Detective Jones parks his car and climbs out, taking a couple of minutes to survey his surroundings, to get a feel of the energy that usually lingers after a crime has been committed. Jones doesn't consider himself clairvoyant or anything like that, but he's just always possessed a strong sense of clarity when it comes to crimes. He rolls his shoulders and pops his neck to relieve some of the stress he is carrying and starts walking over towards the traumatized couple.

"How are y'all doing?" Jones asks in a concerned tone, looking first at the woman, as she clutches her arm sniffling, then at the man, as he keeps a cold calm composure and stares right back into Detective Jones' eyes, almost as if he's issuing a challenge. Jones' internal radar starts going off from the man's standoffish demeanor, and he makes a mental note to check up on him later.

"OHMIGOD! It was crazy as fuck!" blurts the woman immediately, causing the man to shoot her a cold glare, which she apparently doesn't notice as she continues, "We had just dropped off my friend, and were heading back to our hotel, before the gunshots started," she says, as the man becomes visibly upset.

"Okay, so can you tell me your names, along with your friend's, so I can verify a few things?" Jones asks, pulling out his notepad, preparing to take notes for comparison later.

"I'm Nicole Lewis, and my friend's name is Skyla Hayworth," Nikki tells Detective Jones, as she continues to tremble, still scared to death about almost getting killed.

Once Detective Jones had written down the names that Nikki had just provided him, he turns towards Sin and the two men had a brief stare down while Jones awaits his name to come forth.

"I'd rather not get involved with your investigation detective," Sin tells Jones with a smirk as they stand in the middle of the street surrounded on all sides by police and EMS activity.

Detective Jones angrily slams his notepad closed, before taking a step toward Sin and invading his personal space. "That's fine, but I can take your ass to jail for impeding an active investigation," he threatens, as they stare at each other with malice.

Sin smiles at Detective Jones' statement before replying, "Actually, you can't detective, I'm a victim, not a suspect, and the law says that a private citizen doesn't have to divulge any of their personal information unless charged or suspected of a crime, so, I'm not hindering your investigation at all," he states confidently, not breaking eye contact. "So, unless you want my attorneys making a personal call down to your captain and filing a complaint against badge number 2743," Sin says, as his eyes travel to Jones' chest, looking at his badge, hanging from a necklace around his neck. "I'd suggest you make use of your title of 'civil servant' and go find out who the real perpetrator of this crime is, and stop badgering the victims," he growled, leaving Detective Jones steaming mad.

Detective Jones spins around and storms off, making Sin think he just won, but all he did is place himself firmly on Jones' radar. Detective Jones walks over to the black Mercedes-Benz still parked where it sideswiped the other cars and begins to write down the plate number and VIN number as he smiles to himself. "This nigga got me fucked up if he thinks I'm a donut munching pig," Jones thinks to himself, as he begins to settle into his comfortable role as investigator. He lets the crime scene envelope him, and searches through the wreckage of the Mercedes-Benz, looking for hints as to what transpired tonight.

He bags and tags fragments of bullets from the car door, and the casings he finds in the street to bring back to the lab once he is finished here. He starts to walk back over to the couple and stops in front of them, as he looks down at Nikki.

"Skyla Hayworth lives right over there, doesn't she?" Jones asks, surprising Nikki. She nods her head, yes, and he starts to walk off down the street, towards the small house at the end of the street. "Wait! Detective!" Nikki yells suddenly, stopping Detective Jones in his tracks.

"Yes?" he asks, turning around and expecting an afterthought, with a questioning look on his face.

"We've been here forever and I just want to lay down in the safety and comfort of my own bed," Nikki says with a pleading look on her face, as she stares at him. "Do you still need us or are we free to go?" she asks, standing up and brushing the hem of her skirt down against her thick, beautiful chocolate thighs.

"Well, as your gentleman friend has so kindly pointed out, you're not suspects, so yes, ma'am, y'all are free to go," he states with a smile, as he briefly looks over at Sin, before returning his eyes back to the lovely Nicole that he is now infatuated with and dying to know why she would be in the company of this ghetto street thug in a business suit.

"Thank you, detective," Nicole says, as Detective Jones turns back around and starts walking towards the home of Skyla Hayworth, the first time he's been back to this house in over two years.

Chapter Twenty - Six

Skyla

Skyla sits on the couch, sipping from a bottle of wine and smoking a joint, as she tried to collect herself from all the drama that ensued between her and Kian earlier. Not to mention the fact that she was starting to come to terms with the fact that she had been sleeping with the enemy. She had fallen for a trap that was so smoothly laid by her own friend and that devil tongued evil man. She jumps slightly as the doorbell rings, scaring her a little. She quickly put out the joint before getting up and creeping over towards the door cautiously. She stands off to one side of the doorway, not daring to peek through the peephole to see who it is.

"Who is it?" she calls through the door, standing off to one side and waiting for the person's response from the other side of the door.

"Miss Hayworth, it's Detective Jones with PBSO, I handled your husband's murder investigation a couple of years back," Detective Jones calls from the other side of the door, causing Skyla to panic and wonder why he's there. She opens the door and greets Detective Jones with, "Yea, I remember and you did such a bang up job of finding his killer too," she said ironically, while leaning against the door, blocking his view to inside of the house.

"Yes, I remember, how can I forget? What do you want, detective?" Skyla asks, as nonchalantly as she can, watching Detective Jones' eyes trying to peer around her to peek inside the house.

"I'm just here to ask you a couple of quick questions if you don't mind, Mrs. Hayworth," Detective Jones says, as he takes his notepad out of his breast pocket, along with his pen. "Do you mind if we step inside while I run through questions with you?" Detective Jones asks charmingly, as he attempts to step inside the open doorway, only to be blocked by Skyla's body, as she crosses her arms and shakes her head.

"We're fine right here," Skyla says sternly, staring at him as if he's crazy for trying her like she isn't aware of that dirty police tactic already.

"Okay, so I talked to your friend, Nicole Lewis, and she said that they had just dropped you off earlier?" Jones asks, as he prepares to write, looking at Skyla for confirmation to make sure what he just asked her is accurate.

"Yes, that's right, sir," Skyla says, as she places a hand against her chest and releases a deep breath in relief at hearing that Nikki is okay.

"Yes, they had just dropped me off and turned out onto 12th Avenue South, when I heard the shots and ran inside the house," Skyla says, remembering, seeing the flashes from the gunshots she now knew Kian fired.

"Okay, so once you got inside the house, what did you do?" Jones asks, pausing from writing and waiting for her to continue.

"I ran inside and grabbed my two youngest and we all took cover," Skyla tells him, trying to keep herself from shaking.

After asking Skyla a couple more questions about if she saw or heard anything in particular that she thinks would be important, Detective Jones finally puts his notepad away, signaling the end of the questions. "Okay, well that's all for now, you have a good night, Miss Hayworth," says Detective Jones, as he takes a step away from the door towards the driveway. "Oh, and just one more thing," he says, as if suddenly remembering, "Would you mind if I asked the kids if they could remember anything specific? You know how their minds are—," he adds, causing Skyla to narrow her eyes in irritation.

"My children are asleep, detective, and they've been through enough tonight, don't you think?" Skyla snaps, aggravated, cocking her hip and staring at him in annoyance.

"By the way, I noticed the strong scent of marijuana when you opened the door, and you know it has not been made legal for recreational use—" Jones starts to say.

Skyla cuts him off, "and unless you have a warrant detective, I suggest you continue doing such a fine job cracking down on the violence in the city, I see you've done such a great job so far..." she said ironically and with attitude, as she closes the door in his face, before heading back to her wine and weed, with a sigh of exasperation.

She takes a moment to sit and relax as she lights her joint back up and collects her thoughts, then takes a couple of puffs and sips her wine glass. She feels a sense of dread settle over her and finds comfort in her living room as she wishes Maniac was still with her. She can't put a finger on where the bad feelings are coming from, but being with Maniac toughened her up and conditioned her for tough living. One thing she remembers Maniac always telling her was that bad things always happen in threes.

Chapter Twenty - Seven

Kian

After Kian ran out the backdoor of his house that night, he watched all the activity at the scene of the shooting like the other people from the neighborhood. He made sure to stash Maniac's gun in some bushes in case his mom turned troll and told twelve what happened, which he doubts, figuring that all those years his dad had her, he would've at least conditioned her to be thorough. He watches the same detective that he talked to at the precinct the day his dad was killed, walk down the street to his house, after talking to Sin and Aunt Nikki, then snooping around the crashed Mercedes, collecting a few things too small for Kian to see. When Kian saw that Sin was alive, he knew he had to keep his cool until next time, because next time, Kian knew he wouldn't miss.

He releases a pent up breath of relief when the cop finally walks down the driveway and back over to where all the activity is at, goes back over, and takes another look at the Mercedes. As other spectators begins to fade off and return back to their homes, Kian follows their lead and slips off, heading over to Quan's house and knocking quietly on his window. He stands outside for a minute, quietly shifting from foot to foot and debating with himself about whether or not to tell Quan the truth about what him and his mom fought about and finally decides to tell him the truth, in case Skyla has already called Quan's moms.

He sees the curtains inside Quan's room shift and Quan's face appeared against the glass looking confused at finding Kian standing outside his room dressed in black. Quan opens the window after Kian motions him to hurry up and stares at him sleepily, before asking, "What's up, Key? Whatcha doin' out here, bruh?"

"Shit, I got into it with moms, lem'me in, nigga," Kian whispers, loudly enough for Quan to hear but low enough not to draw attention from the bedroom next door belonging to Quan's parents.

Quan sighs before telling Kian to hold up and disappearing from sight, heading through the back door in the kitchen. Kian walks around the back of the house and arrives around the same time Quan does, and the boys head back to Quan's room to settle in. Kian grabs a bunch of pillows and blankets out of the closet and spreads them out on the floor before getting comfortable and laying down. Kian sets the alarm on his phone for 5 a.m. so he can get up and get ready for school early, before Quan's moms wakes up and comes to wake him up for school like she's been doing for years.

§§§§

Kian jolts awake. The beeping from his phone wakes him up from a dream of Maniac reaching out for him from the floor with blood pouring out of his mouth. He creeps down the hallway and washes his face quickly before squeezing some toothpaste onto his finger and scrubbing his mouth quickly with it before rinsing and stepping out of the bathroom and heading back to Quan's room.

Kian puts the extra blankets and pillows away so Quan's moms won't be suspicious and climbed out the bedroom window. He waits for Quan to get ready, since his moms is bound to come make sure he's up for school. Once Quan leaves the house 15 minutes later, the boys walk down to the bus stop a mile or so away. At 6 a.m., the junkies were already up and traveling down the block and they passed multiple corner boys standing on the 12th Avenue South block, bustin' sales early in the morning. When they had walked enough to rub the sleep out of their eyes, Quan finally asks Kian to fill him in with what happened with his moms.

Kian thinks for a second and juggles the thought around in his mind about telling Quan the real truth about what transpired last night. As he weighs the pros and cons of the reasons he should or shouldn't tell Quan about him shooting at Sin in his mind, he comes up with Quan weighing heavily on the good side to be laced up, and slowly proceeds to fill him in from the beginning. Once Kian finishes lacing Quan up, his best homie turns to him with a serious look on his face. The boys stop in the middle of the street and look each other in the eyes.

Quan looks at Kian another moment before taking a deep breath and releasing it, as he reaches out his hand, "I'm with ya, bruh, since day one my nigga, you already know what it is bruh, *till the wheels fall off this bitch.*"

The boys shake up and clap each other on the back. "Say less, bruh," Kian says with a grin, as they continue to head for the school bus stop.

As they pass the corner where Kian had helped Glizzy, they both turn and look, as they see a shadow standing at the entrance of the cut, but as they look closer, they realize that it's not Glizzy and keep it pushing. They get to the corner and kick it with a couple of other kids there, waiting for the same bus for about 10 more minutes before they see the big yellow school bus with flashing lights start pulling down the block.

They board the bus once it stops, and the hydraulic doors slide open with a hiss. Kian and Quan head straight to the back and settle in on the fake leather seats as the bus pulls away from the curb. After a couple of more stops, they watch as one of the rich white kids they had run into when they picked up their schedules from the front office, climb on board from a stop down the street from a second hand looking used car dealership called *Reliable Rides*.

The white boy mugs them briefly before choosing an unoccupied seat a couple rows in front of them, and sitting down, after placing his backpack on the ground. He takes out the white iPod headphones and connects them to his phone before placing the buds in his ears and leaning back in his seat to relax for the rest of the ride.

The school bus makes two more stops, and at the last stop, a pretty blonde girl gets on and looks around, then spotting the white boy sitting three rows in front of Kian and Quan, listening to music on his phone, she smiles before walking down the aisle and sitting down next to him. The students talk, sleep, or listen to music, as the bus heads to John I. Leonard High School, and once it pulls into the bus loop and parks, they proceed out the opened doors and head their separate ways, going to the gym, the cafeteria for breakfast, or the courts to hang out.

Kian and Quan head to the courts to chill, and after about 20 minutes of bullshitting with a couple of other kids they met their first day, and talking for a while, Kian spots Isabella's pretty eyes, as she is walking in from the front of the school where parents can drop their kids off at the front office. He waves her over as she's looking around and from 20 feet away he can almost swear he catches her blush when their eyes meet and she acts shy before heading over his way.

95

"Good morning, shawty," Kian greets, as she smiles and gives him a hug, before whispering her good morning in reply. "What's up with you this morning?" Kian asks her, once they separate and stand there looking at each other in the courtyard of the school.

"Nothing much, just been chillin', ya know?" Isabella replies cutely, as she looks at Kian with her luminous hazel eyes.

"I feel you, I ain't been up to nothing spectacular either, but I'm looking forward to hitting the ground running today, ya dig?" Kian says, looking around for Quan and spotting him talking to an older kid named Luke, that was talking about joining the football team.

"Yea, I can feel that," Isabella replies, before catching sight of a freckled, red headed girl walking out of the cafeteria with a group of friends and waving at her.

The girl says something to her friends before leaving them to go their own way and walking over to Kian and Isabella. "Hey girl!" squeals the red head in delight before hugging Isabella quickly and standing back, looking at Kian with a welcoming smile.

"Jenna, this is Kian," Isabella introduces, while Kian nods his head and smiles as he is taken in by the red head.

"Hey, Kian," Jenna says grinning, as Quan finally finishes his conversation with Luke and walks over to the little group.

"Was'sup, Isabella?" Quan greets smiling, receiving a smile in return from her and turning to Jenna with a questioning look.

"Jenna, this is my homie, Quan," Kian says, introducing his 'day one' nigga to Isabella's homegirl, as the two of them take a moment to examine each other, before smiling in mutual acceptance.

They all settle into comfortable conversation, until the bell rings, signaling the first period. "A'ight, y'all. We'll see y'all later," Kian says to the girls, who wave as they head to their homerooms for the morning.

Kian and Quan walk with each other to their homeroom class, and Quan surprises Kian for a second when he brings up Isabella's homegirl, Jenna, "I think that girl fine as fuck, Key," Quan says with a grin, as they walk down the hallway and open their homeroom door before entering and sitting down at their desk.

"Yea, shawty fine, but you already know, I'm tryna shoot my shot at Isabella, ya feel me?" Kian says with a grin, as he takes out a notebook from his backpack and sets it on his desk. The teacher tells them to open their text books to chapter one.

"I already know bruh, Luke says all the hoes be sweating niggas on the squad! We could have our pick from the cream of the crop," Quan says with glee, as he looks through the textbook for the desired page.

"I already know bruh, but we'll see what's happening with that, just let me figure out this shit with moms, ya feel me?" Kian says, quietly hiding his face behind the textbook cover so the teacher won't see them talking.

"A'ight bruh, say less, I'ma think of something to help you out with this situation, ya feel me? You just gotta give me a lil' time to plot shit out," Quan says, as he finally finds his page and they settle in for the lesson.

"I already know, Q," says Kian, gratefully, thankful to have a nigga like Quan by his side when he's going through a tough time.

Chapter Twenty - Eight

Isabella

Isabella and Jenna sit next to each other in homeroom while Jenna fills her in on all the gossip, as she watches Isabella draw after they got done with the morning lesson. Once they get some free time, the girls chill and the talk eventually moves onto the two boys Isabella introduced Jenna to that morning.

"So, I'm saying, though," Jenna starts, looking at Isabella with a wicked grin. "That boy Kian is cute as fuck," she finishes, waiting on Isabella's reaction to gage if her friend has any intentions for him down the road.

"Yea...he is..." Isabella replies shyly, not looking Jenna in her eyes, but not being able to hide her smile either.

"So, what's going on with y'all?" Jenna asks, causing Isabella to pause from drawing and set her pencil down before answering.

"I don't know, I think he's cute and all, but we just met, ya know?" Isabella says, turning to look at Jenna finally.

"Well, you'd better hurry up and make a decision about wanting to fuck with him or not, girl. From what his friend, Quan, was talking about with that other kid, they'll probably join the football team this year," Jenna says, filling Isabella in from the little bits and pieces she overheard from Quan's conversation with Luke when she had walked over.

"Yea, so what?" Isabella asks, with a little attitude in her voice.

"Sooo...that means that once that happens, all these thirsty bitches are gonna start flocking all over them niggas," Jenna says dramatically, rolling her eyes at Isabella's naivety.

The bell finally rings and the class pack up their books and papers, and everybody scurries out the door heading to their next period class. Isabella and Jenna walk out of the classroom side by side, Isabella still thinking about what Jenna said about Quan and Kian probably joining the football team. Deep down she feels like she's already lost the opportunity she might've had with him since he doesn't seem like the type of boy who would go for a girl like her in the first place. Isabella has always envied the pretty and popular girls who just seem to naturally have all the right talents to accentuate their beauty. They split off from each other in the courtyard as Jenna heads to her next period class, which is math.

"Ughh, fuck my life, I hate math," Jenna complains, before rolling her eyes and stomping off, after waving goodbye to Isabella.

Isabella heads to the gymnasium and walks into the girls locker room to dress out for class. She finds a secluded bench to set her backpack down and she begins to change into her gym clothes as the rest of the girls talk and giggle around her. Once everybody is dressed, they all filed out the doors of the locker room into the gym. Their gym coach, Mrs. Mathis, tells them that they will be in the gym after logging in their times on running the mile, earning a chorus of groans and complaints.

The boys side door to the locker room opens and Isabella unconsciously catches her breath as her eyes land on Kian as he walks out the doors, towards the back of the crowd. She realizes that she's wearing the ugly school issued gym shorts and tries to hide behind some other girls as they all head pass the boys, lining up to do warm up exercises, but Kian spots her and inclines his head slightly in greeting. She acts like she doesn't see him and slides pass, quickly disappearing outside in the humid air of South Florida.

For the next 45 minutes, the girls gym class is stuck outside until finally their gym coach relents and lets them back inside the gymnasium, where they can cool off in the A/C until the bell rings.

§§§§

Isabella ends up playing some volleyball with some of the other girls, to her astonishment, her team won, about twenty minutes before the bell rang. They all head back to change clothes again and they talk about how good the game was. Kelsey, a pretty brunette tells Isabella that she should try out for the volleyball team.

"Yea, girl, you already know they going to put out a tryout sheet, you should definitely sign up," she compliments, making Isabella smile as they enter the locker room.

They dress out and Isabella walks out of the locker room, as she heads to her 3rd period class: science. As she walks down the hallway, she checks her phone for texts and prays that this period will pass quickly, so she can go to lunch. She finds a desk and unpacks her books and notepad as the teacher begins with the lesson. Isabella lets her mind wander off in thoughts of Kian, as she listens to the teacher talk about atoms. As her mind drifts, she wonders if her dad would like him, since he seems like such a straightforward kid and she grins at the thought.

She turns her textbook to the next chapter and starts working on the test the teacher hands out and settles in for the rest of the class.

Chapter Twenty - Nine

Kian

Kian shoots out of the classroom and heads toward the cafeteria for lunch to meet up with Quan as they leave different classes. He spots Quan standing by the lunch room doors and they dap each other up as they walk inside and get in line. They finally get their trays and discover that they're serving chicken fingers. They find a table and sit down to eat, and as Kian begins, Quan tells him that he's pretty sure he's come up with a solution to Kian's home problem.

"So, just come to school in the mornings and shit, then crash at my house at night, my nigga," Quan tells him, taking a bite of one of his chicken fingers, as they both run through it in their minds.

"Yea, but what about all them hours in between school and night time?" Kian asks, pointing out the obvious flaw in Quan's plan.

Quan shakes his head and tells Kian, "That's easy, my nigga, we join the football team," he says with a grin, as if staying after school once they make tryouts, and not having a ride is a simple fix to take care of.

"I told you, shit is complicated right now, bruh," says Kian with a groan at Quan's persistence about joining the football squad.

He looks around the lunch room, searching for sight of Isabella, as Quan begins to talk about the pros and cons of both of them joining the football team together again this year. Kian half-listens to Quan's preaching as he continues to search for Isabella while filling the appropriate "uhh, huh," or "I feel yous," when needed. He finally spots her across the lunch room with her friend Jenna as they near the end of the line to put in their lunch numbers and pay for their food. As the girls exit the line, Kian manages to make eye contact with Jenna and she steers Isabella over to Kian and Quan's table and sits down.

"Was'sup, y'all?" Kian asks smoothly, making both girls smile, and say hi back, as they begin to eat their food. "Damn, Isabella, I seen your ass in gym earlier, but it was like you was ducking a nigga or something," Kian teases with a grin, causing her to blush and shake her head in denial.

"Boy, bye, I ain't seen you, I was complaining about the mile," Isabella says, dipping her head and hiding her eyes from him, hoping he won't think she was ducking him for reals.

They all talked and kicked it for the next 20 minutes, before they all walk out to the courtyard, after dumping and stacking their trays. Quan ends up walking and talking to Jenna, and Kian smiles to himself, as he listens to his homie try to shoot his shot with her. The bell rings and they say their goodbyes before heading their own way to their classes to finish up the school day.

Kian walks to his English class and ends up sitting behind that same white boy that mugged him on the bus as he sat a couple rows in front of him and Quan on the bus. Kian overhears him talking to another white kid about seeing a Mercedes being brought over to a mechanic's shop with bullet holes in it the other day, when him and his father were picking up some cars.

After hearing this, Kian's ears are perked up and he feels like his heart is pumping a little bit faster because from the description of the man and his car, Kian knows that it is Sin. He makes a mental note of it and keeps an ear tuned for the white boy during the rest of the class and begins to prepare a reason to ask him about it later, when the opportunity presents itself. Kian focuses on his school work and waits for the bell to ring, as the time trickles slowly by.

He heads to his next class and he is in his own world as he thinks about his course of action the next time he crosses paths with Sin. He definitely doesn't want to make the mistake of letting him slither away again, or become aware of who it is that got beef with him. Kian thinks about where he can get some more bullets from since he is down to about five now since he had his shoot out with Sin. Glizzy comes to mind. He ponders over Quan's proposal about football and decides that, until he can come up with a better idea about where to stay at, it might just be the best bet. He doesn't just want to stop coming to school, since that will just send a truancy officer over to his mom's crib, looking for him, since he isn't 18 yet. He tries to come up with ways to make money in his mind and his thoughts turn to the metal Folgers can that he saw Skyla knock over that day long ago, after Maniac's funeral and decides that even though it's probably long empty by now, it's still worth checking out. He plans to go and check that out soon, when Skyla's not there and he is able to grab some more of his clothes without her noticing.

The final bell rings and he waits for Quan by the bus loop and they head to their bus, walk down the aisle toward the back, and sit down in their usual spot. The bus fills up and the same white boy from earlier sits in the seat in front of them and promptly puts his headphones in, after catching sight of Kian and Quan talking in their seat. The same blonde girl sits next to him, and they begin to talk. As Kian listens, he learns that the boy's name is James, and his father owns a business called *Reliable Rides.* Kian saves this information at the back of his mind for future reference and tells Quan about his change of mind about the football team and his reasons for switching his decision.

"I think that's smart though, for reals, bruh," agrees Quan, about not getting the truancy officer sent to his mom's house. "Ya moms is already on some bullshit, ain't no reason to add fuel to the fire any more, you feel me?" Quan adds, as the bus finally arrives at their stop and they get up from their seat and walk down the aisle and out of the doors.

They begin to walk down the block as the bus pulls off, and Kian keeps his head on the swivel for Glizzy, as they reach each corner where a hustler would post up at. Quan eventually notices Kian keeping his eyes on a constant sweep and asks him what he's looking for.

"Shit, I'm looking for Glizzy my nigga," Kian replies, once again looking around the corner and catching sight of a figure dressed in a black hoodie, True Religion Jeans, with Nike Infrareds on, leaning against a building, chilling.

Kian looks harder and recognizes Glizzy, before changing directions and heading over to his way with Quan. Glizzy looks over and catches sight of them and straightened up from against the wall, grinning and daps up Kian and then Quan.

"Was' good, y'all boys?" Glizzy asks, as they all post up on the corner.

"Shit, nothin' major, Big Bruh, just maintainin', ya feel me?" Kian says, looking at Glizzy.

"That's was'sup, bruh, and again, I appreciate you," Glizzy says, sincerely thanking him for helping him out when he was getting jumped by the basers.

"It ain't even no problem," Kian says, "Yo, what you do about that anyways?" Kian asks Glizzy.

Glizzy looks around briefly before showing Kian a Glock .40 caliber with a 20 round magazine tucked behind a red Gucci belt with a gold buckle.

"I got the same one at the crib," laughs Kian, disbelieving at his luck with having Glizzy have the same twin of his gun that he needs the bullets for now.

"Say bruh, you wouldn't happen to have extra bullets would you, bruh?" Kian asks, admiring the extension of the magazine.

"Yea, we got boxes of that shit at my uncle's spot, Lil Bruh, what y'all up to right now?" Glizzy asks, making Kian and Quan look at each other, before looking back at Glizzy and shaking their heads, letting him know they weren't on nothing for the rest of the day.

"A'ight, that's was'sup, just lem'me holla at my uncle to see if he's free to head our way," Glizzy says, pulling out his phone and dialing Dice.

"Yeo, Unk, I got the lil homies out here tryna pick up some stones for the slingshots," Glizzy says, joking into the phone. "Yea, it's dry out here, so I'ma just come back to you then," he adds, before hanging up and putting his phone back in his pocket. "Shit, we can just head over to your spot to drop your bags off and walk over to my spot after," Glizzy says, as they start heading back down the street to Quan's house.

Once they arrive, they go around the back and Quan brings his and Kian's books inside the house after putting them in his backpack. Kian slips around the house and grabs his pistol that he had stored in the bushes and puts it in his backpack, walking over to where Glizzy is standing, still waiting for Quan to come back from inside. As Kian rounds the corner, Quan opens the door and steps out, before Kian reaches them. They walk off from Quan's house and head to Glizzy's house. "So, what you lil niggas be doin' in ya free time, when you ain't in school?" asks Glizzy, as he looks down at his iPhone 14 Pro and scrolls through his music playlist, pressing play.

"All these niggas fallin' off, they ain't fallin' back," a voice croaks from the speakers as they turn a corner, Glizzy points to.

"I just be chillin' for reals, but we usually play football," Kian says, nodding his head to the music.

"I ain't become who mama want me to be, but I told her just love me for me," the voice playing from Glizzy's phone raps, striking a cord in Kian.

"Yo, who is that?" Kian asks, pointing to Glizzy's phone in his hand.

"That's that nigga Mozzy," Glizzy says with admiration in his voice, nodding his head to the beat as well.

"I'ma gangsta," Mozzy raps, as they reach the end of the block and Glizzy leads them to the plain yellow house. They walk pass a weight bench sitting on the front lawn as they approach the door. Glizzy leads them inside, and as he opens the door, Kian and Quan are instantly hit in the face with the strong potent cloud of Kush smoke and the sound of rap music blaring in the backroom.

They walk inside and Glizzy leads them into the living room, introducing them to Glizzy's Uncle, Dice and two of his Zoe Mafia Affiliates homies, Haze and Draco, who are sitting on the couch, passing the blunt around and talking about the problem with the chicos that happened earlier.

"What's good, Neph?" asks Dice, as he and Glizzy dapped each other up and he turns to look at Kian and Quan, standing behind him.

"This Kian and Quan, bruh, they was there that day I got jumped, and helped a nigga out," Glizzy says, reminding Dice about the two young boys that had been around that day.

"Oh, word! That's what's up, I appreciate y'all for looking out for my family," Dice says, dapping up Kian and Quan, before turning back to Glizzy and asking about the bullets he had called about earlier.

"So, what y'all need, lil' bruh?" Dice asks looking at Kian, who takes his backpack off and takes out Maniac's .40 caliber Glock model 22.

"They got the same shit as mines," says Glizzy, as he heads towards the kitchen and digs around under a corner tile against the refrigerator, returning with a box of hollow points.

Kian takes the magazine out and Glizzy hands him a black bandana, Kian proceeding to refill the clip the rest of the way up with fresh ammunition. Once he finished, he tries to hand Glizzy back the box, but Glizzy waves him off. "I got a lot more bruh, keep that."

"That's was'sup," Kian says, as he slips the box into his backpack and zips it close.

"Yo, lem'me see that hammer, lil bruh," asks Dice, once Kian has slipped the magazine back into the receiver.

Kian pauses for only a second, and looks at Dice as the room seems to slow down around them awkwardly.

"No disrespect, OG, but I don't hand anybody my pistol," Kian replies wisely, as he looks at Dice and his two homies sitting on the couch with their weapons close by at hand.

"That's the right answer, lil bruh," Dice says with a grin, before turning to look at Glizzy and asks him where he found these boys at.

"Shit, they Dub City material," Glizzy replies, nodding his head at Kian, directing him and Quan to take a seat and chill.

As they chill and talk, Dice asks them what type of shit they be into, and they tell him that they been playing football.

"My pops used to always make us play, since 'Red Light-Green Light'," Kian says smiling, reminiscing about the times Maniac used to bring him, Quan, and Jermaine to football practice.

"What your pops name is?" Dice asks, causing Kian to pause for a second, something not missed by Dice, but still telling them his dad's name was Maniac.

"He got killed two years ago," Kian says, as he shakes his head and sends a vow up to the sky once again promising vengeance against Sin.

"He was a tall dark-skinned nigga with a fade?" Dice asks, knowing exactly who Kian's dad is, having done prosperous business with him before, and having known him for a long time.

"Yea, that was my pops," Kian replies.

"My condolences, lil bruh, I knew your pops personally, and he was always a good nigga in my eyes," Haze says, as Kian nods his appreciation in his direction.

"That shit was fucked up about how he got shot in his crib," Dice says, remembering hearing about Maniac's death through the grapevine in the streets, and feeling sad about his passing.

They all chill and vibe some more and Kian ends up smoking a blunt with Glizzy and Quan, as they kill zombies on call of duty. It starts getting late, and as Kian and Quan prepare to leave. Dice stops them and tells the boys that they are welcome over any time, and to holla at him or his nephew if they ever need anything. They dap Glizzy and Dice up and Kian and Quan walk back to Quan's house. Kian hides the gun in the bushes as he waits while Quan walks inside to see what his parents were up to. When he comes back out, he brings Kian a bottle of Raspberry Kool Aid and some Jalapeno Cheetos from inside since they both got the munchies off the weed they smoked with Glizzy.

"I ain't wanna leave you out here without nothing to eat, ya feel me?" Quan states, handing Kian the items.

"Thanks Q," Kian says, as he unscrews the the cap from the bottle and drinks some of the Kool Aid.

"They still up chillin' in the living room, bruh, so when they go back to their room, I'll let you know," Quan says, filling Kian in, before promising that it probably wouldn't be long before that happened and headed back inside the house.

Kian prepares to settle in for the wait until Quan gives him the OK, and he takes out his phone, messaging Jermaine on Facebook, "Aye lil bruh, lem'me know when the coast is clear so I can come holla at you," Kian types, before pressing Send, then scrolling through Facebook for a while, looking at people from school post about lame shit, hoping that Jermaine will message him back soon.

He sees an Isabella Perrelli pop up on his newsfeed for people he may know and sends her a friend request before his phone chimes, and he sees that he's just received a message from his little brother Jermaine.

110

"Moms in her room, she been in there all day since I got home from school," Jermaine says in his message, as Kian reads and replies, telling him to open the bedroom window so he can climb in.

Kian puts his phone back in his pocket and walks across the street to his house, before circling it and arriving at the back. He knocked at the bedroom window he shares with Jermaine. He sees the top of Jermaine's head pop up, waving in Kian, once he had unlatched the window. Kian climbs up into the room as quietly as he could, and him and Jermaine hug each other.

"How you been, Jay?" Kian asks his little brother seriously, as he searches through his drawers, looking for socks and boxers, before heading to the closet and picking out a couple fits for school.

"Shit, I'm okay, Key, moms just been actin' weird since y'all fought and it's starting to get to Imani since she's a girl, ya know?" Jermaine says, making Kian feel bad for putting stress on his baby sister over his beef with his moms.

"Damn, bruh, that's my bad, but I can't take anymore of that bullshit moms been doin'," Kian says, referring to Skyla's drug use that's making her lazy around the house as well as with her own kids.

"It's worse," Jermaine says sadly, dropping his head in shame, before telling Kian about hearing Skyla on the phone with Aunt Nikki, checking up on her, and promising to come see her soon.

"What the fuck she wanna hang out with that thot so bad for?" Kian asks angrily, before Jermaine interrupts him.

"That's not it, bruh," he says quietly, then tells Kian about how after Skyla got off the phone, he heard her sniffing loudly from inside her room, behind her closed bedroom door.

"So, I know what she was back there doing, obviously," Jermaine says, breaking Kian's heart again, over the deterioration of his family ever since Maniac's death.

"What's in the kitchen?" Kian asks, as he tiptoes out of the bedroom, down the hallway before looking in the fridge and finding it empty except for a half a gallon of milk, an old loaf of bread with green fuzzy mold on some of the slices, and a bag of hard ass baby carrots in the crisper.

He shakes his head and riffles through the cabinets, looking for something to take with him and has to settle for a couple of cans of *Campbell's Chicken Noodle Soup*, the white people's cure for everything. There is very little there, the cabinets are bare. He closes the cabinets and looks around the kitchen for the Folgers coffee tin and ends up finding it in another bare cabinet. He takes it down and shakes it once before opening it and isn't surprised to find that it is empty as well. He sighs in frustration and creeps back down the hallway to the bedroom, where Jermaine is waiting for him by the door.

"So, where the fuck you staying at now?" Jermaine asks, once they close the bedroom door, so their voices won't alert their moms of Kian's presence in the house.

"Shit, I'm at Quan's at night right now, but I got some options I'ma explore once I get a chance, ya feel me?" Kian says cryptically, thinking about Dice telling him to let him know if they needed anything.

"Oh, word? That's good, Key," Jermaine says, happy that his brother isn't completely on the streets without somewhere to lay his head. Jermaine fills Kian in more about what's been going on at home with moms and Imani, before telling him about what he's been doing in school. "I'm thinking about trying out for the football team at school," Jermaine says, bringing a smile to Kian's face, remembering how excited Jermaine would be when Maniac would put the money together for his sons' jerseys.

"That's a good idea, Jay," Kian says enthusiastically, as he prepares to leave and Quan texts him, letting him know that his parents just went to their bedroom to get ready for bed.

"Yea, but I asked moms for the money for the jersey and she said that she ain't got it right now," Jermaine says sadly, as Kian grits his teeth in anger at how deep his moms has fallen in two short years.

"Don't worry, Jay, I got some irons in the fire right now, I'll see what I can do," promises Kian, as he and Jermaine dap each other up and he climbs back out the window, creeps around the side of the house, and crosses the street, heading over to Quan's window and knocking.

Quan's head pops outside and he tells Kian to meet him at the back door. Kian walks around back and Quan leads him quietly through the house to his room, where the boys pull out the extra spare pillows and blankets out of the closet for Kian to use on the floor. Once they are settled, Kian makes sure his early alarm for school is set before rolling over and preparing to go to sleep.

As he lays there on the floor, his mind races and turns over the conversation he had with Dice today about his pops, and wonders if Dice is trustworthy. Before Kian drifts off to sleep, he comes to terms with the fact that he doesn't really have anybody he can trust if he wants to move forward with getting his shit together and fulfilling the promises he made to his little brother about helping him get his football jersey.

He finally decides to take a couple days before stepping to the big homie and asking him to take a chance on a young nigga trying to get his weight up. Kian goes to sleep with dreams of the glorified hood fame running through his mind and could almost swear he felt Maniac's presence smiling down on him with love.

Chapter Thirty

Sin

Sin sits in his traphouse in Greenacres with three of the members of the Cuban Y-Lo Gang, or the Young Latin Organization, as they were also known, as they talk about prices of the guns Sin is buying them. Rampage, the highest ranking member of the group, tells Sin that his baby momma's uncle has two FNs and three Dracos for sale, knowing that her uncle will give them a deal.

"I ain't worried about the price tag lil bruh, I'm just tryna find out where these shots originated from, ya feel me?" Sin says, Rampage nodding his head in the affirmative. He looks over at PJ and Swindle, and they begin to explain their plan for combing information out the streets.

"The only hate being thrown your way, big bruh, came from either ZMA or Maniac's people," Swindle states, looking at PJ for confirmation.

"Ain't no other way, unless you got more past beefs," PJ throws in, as they sit in the living room theorizing.

After Sin and Nikki left from where the shooting went down at, while in one of Cien Fuego's people's whips, they pulled up to the hotel for the night and Nikki got herself drunk in hope of getting over the trauma. After Sin fucked her to sleep, he made plans with Cien Fuegos to pull up to his spot in the afternoon, to lace him up in person, not wanting to speak about business over the open line.

When they woke up in the morning, Sin dropped Nikki off along the way, as he headed to Grove Custom Auto mechanic shop in Delray Beach, to chop it up with the plug. He walked into the office and leaned up against the wall until Cien Fuegos finished his conversation with a middle-aged white man dressed in a shirt, slacks, and tie.

The men pause, and Cien Fuegos addresses Sin. "Amigo, this is Mr. William Deckard, he owns *Reliable Rides*."

Sin nods his head in greeting, "I may be able to hook you up with some wheels," Mr. Deckard suggests, handing him a business card from a stack secured by a gold monogramed money clip. "You're very lucky to be alive, sir," says, Mr. Deckard, looking at Sin. "It's not that often that people survive that type of violence. I was in the Armed Forces, so I know combat and how hard it is to walk away unscathed."

"My pops was in the Corps and he showed me how to shoot a gun, ya feel me?" Sin replies with a smirk, before turning to look at Cien Fuegos.

"How long is it going to take to have the body work and shit finished?" he asks.

"At least three weeks," says Cien Fuegos.

Sin groans and tells the white man he would give him a call later when he got back to his house and tied up some loose ends. Once he left the shop, after talking to Cien Fuegos, when Mr. Deckard and his son were gone, they came up with the idea to hire some young local killers to keep their ears to the street, which led Sin to link up with part of the crew that had a big hood around Greenacres, who were sitting around the table in his trap scheming.

"I'll have my homies look into that situation for you ASAP, bruh," says Rampage, pulling his phone out of his pocket and telling someone on the other end what to look for. He hangs up the phone and looks at PJ. "Wack-O is heading out with the squad now, we'll meet up with them later," Rampage states, before turning back to Sin, "So, what's the job paying?"

Sin thinks for a minute before calling Latoya from out of the kitchen and instructing her to bring him the Louis Vuitton bag from his room. When she returns, he opens the bag and counts out $15,000 dollars and places it in front of the hungry killers.

"Divide this up however y'all gon' do it with ya crew," Sin says, placing the bag back into Latoya's waiting hands and they all watched her ass cheeks jiggle as she sashays away.

"A'ight, that's a bet," says Rampage, dapping up Sin, as they put it in their duffle bag. "We gon' holla at you when we know some more, Big Homie," Rampage adds, as he, PJ, and Swindle take the bag to the whip, and the three of them prepare to leave and hunt their target.

"I got you," Sin replies, as they head out the door and the sound of an engine revving and wheels peeling out can be heard from inside the house where Sin is sitting. He dials Cien Fuegos's number and when he answers, he tells him that he placed an order for take out from a Chinese restaurant around the area, letting Fuegos know that the wolves are on the trail about the situation they had discussed while at the shop.

"Tha's good, my friend, so all we need to do is sit back and they will come to us," Cien Fuegos says enthusiastically, before they make plans to meet back up to see how their newly acquired block has been turning a profit, after Sin picks up some new wheels to slide in.

Sin hangs up and pulls the card for *Reliable Rides* out of a stack of papers and various cigarillo foil packs from the table, and dials Mr. Deckard's direct number. Once he picks up, Sin reintroduces himself and they got down to the business of discussing what type of ride he is looking for. "I want something with a luxurious quality and feel to it that's not too ostentatious," Sin explains, causing Mr. Deckard to pause on the other end of the line as he scrolls through his mental inventory list.

"Well, since we both are connected to our mutual friend, why don't you come over and I'll show you some options that I think you'll like," Mr. Deckard offers.

Sin agrees and they make plans for a 4 p.m. and Sin hangs up the phone, as he leans back in the chair, rubbing his temples. "Latoya!" Sin calls, bringing the beauty back into the room, to stand by the chair and look down at him.

"Yes, daddy?" she asks cutely, batting her eyelashes at him.

"You got anything to do for the next couple hours?" Sin asks, as he searches through the stack of papers on the table for the keys to her car. Latoya gets a wicked grin on her face before lowering herself to her knees and fumbling at his belt buckle.

"Just you, daddy," she replies lustfully, before pulling out his dick and sucking it into her salivating mouth, causing Sin to groan and lean back into his chair as she begins to take him up to heaven.

Chapter Thirty - One

Kian

Kian wakes up as his alarm beeps on his phone, and after yawning and rubbing his eyes for a couple of seconds, he forces himself up and into the bathroom to wash his face and brush his teeth. As he returns from the bathroom, he gets dressed and wakes Quan up, before slipping outside to wait for Quan to go through the daily routine of his moms coming in to wake him up. After Quan is finished getting ready for school and walks outside, the boys head down the street, headed for their bus stop. As usual, life continues to show that activity on the block never stops, as Kian and Quan watch the hustlers catching sales early in the morning from junkies, neither of them having gone to sleep yet. They get to their bus stop after checking for Glizzy at his usual corner. Not spotting him, they end up having to wait for the bus with a couple of other kids who go to their school. Kian watches as a couple of boys with dreads roll up a blunt and prepare to smoke as they wait for the bus to arrive. They finish rolling up and light the tip when they notice Kian watching them and one of them asks if he smokes.

"Yea, I smoke," Kian says, walking over to join them, waiting for his turn as the blunt gets passed around. Once it got to him, he takes a slightly bigger hit than he intended, and ends up swallowing the smoke, causing him to cough, and the two stoner kids smoking next to Kian start to laugh.

"Damn, bruh, I thought you said you smoked before," one of the kids teases as he laughs, watching Kian cough uncontrollably with tears streaming from his eyes.

"I do, bitch," Kian rasps angrily, as he pounds a hand against his chest trying to fight through his coughing fit.

He finally gets himself under control and takes a couple more hits from the blunt before they hear the bus coming from down the street and watch the flashing of its lights. Kian hands the blunt back and they put it out before spraying some Axe Bodyspray on themselves and climbing up the steps of the bus, once it pulled up, heading back to their seats to chill.

Kian feels extra high as he stumbles down the center aisle of the bus before falling backwards into his usual seat at the back of the bus with Quan taking the open seat across from him.

"You good, Key?" Quan asks, looking at Kian's red half-closed eyes and shaking his head, trying to suppress a grin.

"Yea, I'm cool," Kian replies, slowly trying to nod his head against the seat, but having trouble doing so.

"I think you're turning into a pothead," Quan says, laughing at Kian's antics as he watches him roll his head across the back of the seat, listening to the squeaking sound it makes.

"Shit, I'm okay with that," Kian says, happily, pausing briefly before adding, "this shit is great!" causing Quan to laugh.

"Now you sound like Tony The Tiger, bruh," Quan says, as they watch the bus pull up to *Reliable Rides* and the white boy, James, Kian had heard talking the other day, walks into the bus. James looks at Kian and Quan disdainfully, before taking his usual seat and putting on his headphones.

"I feel frosted," Kian mumbles, as he looks out the window of the bus looking at the cars on display at the *Reliable Rides* parking lot.

The bus pulls off and the students all drift off to sleep, talk and chill, or listen to music for the rest of the ride while they wait to get to school. When the bus pulls up into the bus loop and the doors hiss open, they exit and all go their separate ways. Kian and Quan follow a crowd of people into the cafeteria and go through the breakfast line, receiving pancake sticks with syrup, a banana, box apple or grape juice and either white, chocolate, or strawberry milk. Kian chooses strawberry and apple, while Quan chooses chocolate and grape. They type their lunch numbers into the computer and receive free lunch program receipts, which they throw into the garbage container against the wall by the tables.

They choose an empty table and sit down to eat. Once they're settled, they open their milks and Kian begins to devour his pancake sticks, dunking them into his strawberry milk before swiping them through the thick imitation maple syrup and chomping down. Within seconds, the four breakfast sticks are nothing but a memory, which left Kian looking at his tray mournfully, wishing for more. He looks over to the food line, and sighs, seeing that it's closed, before looking back down at his empty tray and then turning his gaze to Quan's.

"Don't even think about it," threatens Quan, making Kian grin at his day one nigga. "So, sign-ups for football and shit is today bruh, you going, right?" Quan asks, anxiously biting down on a pancake stick and chewing thoughtfully.

"Yea, what the fuck else I got to do?" Kian asks, causing Quan to shrug while he eats.

They throw their trays away, and head to the gym to talk to their gym coach, Mr. Garrett, about joining the team. As the boys exit the lunchroom and walk through the open courtyard, they pass a group of white boys standing next to the gym entrance with baseball, football, basketball, wrestling, and even some with track gear, talking. Kian and Quan passes by them to enter the gym, and the group suddenly pauses the ongoing conversation. Kian can feel the stares being aimed at him from the inside of the circle. They

121

pass by in awkward silence and head down the hallway to the men's locker room entrance, walking inside. They knock on the office door, and wait for an answer. After a couple of seconds, Mr. Garrett opens the door and stands in front of them imposingly.

"We're here for the football signups," Quan states excitedly, looking at Coach Garrett with a hopeful light in his eyes.

"Tryouts are in two weeks, but you can put your names down now so you can be at the front of the line," Coach Garrett replies, handing Quan the clipboard.

They put down their names on the last couple of lines available on the clipboard.

"Okay, so you guys are good, just come back in two weeks for tryouts after school," Mr. Garrett says, as he turns around to put the sign-up clipboard back on the desk inside the office.

"Okay, Coach, we'll be there," says Quan, as he practically drags Kian out of the locker room and down the hall.

"I don't know if I'll be able to buy my jersey, Quan," says Kian, as they walk down the hall to their homeroom classes.

"Just chill, bruh, we got two weeks to figure shit out, you feel me? Shit will fall into place," Quan says confidently, strolling down the hall.

"I promised Jermaine that I'd buy his jersey too," Kian adds, forcing Quan to stop in the middle of the empty hallway to turn and look at Kian.

"Bruh, we have two fucking weeks to put something together, okay?" Quan says, seriously, as he stares at Kian, forcing him to look into his eyes.

"All you have to do is figure out what to do in the afternoons after school until tryouts start, and we can come up with an excuse to be at my house late-night," Quan adds, causing the wheels to start turning inside Kian's mind, forcing him to develop a plan.

"You right, I'll figure out something with Glizzy and them so I can get the jerseys," Kian says out loud.

"It's a start, bruh," replies Quan, shrugging briefly, before turning and beginning to head to his homeroom class.

"A'ight, so let's meet up at lunch to go over the basics, so we can have shit established when it's time," Kian says, as he and Quan dap each other up and head their separate ways to their different classes, already eager to get this day at school done and over with.

Kian sinks into his own thoughts as he passes by groups of students mingling in the hallway, talking with friends or waiting to skip class when the bell rings, as he thinks about his next course of action to help himself progress and to make sure his family is always going to be secure.

Chapter Thirty - Two

Isabella

Isabella stands next to Jenna at the snackline counter, while Jenna looks at the display board, "So, can I have two pretzels with cheese, two Minute Maid drinks, and two nutty bars, please?" she asks, handing over a $10 bill and receiving her change back, along with her purchases.

The girls leave the line and head outside to sit under a pavilion in the courtyard to eat. They pass by the tables and wave and smile to different friends, as they walk towards the exit. Once outside, they cross the courtyard and walk underneath the pavilion into the shade and sit down at the blue plastic picnic table. Jenna passes Isabella a pretzel with its cheese sauce, a Minute Maid drink, and a nutty bar, before taking the cap off of the cheese sauce container, dipping the edge of her pretzel and taking a bite. Isabella watches her friend chew the pretzel with delight as she unwraps her nutty bar and nibbles one of the wafers.

"So, what'cha been up to?" Jenna asks, between bites of her pretzel, which she dunks into the cheese sauce and continues to devour.

"Nothing much, I've just been dealing with my dad's job transfer, so now he works nights so I'm just chillin' at home five nights a week," Isabella says, taking a sip from her drink.

Ever since her dad got laid off from his hospital job as an RN, he's been working at JFK Trauma Clinic with shitty hours and pay, leaving Isabella home alone a lot more often.

"What are you sad for, girl? That's good news!" Jenna says excitedly, practically bouncing in her seat.

"Why?" asks Isabella, confused as she waits for her friend to get done dancing on her side of the table.

"Becaaauseee," Jenna sings dramatically, "we can have sleep overs at your house, and then go out to parties," she says, grinning at Isabella.

"I don't know anybody that's been throwing parties," Isabella said, as she shakes her head.

"My parents won't even care if I stay over at your house, so we'll be able to go out," Jenna continues, not hearing Isabella. Jenna asks what days Isabella's dad goes to work, and Isabella tells her that he's only off Sundays and Mondays, so the window is always open for her to stay over.

"There's going to be a party this weekend that we can go to," Jenna says, looking over at Isabella and measuring her briefly before adding, "We'll have to get you some clothes and shit, though."

As they continue to sit and talk, Isabella spots Kian and Quan walking out of the cafeteria. She smiles and waves when Quan looks over and sees her and Jenna sitting at the table, before grabbing Kian's arm to catch his attention. The boys walk over and receive hugs, before sitting down at the table and joining the conversation.

"What y'all out here doing?" Kian asks, looking at Isabella, causing her to blush and look at Jenna for help.

"Nothing, just trying to figure out how we're going to get to the party this weekend," Jenna replies coyly, batting her eyelashes at Quan flirtatiously.

"What party?" Kian asks, looking around the table confused.

"There's a party going on at some kid named Aaron's house, who is a sophomore and has been on the baseball team since he came to John I. Leonard High," Jenna says, filling them in.

"I think I heard something about that earlier," Quan says, trying to think back and remember what he thinks he overheard about it.

Kian looks from Quan, over to Isabella before asking, "So, you going, or nah?" causing her to freeze up, surprised.

"I don't know yet-" Isabella begins to say, before Jenna interrupts her, saying, "Yea, we're going, I'm going to stay over at her house and we'll get ready there, we just need a ride."

Isabella looks over at Jenna, exasperated at her for forcing her into going to a party with Kian, but deep down, she knows that if Jenna wasn't doing it, then she would never gather the confidence to do it herself.

"Shit, let me see what I can do and I'll let y'all know," Kian says simply, as he stands and the 5 minute bell rings, letting students know that they have 5 minutes to get to class.

"Okay, just let us know," Jenna says cheerfully, before grabbing Isabella's hand and jerking her away from the table, leaving Kian and Quan standing behind, watching them scurry off.

"Jenna! What the hell?" snapped Isabella, finally yanking her arm free from her friend's vice-like grip.

"Sorry," Jenna says, watching Isabella rubbing her sore wrist from Jenna's tight grip.

"This could be your chance to get him," Jenna says suddenly, spinning around to look at Isabella.

"What?" Isabella asks, looking cautiously at Jenna, as if she's lost the rest of her marbles.

"Kian, bitch! This could be your chance to get with Kian!" Jenna repeats her intent, crossing her arms over her chest and looking at Isabella with a scrutinizing glare, making her want to squirm.

"He doesn't even like me," Isabella argues, following Jenna to their classroom at the end of the hallway.

"Yea, he does. Why the fuck you think he's always checkin' for you?" Jenna puffs, as she opens the door and they walk inside, taking their seats.

"You just wanna hang out with Quan," Isabella says, trying to poke holes in Jenna's logic so she doesn't feel obligated to go to the party.

"Yea, so what?" asks Jenna, looking over at Isabella as she takes her books and notepad out of her backpack, placing them on her desk.

"Ughhh! You're so annoying!" Isabella complains, shaking her head in aggravation, before tuning out Jenna and listening to the lesson the teacher is beginning to write up on the board. She and Jenna came up with a plan for this weekend during the class period, Jenna taking the role of the mastermind.

"So, I'll just tell my parents that I'll be staying the weekend over there and it's already cool with your dad," Jenna whispers, once their teacher turned her back to them, writing on the board to emphasize her point to the class.

"Yea, but what if they call and want to ask my dad to verify?" Isabella asks naively, Jenna rolling her eyes in disdain.

"They won't," Jenna says firmly. "All we have to do is spring it on them late in the week and they won't have a choice but to go with the last minute plans," she states, causing a sliver of hope to wedge itself inside Isabella's heart, at the chance to really spend some time with Kian, other than in between classes and lunch.

"Okay, let's do it," Isabella says adamantly, surprising Jenna with her reaction.

"We'll hash out the rest of the details later, like what to bring or wear, and I'll need to get some money for alcohol and weed," Jenna adds, bringing a slight sense of apprehension into Isabella's sphere, as well as her excitement.

Isabella sighs and rolls her eyes at Jenna's antics, as she tries to focus on the lesson and Jenna continues to plan for this weekend. Isabella gives a little input when needed, to make it seem as if she's listening, but in reality, she's thinking about how shit will work out with Kian. She thinks of all the different situations that could lead up to them actually being together and she breaks out into a smile without even realizing it, until Jenna startles her, asking her what's so funny.

"Nothing, I'm just thinking," Isabella replies dreamily, as she works on the assignment their teacher has given to them to work on out of their textbook. She's so engrossed with her visions she doesn't even notice Jenna copying all of her answers from beside her.

"Girl, wake your dreamy ass up," Jenna scolds, snapping Isabella out of her daydreams, as she looks around and notices the classroom emptying out, as all the students head to their last period class of the day.

"You were thinking about Kian, weren't you?" Jenna teases, raising her eyebrows at Isabella, causing her to blush.

"No, I was thinking about the plans to go to the party," Isabella lies, swinging her tote bag over her shoulder and walking to the door, Jenna trailing behind her laughing.

They walk down the corridor to the doors and walk into the courtyard. As they pass the cafeteria, they pass a couple of girls from one of Jenna's other class who hands them fliers about volleyball, soccer, track, and softball, also the cheerleading tryouts that were coming up. They tuck them into their bags as they keep walking to the hallway leading to their other classes.

"Are you signing up?" Jenna asks Isabella, as she turns to head to her class. "I'm thinking about volleyball," Isabella replies.

"That might be good, but we'll talk about that later," Jenna says, before hugging Isabella quickly and walking off.

Isabella turns to head down the corridor to her math class as she wonders what Jenna's getting her into at the party. She decides that she won't drink much or do drugs to be safe, as she opens the door and walks inside. She sits down at her desk and settles in, falling into the calming effect of her classroom, letting her worries just fade away. She only hopes that whatever happens with her and Kian, works out in the best way possible because she really does like him a lot.

Chapter Thirty - Three

James

James walks out of the class behind Matthew, as the last bell of the day rings, signaling the end of the school day, as students pour out of their classrooms and flood into the courtyard, heading towards the bus loop or the front office. They follow the flow of the traffic as Matthew texts on his brand new iPhone 14-Pro and walks, somehow managing not to crash into something. James' phone chimes, alerting him to a text message. After he takes his phone out of his pocket to see who it's from, he sighs once he sees it's from his father, but still swipes across the screen, opening the message to read it.

"Need you at the shop," James reads, before placing his phone back into his pocket without replying.

"You going to the party this weekend?" Matthew suddenly asks, catching James off guard and causing him to stutter in his response.

"Wha-huh?" James asks, tired and confused from being at school all day and just wanting to go home to lay down without having to run around doing paperwork or changing oil at his father's business.

"Are you going to Aaron's party this weekend?" Matthew repeats, putting extra emphasis on Aaron's name.

"I didn't even know there was a party," James says lamely, cursing himself for his stupidity, trying to shake the cobwebs out of his head.

"Yea, there is, everyone's going," Matthew says crisply, detaching himself from James' path and drifting off towards a group of kids from their table, whose parents pick them up in the front parking lot.

James continues to follow the opposite flow of the kids, as he makes his way to the bus loop. As he passes through the doors from the courtyard to the bus loop, he fights his way to the edge of the current and finally breaks free. He posts up against the wall, takes out his phone and texts Emily, before locking his phone and returning it to his pocket.

After about 5 minutes, James sees a blonde curly head bobbing its way through another crowd of students and manages to make out Emily's face before grabbing her arm and pulling her over to him.

"Hey you," Emily murmurs, brushing her fingers against his arm, creating gooseflesh, as she smiles and stares at him.

"Hey yourself," James replies, with a goofy smile of his own, before they start walking to their bus.

"How was your day, Em?" James asks awkwardly, walking in stride next to the blonde beauty, feeling like everybody was looking at him scornfully as they passed by.

"It was okay, I just can't wait to get back to the house," Emily says, with a sigh, as she types a reply to something somebody texted her as they walk.

"Yea, I know what you mean," James says, as they reach their bus and he helps her up the stairs, holding her steady from the concrete.

Once she's on the bus, James climbs up the steps and they walk down the aisle to sit in their usual seats at the back of the bus.

After letting Emily slide in first, so she can look out the window, James goes to sit down, and momentarily locks eyes with one of the angry black kids who is always sitting at the very back of the bus. The kid nods his head curtly at James silently, making James feel momentarily insecure from the ice in the kid's eyes which causes him to shiver uncontrollably and avert his eyes quickly, as he takes his seat next to Emily.

The bus pulls out of the school and into traffic and the atmosphere inside the bus becomes rowdy, as the students sing, talk and pull pranks on each other loudly.

"So, are you going to Aaron's party this weekend?" Emily asks, looking over at James sitting next to her with his leg brushing against hers.

"Maybe," James replies, noncommittedly. "What about you?" he asks in return, trying to take the attention off of him.

Emily takes a couple of seconds before responding, "I was thinking about it, but since you're not going..." she says, not finishing her thought, trying to purposely make James curious.

"I didn't say I wasn't going," James corrects her nervously, squirming in his seat.

"There's no reason for me to go if you're not even going to be there," Emily says, pouting her lips, as she types on her iPhone X, replying to something from a group message that she's in, with some of her other friends from school.

"I'll have to check in with my dad and shit, Em," James groans, already knowing that his dad won't let him go to the party *any* weekend, let alone this weekend.

"So, don't ask then, James, just bring your ass," Emily says, grinning wickedly, as she places her hand on James' thigh, "Don't be scared, James."

James feels himself getting turned on as Emily continues to run her hand over his leg, teasing him. As he fights against her seduction, he begins to get really angry that she would think he would be scared to be seen with her at Aaron's party. Hasn't he showed her how he really feels, ever since the start of the school year? James takes a minute to collect his thoughts, not letting Emily distract him with her hand or words, as she continues to belittle him about being at the party. When he closes his eyes and organizes his thoughts one at a time, he realizes that most of the time he's around Emily or his dad he always feels overwhelmed. The feelings are confusing to him. James doesn't know if it's because they both seem to force their will upon him or not, but he doesn't like it at all, and that he *is* sure of.

As the bus pulls up outside the first stop, a couple of students get off and wave their goodbyes, as the bus pulls away from the curb, headed to the next stop.

"So, I'm going to need you to figure out a way to make an appearance at this party with me," Emily states firmly, looking at James seriously, daring him to refuse her this.

James sighs, knowing better than to start an argument with Emily right before they got off at their stops. "I'll see what I can do, Em," he concedes, knowing that it will most likely come back to bite him in the ass later on down the road.

Emily smiles contentedly and goes back to rubbing on James' thigh and responding to texts in her group message. After about 20 minutes, the bus pulls up outside of her mom's salon on K Street and 10th Avenue North. Emily hugs James, as she prepares to get off the bus," don't forget you promised to take me to Aaron's party," Emily says, threatening him with just a look, letting James know she was serious about this.

"I gotchu Em, I won't forget," James promises, receiving a kiss on the cheek before watching Emily's slender frame walk away down the aisle and off of the bus. He sits back down in his seat, as the bus starts to pull off and he catches one last fleeting glance of the blonde beauty standing on the sidewalk, looking up into the bus windows, searching for his face before they are separated.

As he turns around in his seat, James spots one of the black kids in the back seat staring out the window at Emily, instantly putting James on the offensive. He decides to play it cool as the kid catches sight of James looking at him and offers him a smirk which pisses James off more.

"This black kid thinks he could ever have a snowball's chance in hell with a girl like Emily," he thinks to himself angrily, unconsciously plastering a mean mug on his own face, causing the black kid in the back to grin maliciously.

"Who the fuck you muggin', bitch?" he asks darkly, looking at James intensely with ice cold eyes.

James feels his stomach clenching in fear before finally steeling himself and replying angrily, "Not much, just a fucking ugly ass monkey..."

This causes the kid to growl like a wolf deep in his throat, startling James for a second, as he makes to get up and out of his seat.

"Chill, Kian!" says the other black kid quickly grabbing the black kid's shoulder and pressing downwards, forcing him back into his seat. "You can't fuck up before tryouts," the other kid adds, once Kian is back in his seat, staring at James with hatred of his use of the racial remarks.

"Yea, don't fuck up your tryouts, Jackie Robertson," James says, taunting Kian about the Negro Leagues in baseball's past history, purposely mispronouncing Jackie Robinson's name as an insult.

"Pussy," Kian replies disdainfully, as he turns back to his homeboy who kept him contained in the back row, dismissing James without a second thought.

For a second, the dismissal causes James blood to boil, as he stares at Kian in shock at how casually he was just dismissed, as if James was nothing more than a speck of lint on a new blazer. James considers throwing another racist comment at Kian and the other black kid, but decides against it, considering that he wouldn't be able to fight and win against both of them, but also because he can see his father's car lot in the distance, coming up soon at his stop.

As the bus pulls up outside the entrance to *Reliable Rides* and James prepares to get off the bus, Kian breaks off the conversation between him and his friend to look over at James as he slides out of his seat into the aisle and puts the straps of his backpack over his shoulders.

"Pussy," Kian reiterates, staring at James in the eyes unflinching in a challenge of sorts.

James ignores him, as he turns and walks down the center aisle and off the bus, before watching it pull away. James turns and walks into the office of *Reliable Rides*, where his father is sitting behind his desk in his office talking to the dark-skin man with braids, who they had met at the Grove Custom Auto mechanic shop over in Delray Beach, when they had been talking to the owner about getting some of their SUVs worked on.

135

"Jimmy! How was school, son?" Mr. Deckard asks enthusiastically, coming from behind his desk to clap a hand on James' shoulder in a rare show of affection.

"It was good, dad," James says, embarrassed, as he stands there awkwardly underneath the weight of his father's hand resting on his shoulder.

"I need your help showing Mr. Rodriguez around the lot and showing him our selection of luxury vehicles," Mr. Deckard instructs, sending James outside with the man who he figures must be of some importance if his father has him here in a more private setting while conducting business.

Usually, when James gets off the bus at the dealership, his father has him fill out paperwork, so he can get a grasp on how it needs to be done properly. If he is not doing the paperwork then he is either detailing the cars, or in the garage with Eddie, the mechanic, who works for James' father at *Reliable Rides*. Eddie was always showing James how to fix any part of a car in a simple and cost effective way while running a business.

Over the years, his father has been teaching James the ins and outs of the car dealership business while under the tutelage of different teachers that have been purposely placed in James' life, and he has been soaking up everything like a sponge. James knows that his father has been grooming him to eventually take over the family dealership one day, but despite being rich, James finds no sense of joy with cars as his father does.

They walk past a row of family size utility vehicles as they head towards the front of the lot, where a line of Acuras, Corvettes, and Cadillacs sat waiting to be purchased. As James stands off to the side, Mr. Rodriguez walks around the assembly and inspects each vehicle with a critical eye. James does his best to fill him in on each of the vehicles as best as he can from a mental rolodex. After a while, Mr. Deckard comes out of the office and heads over towards where James is currently in the process of filling Mr. Rodriguez in about the benefits of owning a 2020 Cadillac Escalade and purchasing it from *Reliable Rides*.

"We also guarantee a one year service plan for everything from tire rotation to oil changes or custom parts being ordered," James says, reciting one of his father's golden business mantras when dealing with an important client that he wants to keep around.

When Mr. Rodriguez spots Mr. Deckard approaching, he walks away from the pearl colored Escalade that he was just admiring, and sticks his hand out, surprising Mr. Deckard for a moment, causing him to stop in place.

"Your son drives a hard bargain, Mr. Deckard," Mr. Rodriguez says with a grin, as he motions to the Escalade.

"That he does," replies Mr. Deckard, coming forward to shake Sin's hand, as they head back inside to close the deal on the truck he has decided to buy.

Once they got inside, James is made to fill out the paperwork, leaving the most important parts for his father to complete, since it's too complex for him at this stage of his business management training. After all the paperwork is finished, they stand outside and watch another happy customer drive off the lot in one of their *Reliable Rides*, after sticking one of the company bumper license plate borders around the temp tag in the back, of course.

"You did a good job today, Jimmy," Mr. Deckard says, proudly thumping James on the back.

"Thanks, dad," James replies, thinking about taking advantage of this situation and asking for permission to go to the party this weekend, so he can keep his promise to Emily.

"Hey, there's a little get together at Aaron's house this weekend, and I was wondering if I could go," James asks, adding a couple white lies into the mix for added benefit.

"I need you here, Jimmy," Mr. Deckard replies expectantly, causing James to become upset at his father for always trying to keep him on a short leash.

"It's just a get together for the guys who're going to try out for sports at school, dad," James explains, knowing that sports isn't something his dad will turn down.

Mr. Deckard sighs before turning to look at James with a level look, "Look at you! Asking right after making a sale on the lot, you *are* getting good at business after all, I've made a businessman of you. Okay, you can go, but I'm going to need your help during the week and you'll have to find your own ride, there and back, since I'll be tied up with shit here at the dealership," his father explains, causing James to agree quickly, before he can change his mind.

"Yes, sir," James says, excitedly, taking out his phone to let Emily know that he will be able to keep his promise to her for sure now.

"I also need you to go around and spray some water on the cars to knock some of the salt from the ocean off of them before we head home, Jimmy," his father says, before turning to walk back inside of the office to finish taking care of some of the last minute paperwork, and to send off some company emails, like any other day.

James shoots off his text to Emily before heading over to the garage and grabbing the hose, eager to get the work he was assigned finished as soon as possible, so he could call Emily and talk to her about the party coming up.

Chapter Thirty - Four

Kian

After getting chewed out by Quan for the rest of the bus ride home for messing with that dumbass white boy, James, they got off the bus at their stop and walked through the hood, heading back towards Quan's house slowly. All day, Kian had been rolling an idea around in his mind that would help him out with his current situations all across the board. They pass by the familiar street where Glizzy is usually posted up at and stand there confused for a second at seeing a crowd circled up around two individuals preparing to fight in the center of a ring of bystanders.

They walk over and have to push and shove their way through the raucous crowd to see what is happening in the center. As they break through, they see that everyone has their camera phones out and are recording. There are two skinny base heads gearing up, preparing to fight.

"In this corner, we have Porky! The Human Spider Monkey!" Kian hears a familiar voice yell, before going on to introduce the other fighter. "In the other corner, we have Bastos! The Cannibal! Let the Baser Wars BEGIN!" Kian hears Glizzy add, as he caught sight of him standing on the hood of a car parked close to the curb beside the ring of spectators circled up to watch and bet on the junkies tearing into each other.

Somewhere nearby, a whistle sounds off and the junkies run full speed at each other, screaming and yelling, before colliding in a tangle of flying fists and feet. Kian watches the spectacle unfold before him and can't stop himself from laughing as Bastos howls like a jackal and bites Porky on the leg, shaking his head and growling like a Pitbull. Porky screeches and begins to try to

139

scramble away, as he pounds Bastos on his head with his fists clenched.

Porky unlocks his teeth from Bastos' leg and they start landing punches on each other, trading blow for blow while making wild animal noises. Kian notices that Bastos is favoring his left leg and sees a trickle of blood running from his knee to his ankle as they keep swinging at each other with wild haymakers. Kian watches as a couple niggas standing close to Glizzy with black bandanas are collecting money from people's hands as they place bets. The crowd roars as Bastos lands a punch on Porky, causing him to stumble, but not fall, windmilling his arms to keep his balance.

"Last call!" yells one of the men by Glizzy, holding one of his hands in the air and waving it around to draw attention from any potential gambler.

"Give me $20 dollars," Kian tells Quan, earning him a confused look in return. "Scared money don't make no money, Q," Kian adds, as he snatches the $20 dollar bill from Quan's hand before pushing his way through the crowd and towards Glizzy.

At first, when Glizzy spots somebody shoving their way forward towards him, Kian watches his body language and sees him straighten up, tightening his core as one of his hands drifts toward his waistline. As Kian draws closer and lifts his head, looking for the bookie, he locks eyes with Glizzy and shoots him a smirk, earning a laugh in response. He places his bet on Porky and finds his way back over to Quan, who is now cheering along with the rest of the crowd, watching the fight. After a couple more minutes, Porky and Bastos are beginning to visibly get tired, and begin to launch kamikaze attacks on each other, screaming like banshees as they claw and swing at their opponent's exposed head and face. Porky lands a right hook on Bastos, knocking him to the ground on his ass.

Porky growls, as he races across the small open space inside of the circle, and dives on top of Bastos in a flurry of thrashing arms and legs. After a minute or so with no defense, maneuvers coming from Bastos, Glizzy sends the two bookies into the center of the ring to break up the fight and separate Porky from his advisary. They pull a squealing Porky off of the prone form of Bastos and lead him over to Glizzy, who hands him a small baggie containing multiple small white rocks for the main prize. After receiving his prize winnings, Porky raises his arms to the sky and howls triumphantly before returning to Bastos sleeping form and slapping him in the face repeatedly. Bastos groans and sits up, rubbing his head and looking around the rapidly shrinking circle for a moment before Porky catches his full attention by dangling the baggie of crack rocks in front of his face, causing him to break out in a smile and jump up as if nothing had even happened to him.

Porky helped Bastos off the ground and they disappeared around the corner of an alley way to go and get high, arguing with each other along the way about who gets to go first on the pipe. Kian and Quan walk over to where Glizzy is standing in between the two black clad bookies, as one of them doles out the winnings to the few people who had picked the right fighter to bet on.

"Waz gud, bruh?" Glizzy greets, giving Kian dap.

"Not shit, bruh, just waiting on my winnings," Kian replies with a smile, as he turns toward the bookie, waiting for the return on his investment.

"You made yourself a lil' quick buck, huh?" Glizzy asks. "That's was'sup, lil' bruh," he adds, giving Kian a nod of approval.

"You know what the Romans said," Quan says, suddenly. "Fortune favors the bold..."

"Yo, how much you gave me, jit?" asks the bookie, looking at Kian.

"A dub, bruh," Kian replies, as the bookie searches through his pockets, pulling out a knot of bills and handing Kian two hundred dollar bills.

"'Preciate ya," Kian says, handing one of the bills to Quan and pocketing the other.

"So, what y'all niggas up to?" Glizzy asks, sitting on the hood of the truck and taking a foil blunt package from his jeans pocket along with a bag of weed.

Kian watches Glizzy split the 'gar and fill it with weed, before rolling it closed back exactly the same way it came expertly, and then firing it up, the potent trail of smoke spiraling up from the tip of it.

Kian and Quan glance at each other quickly before Kian turns back to look at Glizzy, "Not shit, bruh..." he replies, trailing off.

"Say less," Glizzy says, as he hops down from his seat on the hood of the truck and starts walking to the passenger side before opening the door and getting inside. The bookies jump into the truck at Glizzy's signal, one of them jumping behind the wheel. "C'mon y'all," Glizzy says, waving at Kian and Quan to get inside the truck as they stand on the sidewalk, lost in the sauce.

They climb into the backseat and the truck pulls off around the corner, YNW Melly and Kodak Black's newest hit blasting out of the speakers, repping the South Florida area with their quick wit and lyrics. Glizzy passes the blunt to the driver who takes a couple of puffs before handing it back over the seat to Kian. Kian raises the blunt to his lips and inhales deeply before passing it on, holding the smoke deep within his lungs. He watches as Quan takes a deep pull and finally lets loose a noxious cloud of smoke, coughing once it had been expelled. Kian rubs the tears that are now streaming from his eyes after taking a puff of the strong marijuana filled cigar and watches as Quan begins coughing uncontrollably.

"Damn! Y'all niggas got baby lungs!" teases Glizzy from the back seat, raising a chorus of laughter from the other homies inside the car, playing the peanut gallery, watching Quan's coughing fit.

"We can definitely fix that," comments the driver with a grin, as they pull into the driveway of Glizzy's Uncle Dice's stash house.

As they all open their doors to get out, a thin curtain of smoke seeps from the opened doors, before the five men walk up the walkway and Glizzy knocks on the door. After a couple of seconds, it is opened from within by Dice himself, who grins at seeing Kian and Quan standing behind Glizzy.

"Look who I found," Glizzy says, throwing a look over his shoulder at Kian and Quan.

"What's good with y'all?" asks Dice, as he daps each of them up and they pass him to enter the house, where loud Hip Hop music can be heard playing in one of the back rooms.

They walk into the living room and sit down on the couch as Glizzy heads into the kitchen and returns with a 12 pack of Heinekens from the refrigerator. Kian is just taking a sip of his when the blunt is already being passed back to him. He takes a quick puff before continuing the rotation and is finally able to take a good swig of his beer, sighing in appreciation as the cool liquid quenches his thirst and kills the cottonmouth he had been experiencing.

"How y'all was doing out there, Z?" Dice asks his nephew, as he releases a billowing cloud of smoke.

"We did alright, Unk, we still got a couple of niggas holding it down, and we made a couple of dollars off of the fight," Glizzy says, holding out his hand to the bookies, who produced two bundles of cash each and handed it all over to Glizzy, who in turn passes it to Dice.

Glizzy passes off the now half-smoked blunt before pulling out another foil pack and rolling up two more blunts to smoke while Dice counts the money. Kian can't pull his eyes away from the stack of bills in Dice's hand as he counts through it all, a feeling of anxiousness settling itself inside of him. He knows that the money being counted can't be much more than two thousand dollars or so, but other than the stacks upon stacks of money he has seen Maniac count in the past, this is still one of the moments that he knows is going to stick with him for a long time to come. Kian can feel the hunger for the block rising inside of him as the thought of being affluent floats through his mind and how that would be or feel. It was teasing him.

"There's $1,850 here nephew," Dice, says, breaking through Kian's trance, as he divides the money into slightly varying size stacks before handing back over to Glizzy who pockets it. One of the phones lying on the coffee table rings and Dice reaches for it, presses the green accept button on the screen and holds it up to his ear. "What's good?" he asks.

After a minute of listening, he tells whoever is on the other side of the call to send them in and after another minute or two, there is a knock at the front door. Dice gets up to answer it and Haze walks into the room with a white girl following behind him wearing a black halter top, white leggings, and sandals, showing off her pretty little feet and pink toes.

"What's poppin', y'all?" Haze asks, passing out daps to everyone there.

"Not shit, bruh," Kian replies, as he leans back against the couch.

"Yo, I need an L," Haze says to Dice, walking deeper into the living room and finding a seat. Kian tries to hand him one of the blunts that is still being passed around, but Haze shakes his head, "Not one of those L's, bruh," he says with a smile.

"He's looking for one of these L's," Dice says, walking over to a cabinet with books and movies stacked up on the shelves. He slid it over, revealing a secret hole in the floor. He bends down and pulls it out of the floor with his fingers through the slats and reaches down into the hole, pulling out two medium-sized vacuum sealed packages from inside and tossing them over to Haze. He slips the grate back into place to cover the hole, and stands up before grabbing ahold of of the sides of the cabinet and sliding it back across the floor to cover up the hole.

Haze holds the vacuum sealed packages up, showing Kian and Quan the weed inside, behind the clear plastic wrapper. "This shit right here will blow a muthafucka's socks off," Haze says.

"$15 dollar grams all day long, baby boy," Glizzy chimes in, showing them a Ziploc bag stuffed full of other smaller baggies of weed.

"I know how to sell weed, nigga," Kian says, puffin out his chest, not wanting to look green in front of Dice or Glizzy. "My pops used to sell it," Kian adds proudly, looking around the room defiantly, daring someone to challenge his statement.

"Amongst other things, that is,"Dice says, with a grin, coming over and taking some money from Haze, who tucks the packages under his shirt and stands up to dap up Dice before leaving.

"A'ight y'all, I'll get up with you later," Haze says, dapping up Glizzy, Kian, and Quan, before walking over to the door and opening it, the white girl hot on his heels. Haze stops on the threshold and looks back over his shoulder at Kian for a second and Kian can see the wheels turning inside his head. "Like I said before, Lil' Bruh, I knew ya pops and I always respected him," Haze says honestly, catching Kian off guard momentarily before pushing on. "So, if there's anything I can do for you, just holla at me or my homie," Haze added, nodding his head at Dice.

Kian looks between them for a second and nods his head at Haze before saying, "I appreciate y'all for that, Big Bruh, for reals." He watches as Haze and his company slip out of the door, closing it behind themselves.

After Haze had left, Kian and Quan chill with Glizzy and Dice for a while longer, smoking and chilling, before Quan reminds Kian that he's got to get back to the house. Kian pauses in the middle of asking Dice about some of the stories about his dad, Maniac's operation in the hood, and looks at Quan, "You can go if you want to bruh, I know ya peoples will start buggin' if you playing with them."

"Alright, Key," Quan says, as he struggles to stand up without tipping over from being high off all the weed smoke. "You finna stay here for a while longer?" Quan asks, holding onto the arm of the couch for balance while looking at Kian with red tinged eyes.

"Yeah, bruh. There ain't no reason for me to go back right now while your people still up, ya feel me?" Kian says. "It wouldn't make sense for me to wait outside for them to go to sleep."

"Yeah, I feel you," Quan replies, as he begins to struggle his way through the living room to the front door, preparing to leave.

"Wait, why the fuck is you waiting for his peoples to go to sleep?" Glizzy asks, confused, looking between Kian and Quan, searching for an answer.

For a second, both boys silently look at each other, urging the other to answer Glizzy's question. "Sit down, lil' bruh," Dice says firmly to Quan, sending him shuffling his way back across the tight living room to his seat next to Kian on the couch. Kian sighs and lowers his head, slightly embarrassed by his situation and not wanting to tell Dice that he's been having to sneak into Quan's window at night for a place to sleep.

"Spit it out, Kian. We family," Dice says, sternly yet gently, as Kian raises his head and looks Dice in the eyes with difficulty.

"Me and my moms got into it cause she was doing some junkie shit, and she kicked me out," Kian says, only telling Dice half of the story out of caution, not knowing if he has ties in the streets with Sin or not.

Dice just stares at Kian for a second before shaking his head and telling Glizzy to fire up another blunt. Glizzy obliges his uncle and rolls up a mango Swisher Sweet with some type of weed he tells Kian is called Girl Scout Cookies. "This that shit that Haze just copped," he states, juggling the ziplock bag stuffed to capacity with 1 gram and 3.5 gram baggies of the potent weed. Kian takes a second to try and count the baggies inside to calculate how much that Glizzy can make just off of weed and has a hard time coming up with a figure. Glizzy passes Dice the blunt, who fires it up and after taking three or four gigantic pulls, passes it.

Kian watches as Dice blows a ring of smoke that hovers in the air perfectly and for a second, forgets about what they were just talking about as he takes the blunt from Quan's outstretched hand and tries to copy Dice's smoke ring, failing miserably. Kian finally realizes that Dice is leaning back in his chair, studying Kian intensely as they all chill in the living room and smoke.

"So, you need a place to lay ya head at, huh, Key?" Dice finally speaks up, filling the cloudy room with the sound of his baritone voice.

Kian is momentarily taken aback for a second, thinking Dice is just fucking with him until Glizzy looks at Kian and impatiently asks, "Well, nigga, was'sup?"

"Yea, that would help me out a lot just for a lil' bit when I ain't at school or practice, ya feel me?" Kian admits.

"What type of sports y'all play?" Dice asks in surprise, looking back and forth between the two boys, trying to guess.

"We play football," Quan states proudly, sitting up a little higher up in his seat, not wanting to be left out of the conversation, especially when its about his favorite sport.

"What positions y'all play?" Glizzy asks, getting up to adjust his cargo pants and belt because his gun had fallen inside his pant leg from the way he was sitting.

"I play QB and Key plays wide receiver," Quan replies quickly, getting into the conversation, a light shining in his eyes at the mere mention of football.

"Y'all ain't raw though," jokes Glizzy, getting Quan riled up on purpose.

"Shit! Who, my nigga?" Quan replies, sitting forward on the couch leaning towards Glizzy seriously. "I've been playing football ever since I could walk all the way from 12th Avenue Flea Market on up, you can't tell me we ain't raw!" Quan argues, defending he and Kian's reputation they poured blood, sweat, and tears into in order to hone their skills.

"A'ight, a'ight, lil' nigga, I was just checkin' ya temperature," Glizzy says, laughing and holding up his hands to signal his surrender.

"So, if you stay here, how you gonna spend ya time?" Dice asks, looking at Kian with a serious expression on his face, judging his response.

"I ain't 18 yet, so I still gotta go to school until I can drop out, at least," Kian begins. "Then its two weeks till tryouts, so after I make the team, I'll be staying after school for a couple hours at least 2 to 3 days a week," he adds, putting the pieces together in his head, "and when I get back, I'ma be out getting money!"

Dice only takes a second to make up his mind about taking in Maniac's son before he turns to Glizzy, "Take them to Quan's crib and drop him off, and when you come back, bring lil' bruh's shit over."

"I gotcha, Unk," Glizzy replies, grabbing some car keys off the coffee table and standing up, "C'mon y'all boys," he says, leading them over to the door.

"A'ight, Quan, I'll holla," Dice says enthusiastically, before Quan walks out the door behind Glizzy and Kian, closing it behind him, leaving Dice inside the living room with the two bookies to discuss business.

Glizzy presses the automatic door unlock button on the key fob and the Infinity QX37 beeps, the head lights flashing briefly as he climbs into the driver seat and puts the key inside the ignition, starting the engine. "Shotgun!" Kian calls childishly as he heads over to the passenger side of the whip and climbs inside, leaving Quan to get into one of the back seats.

"Kissin', laughin', expensive passion, sittin' in mansions, glistening, flashin', drippin' in fashion, this is compan'ship...You don't know what I'll do to youuuuu!!!" Blasting out of the speakers they can hear Revenue Rob's new joint, repping out of Riviera Beach, also known as "Da Raw", to the fullest in his song called "Compan'ship", released as he just got out of the FEDs, hitting hard on the bass as Glizzy backs out of the driveway into the street and pulls off headed to Quan's house.

Chapter Thirty - Five

OG Dice, ZMA

Dice listens to the Infinity start up in the driveway, music pumping out of its speakers before he hears it back down the driveway and speed off down the street, the music fading as the distance grows. He turns to Yeyo, who is sitting in the room on a Lay-Z-Boy recliner and asks for an update from him and Champ about what they saw while they were out on the block with Glizzy earlier.

"It wasn't no chicos around or nun' when we was making them juggs fight, Big Bruh," Yeyo says, looking at Champ to see if he has anything to add.

"It was just the regular flow that we usually see," Champ says, after a moment of contemplation to see if he can unearth any submersed memories from earlier that he didn't notice right then.

"Y'all ain't see no weird cars or nothing keep coming around or one of your regulars who bought more than usual or was acting a lil' bit extra or nun'?" Dice asks, sending both youngins' back to thinking, not wanting to miss something critical that could end up helping them out in the long run.

After thinking for a couple of minutes, both Yeyo and Champ shake their heads and tell Dice that nothing stuck them as being out of the ordinary and he tells them to stay aware of their surroundings when out in the jungle. "There's always going to be another beast looking for the position at the top of the food chain," Dice schools, pulling out a bottle of Hennessy and pouring a glass for himself to sit back and relax with at the end of a long and busy day.

"How much y'all make off that fight?" Dice asks, taking a sip of his cognac and smacking his lips in appreciation.

"We cleaned up like 600 or something when we wrapped it up," Champ replies, remembering how much the total was when he and Yeyo had handed over the money they made to Glizzy earlier.

"Did them lil' niggas bet anything?" Dice asks suddenly, confusing both Yeyo and Champ for a second about who he's referring to.

"Who?" Yeyo asks, looking at Champ like he would have a better idea about who Dice is asking them about.

"Them lil' niggas, Kian and Quan," Dice answers.

"Ohh yea," Yeyo says, "That kid, Kian bet a dub and won back $200," causing Dice to grin.

"He got good instincts too then," Dice says talking to himself as he takes another slow sip in silent contemplation about the young nigga he plans to take under his wing.

"You really planning to fuck with them jitts, Big Bruh?" Champ asks, as he freaks a Black & Mild while still in the plastic, causing the plastic to make a loud crinkling sound as he rolls it in between his hands to loosen up the tobacco.

"Yea bruh, I knew his pops back in the day and he was always a thorough nigga," Dice says in warning, letting them both know that the topic was closed for discussion where he was concerned.

"Why you wanted to know if they won off the fight?" Champ asks, as he applies the fire to the tip of his Black & Mild, puffing it to life a couples times to get the cigar to burn evenly.

"I wanna see if he's smart enough to do some gymnastics with it," Dice says with a grin, hearing the sound of an engine approaching from down the street.

"Shit, if you say his daddy was Maniac, then I guarantee he is," Yeyo replies, as they all hear the sound of the car doors slamming shut, followed by feet shuffling over the front porch.

There is a brief knock at the door which Dice knows is his nephew from the rhythm of the knock before the door is even opened. Glizzy and Kian walk inside, each carrying a backpack. Dice just stares at the two nearly empty backpacks for a second before turning his gaze to Kian, " Is that all ya shit, lil' bruh?" he asks with a growl of anger.

"Yea, OG, this it," Kian replies sheepishly, shuffling his feet awkwardly under Dice's look.

"Ain't no fucking way..." Dice mumbles under his breath, going into the hallway in the back and entering one of the bedrooms. He walks into the room and heads over to the closet and opens the door, exposing a stack of plastic tubs of Fruit of the Loom boxers and Nike socks still in the plastics. Dice goes back and hands Kian the clothes, Kian sifting through it to find some Nike and Adidas shirts with a couple pairs of cargo shorts and jeans. Dice looks down at Kian's beat up Nikes and asks what size he wears.

"Ten and a half, or eleven," Kian replies, looking at his shoes with scorn.

Dice turns around and walks back into the bedroom and grabs a pair of 11.5 black Nike Airforce 1's which he brings back and gives to Kian. Kian looks down at all the shit for a second before looking back up at Dice speechless. "In this house we treat everybody like family, lil' bruh," Dice says wholeheartedly.

153

Dice watches Kian fight off his emotions for a second, as he processes the kindness he's just received. "Aye-yo, I damn sho appreciate y'all, Big Homie, for reals," Kian says, looking around the living room at Glizzy, Yeyo, and Champ gratefully.

"Ain't no problem, lil' bruh. Here, let me help you get ya self situated," Glizzy says, walking over and taking some of the clothes out of Kian's hands and lifts up the Airforces with his free hand. "We only got two rooms here, lil' bruh, so you gon' have to pull out the couch later when we shut down, but you can put all your shit over here," Glizzy adds, stepping around Dice and walking over to a corner by the couch and placing the items on top of a milk crate sitting on the floor.

"A'ight, I appreciate you," Kian says, tiptoeing his way through the small living room to where Glizzy is standing and handing him the rest of the clothes that Dice had given him.

"What time you gotta be at the bus stop?" Dice asks, as he heads back over to his seat and sits down, picking up his glass of Hennessy and taking a big sip.

"At like, 6:15," Kian says, after thinking for a second.

"Where it's at?" Dice questions, as he picks up the remote and switches on the LED TV to a football game, Miami against Baltimore, already well into the third quarter with four minutes left on the clock.

"It's on 6th Avenue South and M Street," Kian says, as Dice pauses for a second, mentally following the street route in his head that he could take to get there.

"That's like a mile or so away, right?" Dice asks Yeyo and Champ, looking over in their direction, since they work in that area on the blocks around the vicinity of Dice's Stash house.

154

"Yea, Big Bruh, that's around the corner from the block," Champ replies, nodding his head.

"That's not bad," Dice says, as he calculates the distance from where Yeyo and Champ usually are posted at when Glizzy is off his shift, seeing a future plan for expansion when the time comes to acquire more blocks that the chicos don't already control. "How long it used to take you to walk back to Quan's spot?" Dice asks Kian directly and watches Kian's eyebrows raise in confusion, as he is trying to follow Dice's train of thought.

"Like 20, 25 minutes maybe? I guess..." Kian answers, trailing off.

"A'ight, that's cool," Dice says before continuing, "If you ever need a ride or anything, just hit me or Glizzy up and we'll slide through and get you.

"I got you, Big Bruh," Kian says, taking out his phone and holding it out to Dice for him to program his number into it.

Dice grabs the phone and types his personal number into the keypad before saving it under 'Dice'. He then puts Haze's number into the phone as well and saves it. Dice begins typing on Kian's phone again, sending a text to Haze, letting him know whose phone number this is and to lock it in on his side. After typing the message to Haze, Dice thinks for a second before typing "Call Dice" into the message box and finally presses send. Kian's iPhone 'Whoops' as the message is sent and the blue box appears at the bottom of the screen. After a second sent, an icon with the time appears under the text that Dice just sent and a minute later his Galaxy rings with Haze's number and ringtone. "That's my dawg, that's my dawg fo sho'" Lil' Baby croons from Dices phone.

"Yo," Dice says, answering his phone, the ring tone cutting off midverse, "Yea, I sent that, just lock it in for future reference, ya feel me?" Dice tells Haze on the other end of the line.

"I got you homie," Haze replies, before hanging up to continue to work his jelly with his business and distributing ounce bags of weed from the two half pound bags of Girl Scout Cookies he bought from Dice earlier with their cut of the money from their soldiers pushing ZMA products out in the trenches.

Dice hands him back his iPhone as he places his own phone back in his gym shorts pocket and Kian looks down at his screen for a second, reading the text that Dice just sent to Haze. "So, what y'all got planned for the rest of the night, Z?" Dice asks, throwing a look over at Yeyo and Champ standing up from their seats.

"We got some business to take care of on the North Side, bruh," Champ answers with a grin, bumping his shoulder into Yeyo's arm and getting a laugh from him.

"We bouta slide off wit some lil' freaks," Yeyo says, causing Glizzy to search his pockets for his phone to scroll through his Facebook.

"I feel that," Dice replies, nodding his head in admiration of being a man in his mid 20's. Dice turns to Glizzy waiting on his nephew to look over at him after playing on his phone, sending messages. "What bout you, Neph?" Dice asks Glizzy.

"I'm finna go back out and spin the pavement, unk," Glizzy says before turning to look at Kian, "And you're coming too, so bring ya heat," Glizzy says to Kian, who begins to search through the backpack in the corner that he set down.

After feeling the weight of one of the bags, Kian slings it onto his shoulder and walks over to where Glizzy is waiting at the door. Yeyo and Champ walk out and Glizzy turns to look at Kian before following after them.

But Dice's voice stops him short, "Stay on point Neph, and make sure lil' bruh do right, he still a minor, ya feel me?"

"I'm hip," Glizzy replies as he walks out the door after Yeyo and Champ.

"Yo, Key!" Dice calls, as Kian trails after Glizzy, stopping him in his tracks. He turns to look at Dice, sitting in his chair. "Welcome to ZMA, lil' nigga," Dice says, raising his glass to Kian in salute, causing Kian to smile in gratitude as he raises two fingers to his eyebrow in response, returning Dice's salute.

"My pops called me Kilo, Big Homie," Kian replies, as Dice returns his smile. Dice watches as Kian steps out of the door and it closes softly behind him, leaving Dice alone in the living room, watching the end of the game and sipping the rest of the Hennessy from his Versace Bourbon glass.

"I'ma make sho your seed flourishes, Maniac," Dice says, quietly sending a promise up into the universe, hoping that it will reach the ears of his sandbox soldier wherever he is now residing.

He leans back into the comfortable chair and sets his empty glass down on a nearby end table before closing his eyes and sighing. After a couple of minutes of relaxing against the soft padding of his chair, listening to the drone of the sportscaster on TV mixed with the lull of the music playing in the back of the house finally sends Dice off into a deep sleep.

While he sleeps and his dreams begin to form, the Hennessy and weed loosens up past memories of when Dice and Maniac were as thick as thieves back in their youth, when they used to run the streets together. Back when they were both ambitious, free-spirited young men, before the creation of the Zoe Mafia Affiliates family. Something that they had both had a separate influence on. Helping to create what it was today. A Family.

Chapter Thirty - Six

Glizzy, ZMA

Glizzy starts the Infinity and whips out the driveway, headed over to Military Trail and 10th Ave North, where he sometimes posted up on the block serving junkies and basers. Kilo, formally known as Kian, is chilling in the passenger side scrolling through his phone, having just connected it to the Bluetooth inside the whip.

"I just took the doors off a Lamborghini, so I'm riding, and I'm sliding sideways and she call me Zaddy," Young Thug raps, as they slide through the Greenacres streets. They pass blocks where drug activity runs rampant, junkies slowly trudging through the streets searching for a fix, a lick, or a way to feed the monkey on their back, one way or the other. Niggas chilling on the corners waiting for a customer to come shop with them. Some look at the Infinity a little longer when it cruises by with a look of envy on their faces, dreaming of the day when they finally manage to crawl out the mud to the top, to live a life of wealth and luxury. They round a corner and pull over to the curb, where three young niggas are standing against the wall of a building.

Glizzy rolls down his window, "Aye, was' good, y'all boys?" he shouts, causing the youngins' to raise their heads to look up at where the yell came from. "Was good, Z?" replies Yank, a 20ish year old ZMA member who reports block activity to Glizzy, who then relays it to his Uncle Dice.

"Not shit, just showing lil' bruh around while checkin the temperature, ya feel me?" Glizzy says, causing Yank and his two homies to crane their necks, trying to look pass the tint on the windows into the interior of the truck. Glizzy puts the truck in park and turns to look at Kilo. "Let's jump out here so you can get to know the Zs," Glizzy says, opening his door.

Kilo opens his door and jumps down from the passenger side before walking around the front of the truck with his backpack on his back, that Glizzy knows contains his pistol. "This is Kilo," Glizzy says, introducing Kian to Yank and his two homies, Iceberg and Sike.

"What's goodie, lil bruh?" Yank asks, reaching out to dap up Kilo, who then turns to dap up Iceberg and Sike as well. "That's Iceberg and Sike," Yank says, pointing to each in turn, when their name is said, Kilo nodding his head at them in acknowledgement.

"What's shakin' out here?" Glizzy asks, as he scans the block looking for anything out of the ordinary, like Dice has been instructing the members of the ZMA to do lately.

"Not shit, bruh, just the usual ebb and flow, nah mean?" Yank says in his New York accent, as he slides his hands into the pockets of his Nautica Jeans.

"Still been jumping?" Glizzy asks, pulling out his phone and checking the time, seeing that it's already 20 past eight.

"Yea, a lil' bit," Iceburg comments, taking a Newport short from behind his ear and firing it up.

"Lem'me get a buss down, Berg," Sike calls, looking over at his homie, puffing on the Port.

"Damn, Sike, how you gon' buss down a short?" Iceberg complains, passing the Newport over to Sike, who is slouching against a concrete parking barrier.

159

"A'ight, so y'all still straight then? You don't need to re-up?" Glizzy asks Yank, ignoring Iceberg and Sike squabbling over how many pulls is a fair bust down on a Newport short.

"I mean we got about 7 g's left if you added it together, na'mean?" Yank replies, shrugging his shoulders as he turns his head to watch a scraggly looking dude in torn Army pants and a yellow and brown stained wife beater shuffle by like a zombie, as he mutters to himself and pushes a stolen, rusted shopping cart with only three functioning wheels.

Once the jugg had passed by and no longer presented a threat, Yank looks back over at Glizzy, "But we still got a lil' bit left on shift so we might not hold out after all," Yank advises.

"I gotchu, bruh," says Glizzy, earning a nod from Yank, who he daps up briefly, before turning to Kilo, "I gotta hit this spot right quick so I can get them right." Glizzy and Kilo jump back into the Infinity and close their doors. "What you need? Hard or soft?" Glizzy asks Yank.

"Both, my nigga," Yank replies with a playful grin, exposing his teeth; four golds to the top, which glint from the street lights beginning to cut on.

"Say less," Glizzy replies, switching the whip from neutral to drive and skirting off, accelerating down the street. As he focuses on the road, trying to be aware of the night street walkers, he can feel Kilo looking over at him. "What's good lil' bruh?" Glizzy asks, taking his eyes off the road for a second as he chances a look over to where Kilo is sitting.

"Where you said we was heading to?" Kilo asks, glancing over at Glizzy, waiting on his answer.

"We finna shoot over to this spot in West Palm Beach real fast so I can grab some shit for the corner boys," Glizzy replies, swerving around a pack of wild dogs chewing on something in the middle of the road.

"Why you ain't bring it with?" Kilo asks, looking out his side of the window at the abandoned building, chain link fences and burglar bars covering all the windows as they fly by, through the hoods of downtown Lake Worth.

"Because the number one rule out here is to never get caught slipping whenever you can help it, because it ain't promised that a nigga gon' get another chance, ya feel me, lil' bruh?" Glizzy states seriously as he switches lanes, leaving the hood and jumping on the I-95 North bound ramp.

The inside of the truck is quiet except for Quavo rapping softly, as Kilo digests what Glizzy just told him about second chances and how Quavo's own Nephew, Takeoff wouldn't be getting any second chance, as he had just been killed.

"Always rep the Gang! Gang! Gang! Gang!" Quavo spits, as both Glizzy and Kilo bob their heads to the beat.

"So, why you ain't bring none when we left your uncle's spot?" Kilo asks, confused that Glizzy would be up to take a 20 minute excursion, running somewhere to pick up drugs and back just to stay in the same area of operation.

"We don't keep a lot of shit at Unk's spot," says Glizzy, changing lanes again, now drifting into the cruise lane and setting the cruise control on the dash.

"We keep a couple of guns, pounds and some soft over there, but not enough to feed the streets with," Glizzy says, filling the silence between them.

"You should never bring dirt where you lay your head at," Glizzy explains, gaining a nod from Kilo in understanding.

"Yea, I'm feelin' that, bruh," Kilo says solemnly. "My pops got smacked while he was serving out the crib," he adds, catching Glizzy off guard.

Glizzy doesn't reply for a minute as he thinks about all of the shit he has heard about the Legendary Maniac out in the streets of Southside L-Dub and wonders at the mysteries of the universe that have now placed this broken young nigga in his path, the legacy of a street legend sitting beside him as they head to Tamarind Avenue. It takes a second for Glizzy to gather his thoughts and he sighs before saying, "Your pops ain't get smacked cuz he was thuggin' out ya crib, Kilo," causing Kilo to look over at him with a questioning expression on his face. Glizzy sighs again before continuing, "He got hit cuz he got complacent and stopped moving around, which is a safety precaution when you in these streets."

"What you mean?" Kilo asked, a slight edge to his voice, ready to defend Maniac's name if necessary.

"He got married and had kids," Glizzy says evenly, stating the obvious. "When you have obligations like that, you stop being hard to find because you're constantly on the go; 24/7, you following me?" Glizzy asks, looking over and seeing that Kilo is thinking about what he is being told, about Glizzy's jewels being dropped.

"Yea, I'm following," Kilo answers finally.

He reaches down to the floor board where his backpack is resting at and unzips it before extracting his .40 caliber Glock wrapped in a shirt. Glizzy's body instantly reacts to the sight of the gun, his body tensing and awareness tightening, his palms sweating as he

162

grips the steering wheel. He begins to calm himself, focusing his breathing to help, his soldier instincts kicking in as Kilo finishes unwrapping the shirt from around the black gun and places it on his lap as he leans back in his seat. Glizzy's right hand drifts unconsciously out of the 2 O'clock position on the wheel and ends up residing comfortably on his right thigh, in easy reach of his own weapon.

"I ain't neva gon' let a nigga get the drops on me, I'll neva get caught slippin'..." Kilo promises quietly, as he looks around for his phone for a second and changes the song.

"Shawty know I kill people, real people, in the trenches where it's real lethal, totin' real regals..." Trippie Red says from the Bose speakers, as he speaks to Kilo's soul.

Glizzy spots flashing red and blue lights in the distance and takes a little of the pressure off of the gas pedal, before they draw even to the lights. He turns the A/C on, then switches it to the heat, before turning the FM radio on, causing Trippie Red's voice to cut off before he switches to AM and back over to high heat, Kilo staring at him in confusion.

"What the fuck you do tha..." Kilo begins to say, but he notices the sight of a 12 inch panel dropping out of the dashboard, stopping him mid-speech.

"Put your heat in there," Glizzy instructs, Kilo following his directions quickly as Glizzy takes his own pistol off of his hip, a twin of Kilo's with the exception of the extended 20 round magazine, and sets it on top of Kilo's gun after taking the mag out.

He closes the box and turns the music down as they come abreast of a state trooper, posted on the side of the highway with a car pulled over in front of him. Glizzy stares straight ahead with his eyes on the road, "What he doin'?" he asks Kilo, without looking over at the cop or Kilo.

"They sittin' there in the car with the door open, typing on the computer," Kilo replies, peering out the window at the police car.

As they drive a little bit further, both vibing to the music, Glizzy realizes that this lil' nigga is way ahead of his peers. As he thinks about his Uncle Dice's decision to take Kilo in, he wonders about his place in the Zoe Mafia Affiliates family. He knows that either Dice will end up stepping down or the ongoing situation brewing with the chicos might have dire ramifications if not handled correctly.

Glizzy exits the highway and steers around the curve, now entering the neighborhood called Downtown because of how close the blocks are to Clematis Street, where the upper class party at. Tamarind Avenue is notorious for drugs and violence. It also is convenient to the party and club patrons Downtown so that they might be able to acquire their flavor of fix a couple blocks away from the club scene on Clematis Street.

They ride down the streets, which don't look much different from that which Kilo is used to seeing everyday when he steps out the front door in South Side L-Dub. They pull into a parking spot by the curb in front of a little house painted a light brown with a chain link fence round it with a Pit bull inside on guard duty. They get out of the Infinity and walk towards the gate, the dog growling viciously at them as they approach.

"Shut the fuck up, Mafia!" Glizzy yells at the Pit, causing it to settle down just a little bit while Glizzy unlatches the gate and steps inside, Kilo hesitating on the other side of the fence still. "You good, bruh, he trained and shit," Glizzy promises, walking up the sidewalk to the front door to knock.

He waits while Kilo eases into the yard, closing and relatching the gate behind himself and creeping around, Mafia still growling at the intruders faintly. Glizzy knocks on the door and waits as a latch on the inside is thrown and part of a face appears on through the opening. "Fuck you want?" a voice barks from the other side of the door, struggling to make out who Glizzy and Kilo are and probably wondering what they are doing on the door step, banging on their door like the damn police.

"Watch who you talking to like that, Pee-Wee! Dis Glizzy!" Glizzy snaps, leaning closer to the open portal on the door so Pee-Wee can see them clearly.

"Oh shit, my bad, Z!" Pee-Wee replies, closing the door slot and relatching it before Glizzy hears multiple locks being undone from inside and the front door is opened, revealing Pee-Wee's big frame, standing to one side of the doorway with a pistol in his waistband.

As they step inside, Glizzy looks at Kilo and says, "Welcome to the dungeon, Jit."

Chapter Thirty - Seven

Kian, known as Kilo, ZMA

Kilo follows Glizzy over the threshold into the ZMA Downtown trap house, passing by Pee-Wee's 275 pound frame as he glowers down at him with a suspicious look. "Who da fuck is dis jit? We don't allow strange ass niggas up in here!" Pee-Wee says cautiously, while Kilo mugs him.

"You let in whoever the fuck I *say* to let in nigga!" Glizzy snaps, turning around to glare at Pee-Wee, causing him to take his eyes away from Kilo to stare at Glizzy in disbelief.

"When Dice opened this spot, he said not to let any question mark ass niggas up in here that ain't green lighted by him personally," Pee-Wee argues loudly. This gaining the attention of the other occupants inside the house, bringing someone into the foyer where Kilo, Glizzy and Pee-Wee are standing.

"Fuck you niggas cryin' bout?" asks a slim, yellow-skinned dude with medium length dreads hanging in his face, as he saunters into the entryway, a snub nosed revolver clutched in his hand.

"Fuck out of my face, Pee-Wee," Glizzy warns. "This is Kilo, he's Dice's protege," Glizzy tells Pee-Wee, getting a look of shock in return from the big man.

"Ain't no muthafuckin' way!" laughs the skinny light-skinned dude as he squeezes past Glizzy and Pee-Wee blocking the entryway and walking over to Kilo. "What's poppin', Z? Dey call me Raw," he says in introduction, as him and Kilo dap each other up. Raw was named after Riviera Beach, what is called "Da Raw" in Palm Beach

County and its surrounding areas, so Raw was representing his hood to the fullest.

"A'ight bruh, like Glizzy said, they call me Kilo," he says finally feeling like he is now able to live up to Maniac's expectations when he first gave him that nickname.

Pee-Wee finally gives up trying to argue with Glizzy as Raw turns back around and leads them from the foyer of the house into the living room, where Kilo's senses are assaulted by the smell of burning Marijuana. As his eyes adjust to the dim lighting and smoky atmosphere, Kilo can make out a silhouette, despite the darkness inside the room.

"Who you got there, Raw?" a feminine voice purrs, somewhere off to the side of the spacious room, drawing Kilo's eyes, where he can make out the tip of a burning blunt.

"What's good with you, Luna?" Glizzy asks smoothly, stepping past Kilo with a charming smile plastered on his face.

"Glizzy!" the voice exclaims in excitement and surprise before Kilo hears a rustling sound of fabric moving and a light is turned on, momentarily blinding him and causing his eyes to have to readjust to the light.

When his vision returns, Kilo discovers that the voice belongs to a beautiful caramel-complexioned woman, the type of complexion known as the White Haitian. "How you doin', ma?" Glizzy asks, stepping forward to give her a hug when she holds her arms open in invitation.

"I've been good," Luna replies, flashing a beautiful smile before turning to look at Kilo," and who do we have here?"

"This is Kilo, ma, he's staying over at Unk's place at the moment," Glizzy answers, drawing a questioning look from the light-skinned exotic beauty.

"It's been a long while since he's let anyone stay over there," she says, before turning to business. "So, what brings you all the way out here? And don't say it was just to see lil' ole me," Luna asks, teasingly.

"I need a four way," Glizzy answers, as he picks up a couple of the pre-rolled blunts laying on the coffee table and stashes them in his pockets after handing one over to Kilo, "Fire that bitch up, lil' bruh."

"I got'chu," Luna replies to Glizzy's order, as she looks over at Pee-Wee and asks him to get whatever Glizzy needs, sending him off into the back of the house with a petulant expression on his face.

"So, what's been going on with y'all lately?" Glizzy asks, as Kilo applies some fire to the tip of the blunt Glizzy handed him and draws the potent smoke into his lungs.

"Not shit, just been having to deal with some petty bullshit with a local clique around here that's been causing problems lately, trying to move into where they don't belong," Luna answers, sitting back down on the couch and crossing her thick legs sexily, picking up her own blunt, relighting it and taking a good deep intake of the sweet smelling potent weed.

"It's been serious?" Glizzy asks automatically, ready to ride against anyone who tried to move against ZMA.

"There's been some shootings, robberies, but besides that, nothing really too serious. Some corner boys getting stripped and robbed..." Luna says, lacing Glizzy up on the situation as Pee-Wee returns carrying a Nike backpack.

Pee-Wee tosses the small bag to Glizzy, who catches it out of the air before turning his gaze back to Luna, as he accepts the blunt from Kilo. "Do you know who they are?" Glizzy asks, puffing on the blunt.

"Yea. They call themselves the Cuban Y-Los, a Cuban crime wave out of 22nd Ave in Miami," Luna says with a malicious grin. "I plan on making sure they end up on the endangered species list, soon as I can for thinking that they have the clout to fuck with my operation."

"Yea, let me know what's up with all of that shit, shawty," Glizzy says before nodding his head over at the door, "But for now, I gotta jet, ya feel me?" Kilo and Glizzy walk back to the foyer with Luna trailing behind them, and as they approach the door they turn back around to face her.

"You better come back out here to see me soon, ya hear?" Luna tells Glizzy, as she leans back in to give him a hug before turning to look back at Kilo. "You too, handsome," she adds, a gorgeous smile spreading across her face.

"I got'chu," Kilo replied shyly, slightly overwhelmed by the beauty in front of him.

They walk out of the door and down the sidewalk, Mafia growling at them all over again from his doghouse this time, all the way in the corner of the yard. Glizzy opens the gate and they walk through, Kilo re-locking it behind himself after he exits. They jump into the truck and Glizzy opens the stash box in the dash board again to put in the drugs while extracting their guns. "Them niggas might have someone watching this spot that Luna was speaking about," Glizzy explains, as he hands Kilo his Glock and grabs his own, replacing the magazine back into the handle, and charging a round into the chamber.

Kilo places the pistol on his lap as Glizzy cuts the truck on and pulls off into traffic. Kilo reconnects his phone to the Bluetooth. "Yea, I'm the only one to get the job done, I don't know a nigga who could cover for me," Drake spits as 'Believe Me' begins to play through the speakers.

Glizzy hands Kilo the blunt with about half of its length remaining and reaches into his pocket, extracting the cigarillos he had grabbed from Luna's trap and saved for the ride back. He throws them into the center console and reaches for a lighter resting in the cupholder. "Fire that bitch back up, lil' bruh," Glizzy says, handing Kilo the lighter.

Kilo applies the flame to the tip and puffs on it a couple times, drawing the potent marijuana into his lungs. As they ride down the street, Glizzy keeps his head on swivel for anything suspicious, aware that the wolves might be lurking. "Be on point, lil' bruh, niggas round Downtown notice when someone ain't from here," Glizzy warns, as they get caught at the red light coming up on 13th Street, where Tank and Tommy's corner store is located and a lot of hustlers are there selling dope of all flavors, where there are a bunch of tricked out dunks riding on "30's and candy paint, playing music while the niggas hustle.

As they wait for the light to turn green, Kilo watched the parking lot of the store to see if they draw any unwanted attention from the niggas chilling over there hustling. The light finally turns green and Glizzy turns the music down and tries to act inconspicuous as they begin to draw closer to the store parking lot. They pass by and some of the men in the parking lot turn and look at the passing Infinity truck, staring at it until it's passed far enough to where they can't see it anymore. Kilo sits back in his seat feeling like there is a dark cloud hovering over that parking lot, the ominous feeling settling itself in his chest.

They turn the music back up and pass the blunt back and forth while they ride. They cruise on I-95 back toward Lake Worth, where Sike, Yank and Iceberg are still posted up, under the glow of the street lights. Glizzy pulls up to the curb and puts the infinity in park before opening up his door and hopping out, Kilo following suit behind him.

"Welcome back, Z!" Yank says in greeting, as him and Glizzy dap each other up.

"Took you long enough," Sike interjects laughing, as he draws a glare of warning from Glizzy.

Glizzy leads Yank over to the whip and they both climb inside, Yank climbing into the passenger seat where Kilo was just sitting at. Kilo posts up next to Iceberg and Sike on the block, firing up another blunt while Glizzy gives Yank the drugs that he needs for the rest of their shift. When Glizzy and Yank sit in the truck handling business, his phone rings and Kilo can hear a female voice asking Glizzy to come see her. Iceberg passes the blunt back over to Kilo, "That shit some gas," he compliments, coughing slightly and rubbing at one of his eyes.

"It's some shit bruh picked up while we was cycling back," Kilo replies, looking at the blunt as he holds the smoke in his lungs.

"Who y'all went to go see? Haze?" Sike asks, holding his hand out for the blunt.

"Sit ya impatient ass down somewhea', Sike," Iceberg says, laughing at his homie.

"Nawl, we went to go see a bad ass foreign looking White Haitian bitch," Kilo says, finally handing Sike the blunt.

"Ohh, yea? Y'all went to go see that 'Baby'!" Iceberg growls, shaking his head at Kilo and laughing.

"Yea, bruh, everybody stuck on her," Sike comments, looking down at the ground in longing.

"An she ain't passin' out none of that pussy, either!" Iceberg adds, shaking his head at the injustice of it all.

"Shit, she looked super-friendly around Bruh," Kilo says nodding his head over at Glizzy, still sitting in the car with Yank, talking on his phone to the bitch on the other end.

"That's cuz she vibe with son," Iceberg says, grinning. "I wouldn't be surprised if Glizzy already smashed Luna fine ass! Bruh a pussy monster."

"If that hoe on the phone work some magic, I guarantee that he gon' slide to go see what she talkin' bout," Sike says, Iceberg nodding his head in agreement with his assessment.

"Yea, bruh gon' go see what that pussy like, fuck driving around bringin' niggas packs and shit who stuck on the block all night," Iceberg adds.

Glizzy and Yank finally jump back out the truck and walk back over to where Kilo, and the homies are chilling, still passing around the blunt clip between themselves. Glizzy looks over at Kilo. "I got some shit to take care of, lil' bruh, you good here for a second?" Glizzy asks, looking at Kilo with a pleading look on his face.

Kilo thinks for a second, not really wanting to be stuck outside posted up on the block all night at 11pm but figures that Glizzy don't mean no harm by shooting off like this. "Go on, bruh," Kilo says, sighing in resignation, as Glizzy grins and man-hugs Kilo.

"My nigga!" Glizzy says, as Kilo pushes away from him, shaking his head and laughing.

"Take yo ass on, Z," Yank says with a smirk on his face, as Glizzy turns around and starts to head back to the Infinity sitting at the curb, still idling.

He jumps into the driver's seat and shuts the door and for a second seems like he's searching for something inside the truck. Glizzy rolls the window down and hollers for Kilo, "Come here right quick, lil' bruh," Glizzy yells, drawing Kilo over to the passenger side window. "Hold this down, I ain't tryna be ridin' dirty around with all this shit, ya feel me? Stash box or not, it's safer to leave it here," Glizzy says, handing Kilo two bundles, one containing a bunch of cocaine powder, the other a jumble of hard white rocks.

"Why you don't just leave it in there?" Kilo asks, looking around cautiously first to see if anybody is watching before grabbing the two packages and stuffing them into his waistline quickly.

"In case they got a dog," Glizzy explains, before nodding his head as Kilo steps away from the window. "I shouldn't be gone long," Glizzy says, before handing over the blunt from the ashtray. "Here, take these too," he says before putting the truck in drive and pulling off.

"I told you," Sike snickers from the background, as Kilo watches the Infinity disappear around a corner, earning reproachful looks from Yank and Iceberg.

"Shut your ass up, Sike, lil' bruh straight," Yank says, as he takes a pack of Newport 100's out of his pocket and begins to slap the box against his open palm. He takes one out of the box and sticks it in his mouth before putting the box back into his pocket and lighting the cigarette.

"Lem'me see that fire real quick," Kilo says, taking the red Bic lighter from Yank and lighting up one of the blunts Glizzy just handed him before pulling off. "At least I got this," Kilo says, sucking in his breath to hold the smoke in before taking another puff of the blunt, causing the marijuana inside to crackle as it burns.

"At least there's that," Yank agrees, reaching out to take the blunt from Kilo and handing him the Newport 100.

"What's this for?" Kilo asks, looking over at Yank confused, as he hits the blunt. "You ain't never smoked a Port with an El befo', Jit?" Yank asks, as Kilo hits the cigarette a couple times, before handing it back.

"That mofo gon' boost ya high, dawgs," Iceberg says, getting a grin from Kilo in approval, feeling the effects of the Newport, as the tobacco mixes with the marijuana.

They continue to chill on the block, talking, rapping, while they sell their various array of drugs as different levels of low lives approached, as the night went on. Kilo watches how the block boy ZMA members hustle, Yank explains to Kilo that the way they all eat is to have different flavors for the juggs who come to shop with them. Yank sells hard and soft cocaine. Iceberg sells heroin, and Sike sells the Flakka for the block. They pushed the ZMA products and they all ate lovely, what type of arrangement was better than that? Yank asked Kilo.

After about two hours, Glizzy hit Kilo's phone with a text, "I'm on the way, lil' bruh..." Kilo reads, before then typing back a thumbs up and returning his phone back to his pocket. As he waits for Glizzy to return, Kilo tried his hand serving a few buddies, letting Yank and his boys show him how it's done, not even realizing that he is sinking deeper and deeper into the hustla's mentality and addiction to the streets. It is only the very first sale that either pulls you in or pushes you out, and Kilo was being pulled way in.

Chapter Thirty - Eight

Detective Jones

Detective Jones sits at his desk as the night crawls by rereading a report about somebody named "Sin City" that they have finally managed to squeeze out of a rat in Greenacres. He doesn't even notice that he's been sitting at his desk for more than four hours before he's startled back to reality when somebody slaps a manila folder down next to him.

"What the fuck?" Detective Jones exclaims, jumping in surprise as the folder lands next to his arm resting on the fake wooden paneling of the desk.

"This just came in," says a night duty sergeant blandly, before spinning on his heels and walking away back to his post to try and pass by the time of the graveyard shift as easily and lazily as possible.

Detective Jones opens the folder and intakes his breath, once his eyes landed on the crime scene photos laying before him in vivid color, showing an black man in his mid 20's laying on the ground with gunshot wounds to his chest. But the most significant thing about the pictures that draws Detective Jones' eyes in is the grisly letters carved into the young man's forehead. "FUCK ZMA" Detective Jones reads from the pictures of the vic before turning on his desktop and searching for anything through the police database for mention of ZMA.

He scrolls down the search program after typing in the hits and comes across a recent report, detailing multiple accounts of gang and drug activity connected to a local gang called the Zoe Mafia Affiliates, a sub-gang branched off of the much bigger and well known Zoe Mafia Family, whose murder rates makes anywhere else look like Disneyland. Jones settles in as he begins to read through the reports of this gang so he can catalogue as much information as he can. After he finishes reading the reports, he picks up the phone sitting to the left of his desk and dials the night duty sergeant's extension who originally brought him the report.

The phone rings a couple times before finally being picked up on the other side with a sigh of exasperation. "Yes, detective?" the night sergeant asks drowsily through the phone, stifling a yawn.

"Sorry for bothering you," Detective Jones replies cordially before continuing. "I was trying to find out where this particular murder victim was found?" Jones asked, as he scans the report looking for anything specific that might jump out at him, but it looks as though the officer who filed the report wasn't very smart and forgot to put the location of the incident in the report.

"It was called in over in the Greenacres area off of 10th Avenue and 57th," the desk sergeant replies impatiently, wanting to get off of the phone and back to the new show he has been streaming on Netflix on his phone.

"Okay, thank you," Detective Jones says before hanging up and reaching for his notepad, always reliably in his breast pocket. He takes it out, flips pass the various pages of notes as he searches for a blank page near the back. As he is flipping through the pages, his eye catches on the tag number of the Mercedes that had been shot up a while ago around the Federal Highway part of Lake Worth and not even sure why he feels this is relevant to his current investigation, but he looks at that page again.

Detective Jones sits his notepad down, still on the same page as the Mercedes license plate number and opens up the homepage of his computer before logging into the Palm Beach County Sheriff's Office server, using his badge number and password. He clicks on the icon that goes to the Department of Motor Vehicles so he can run the tag number involved in vehicle crimes such as carjacking, fleeing and eluding, vehicular manslaughter and so on, and he types the Mercedes license plate number into the search box and clicks on search. He doesn't have to wait long before he's looking at the name, address and other personal information belonging to one Sintero Rodriguez residing in Wellington's Black Diamond area from the information displayed on the screen. Detective Jones notices that the address on the drivers' license is different from that of where the Mercedes is registered to, raising suspicion and prompting him to dig even deeper.

Before long, he discovers that within the last month, Sintero Rodriguez has purchased a brand new Cadillac Escalade from a car dealership called *Reliable Rides*, and he scribbles a new note in his notepad to call tomorrow and talk to someone over there for more information. As the night slowly crawls by, Detective Jones alternates between reading reports from the Greenacres area and searching through the database, looking for anything that seems likely to jump out at him and put him on the trail of where all of the drugs are coming from around that area. He notices that for some reason there has been an unusually high number of arrests involving Hispanic and black people for drugs and guns which seems to have a high probability of being gang related by photos and notes of their tattoos or the colors they were seen wearing and repping.

Detective Jones sits at his desk and tries to fit the pieces together as he continues scrolling through and reading the reports, as he learns more about the flood of drugs being distributed throughout the Greenacres and Lake Worth areas. Overtime, Detective Jones begins to see a conspiracy for a takeover taking place amongst the rival gangs supplying drugs to the surrounding areas to be able to finance a war for control of Greenacres, Lake Worth, and the Downtown areas. And for some reasons that Detective Jones cannot quite understand at the moment, he has a hunch that Sintero Rodriguez has a lot to do with what's going on in these areas.

"I tried to be civil with you motherfucker, but no, you wanted to be all tough and shit in front of your bitch," Detective Jones says to himself, thinking back to the not so distant night when he got the call about the Mercedes and had to deal with a motherfucker treating him without the proper respect befitting an officer of the law. "I am coming for your ass, punk," Detective Jones declares with so much passion; that which he never felt for his own family and ex-wife.

Chapter Thirty - Nine

Isabella

Isabella sits on her bed listening to Arianna Grande as she scrolls through her newsfeed on Facebook idly, passing the time reading post from people who go to her school talking about the party tonight. Earlier, Jenna had Facetimed her and explained her plans about how she'll get her parents to let her sleep over at Isabella's house so they can sneak out to the party after her dad goes to work.

Isabella sees that she has over 100 friend requests and decides to go through the list to see if she knew anyone for real that's sitting on the wait list. As she scrolls through all of the different profiles checking to see if she knows any of the people who sent her a friend request, her mind drifts off and she finds herself hoping that she'll see Kian at the party tonight. When Isabella had seen him at school over the last couple of days, which hasn't been very much, she's noticed that he has been very distant lately and it's almost as if he's been avoiding her since he hasn't been checking up on her like he used to. It never crossed her mind that he might be going through a lot with the move in with Dice and being away from his siblings. So, it comes almost as a shock to her when she runs across his profile sitting in her friend request box with a sent friend request from over a month ago, judging by the date it says it was sent on her screen.

"Ughh! Fuck my life!" Isabella groans, before accepting his request and continuing on through the list of friend requests, most of which are probably from guys just trying to get into her pants, all of which she declines. Bing! her phone chimes, alerting her to a text message from Jenna, "It's a go, bitch! Make sure you have your clothes and everything ready. I'll bring the party favors!" Jenna's message reads, sending a wave of butterflies fluttering through Isabella's stomach at the thought of being at the same party as Kian's fine ass.

Isabella thinks for a second about what she should say back to Jenna, before deciding against answering and jumping out of her bed and heading over to her closet to pick out an outfit for tonight. She searches through her clothes looking for the perfect choice between classy and and not too slutty and yet something that will catch Kian's eye for sure. Isabella brings out some choices before realizing that Jenna will probably veto her choice regardless of what she picks and gives up, settling for a hot shower while she anxiously waits for her dad to leave.

She heads into the bathroom and turns the water on to let it warm up before getting undressed and stepping under the hot spray. After about 5 minutes, she begins to relax under the soothing pressure of the hot water massaging her scalp and shoulders.

"Izzy?" she hears her name being called faintly from the other side of the bathroom door before knocking and calling her name again. "Isabella?" her father calls through the door as he tries to gain his daughter's attention.

She shuts the water off and is instantly bombarded by the cold pumping through the air vents from the bathroom ceiling, raising goosebumps on her skin as she shivers. "Yea, dad?" Isabella yells from her hiding spot inside the bathtub, not daring to step out to face the cold air.

"I'm going to work now, just wanted to let you know, sweetheart," her father calls to her. She knows she has her daddy wrapped around her little finger. He adores her.

"Okay, I love you!" Isabella replies quickly, before turning the hot water back on and finishing her shower. She steps out and dries off quickly before wrapping herself in a big, fluffy towel and returning to her bedroom.

She texts Jenna back and lets her know that her dad is gone and Jenna replies back almost instantly, letting her know that she'll be getting dropped off in about 20 minutes, raising another wave of anxiety in Isabella. She sets her phone down on the charger and listens to music on the iheart radio app while she throws on a tank top and sweatpants before climbing into her bed and turning on 'Queen of the South'. About halfway through the show, Isabella's phone rings and when she picks it up she sees that it's Jenna calling.

"Hey girl," Isabella says when she answers, pausing her show so she can hear what Jenna is saying on the other end.

"Hey Iz, I'm bout to pull up into your driveway now," Jenna says briefly before hanging up.

Isabella gets out of her bed and heads to the front door to wait on Jenna's arrival, but as she approaches the front door, she realizes that Jenna's waiting outside already.

"Heeeey!" Jenna squeals, when Isabella opens the door and finds her friend waiting on the other side dressed in sweatpants and a sweater with her backpack over her shoulder.

"Hey Jenna, come on in," Isabella says, stepping back to allow Jenna's entrance into the house and waving at her parents in thanks as they are waiting for her to make it inside safely.

The girls close the door and wait, watching the car's headlights back out and pull off, before they head to Isabella's room. Isabella braces herself as she watches Jenna inspect her chosen outfits laying spread out on one side of her bed.

"What the fuck are you aiming for? A celibate nun?" Jenna asks sarcastically, turning to cast a disapproving look at Isabella over her choice of clothes.

"What? Those are cute!" Isabella argues weakly, as she tries to hide her embarrassment over her failure to pick something that Jenna would approve of.

"Thank God I'm here to save you from yourself," Jenna chides, causing Isabella to sink into her covers, trying to hide her shame. "We still got a couple hours before the party starts so that gives us plenty of time to get ourselves together," Jenna adds with a flourish, as she tears through Isabella's clothes looking for just the right fit to hook her homegirl up with.

After helping pick out Isabella's outfit, they start on each other's hair and nails, taking turns, before moving on to makeup. They both hate how boys never understand how much they put into their looks and upkeep, just to look pretty for the boys who don't tend to appreciate it. "Bring that ass here, girl," Jenna teases, as she pats the seat in front of the vanity mirror Isabella has in her room. One that her daddy had bought her right after her mother had disappeared, to show her something to remind her how special she was. She had always loved that vanity. Isabella walks over and subjects herself to Jenna's ministrations for about 30 minutes before finally being released from her friend's clutches. "You look fucking amazing," Jenna states proudly, "If I was Kian, I would definitely try to fuck," she jokes, before searching through her backpack for a moment.

Isabella watches as Jenna pulls out at least 10 bottles of Smirnoff Green Apple Winecoolers out of her backpack before bringing out a bigger bottle of Hypnotiq last. "You ready to get litty?" Jenna squeals in excitement, making Isabella wonder what the fuck she's gotten herself into when she let Jenna talk her into going to this party.

"Are you sure we should be drinking before we get there?" Isabella wonders hesitantly, trying to stall so she can figure out a way to talk Jenna out of making her drink all of that alcohol.

"Of course," Jenna replies, looking at Isabella as if she had grown two heads. "It's called being ahead of the curve," Jenna explains. "Nobody who's smart waits to bring their shit to a party, because the people who don't have access to get their own will be all over you, trying to mooch off of yours," Jenna adds, lacing Isabella up on high school party etiquette.

"Okay, I get it," Isabella says, as Jenna twists off the cap of two winecoolers and hands her one of them. "Bottoms up, bitch!" Jenna says, before turning her bottle almost upside down and taking big gulps from her drink while Isabella stares at her in astonishment. After about 5 or 6 chugs, Jenna finally relents and tilts her bottle back down so she can get a breath of air while Isabella is almost afraid to look to see how much is left.

"Your turn," Jenna prompts with a smirk, already feeling better, as Isabella steels herself and slowly raises the bottle to her lips, only to discover that it tastes more like a Green Jolly Rancher than an alcoholic beverage.

She takes a couple more sips, each bigger than the last, earning a laugh from Jenna when she realizes her shy ass friend likes the taste. "You really thought I'd give you something strong, Izzy?" Jenna accuses playfully, making Isabella feel a little bad for not having more trust in her friend.

"My bad, I guess I was expecting some fireball or something equally crazy from your crazy ginger ass!" Isabella says, laughing.

"Next time I got'chu," Jenna replies, as they continue to sip on their winecoolers and watch 'Queen of the South', waiting on the clock to wind down to party time.

After they each drink their 5 winecoolers, Isabella realizes that she feels a little bit tipsy and turns one of the bottles over to read the alcohol content, seeing that it's only 5% for the Smirnoff Green Apple Winecoolers.

"So, if these are five percent alcohol, how much does that have?" she asks, pointing to the blue Hypnotiq bottle sitting on the nightstand.

"Shit, probably like 30, I hope!" says, Jenna with a grin, before being distracted by the beeping of her phone.

Isabella watches as Jenna unlocks her phone and begins typing something on her screen for a minute before relocking her phone and turning to look at Isabella with an excited expression. "The party's already started and I just ordered an Uber to take us, so get your shit together, cause it'll be here in 10 minutes," Jenna says in a rush, as they begin to pick up all of the empty bottles from the Winecoolers and putting them into a plastic grocery bag that Isabella got from the kitchen to hide them in, so her dad won't accidentally find them.

They each get a purse and put whatever they are taking with them to the party inside and Isabella watches as Jenna somehow manages to stuff the Hypnotiq bottle inside her purse to carry. Isabella leads Jenna to the front door after turning off all of the lights and making sure all of the doors are locked, before heading outside and getting into the backseat of the Uber. The Uber pulls out of the driveway and proceeds down the road while the girls sit in the backseat and talk about everything except the party, hoping that it's jumping by the time they get there.

After about 15 minutes of riding in the Uber, Jenna checks her phone and sees that they are getting close. "We're here," Jenna squeals excitedly, jumping up and down in her seat with a hand on Isabella's shoulder. The Uber driver pulls down the block and parks while Jenna completes the transaction and gives the driver a 5 star rating, after referencing the movie *Stuber* and laughing.

"Thank you," Jenna and Isabella say in unison as they exit the car and walk up the driveway of the spacious house in front of them to the front door to knock.

As they approach, Isabella watches as Jenna sends a quick text to some of her friends who are supposed to be there already. "I let them know we are here," Jenna says, before stepping forward and knocking on the door.

They wait a couple of seconds before the door is opened by Aaron who has a big grin on his face. "What's up guys! Come on in!" Aaron says, opening the door for them and stepping aside so they can enter the house. Isabella walks into the house and can hear loud music being played from a speaker towards the back among the sounds of people talking and laughing. "There's food and drinks in the kitchen, beer pong, a pool table, and a swimming pool on the back patio," Aaron says, as they walk deeper into the house.

They pass groups of people smoking and drinking out of red Solo cups while they stand around and chill, or even just walk around mingling with friends. Jenna leads them out to the back of the house where there is a patio with a screened in pool in the backyard to the beer pong table where a pretty blonde girl stands next to her boyfriend. "Hey Emily!" Jenna gushes, the girl Emily turning around in surprise.

"You came! How are you, Jenna?" Emily asks, as they hug each other and Emily turns to Isabella. "Hey Izzy! I'm glad you came! Do you want something to drink?" Emily asks her with a smile.

"I'm good, thanks," Isabella refuses politely, not wanting to drink any more alcohol at the party than absolutely necessary.

"James, you goin' to play?" Emily asks, turning to her boyfriend as a spot opens up at the table.

"Yea," he replies, as he walks around the side of the ping pong table and grabs a ball out of the fish bowl sitting on the edge. "I got $5 dollars a game!" James calls loudly with a grin on his face as he slaps a bill down on the green table.

"I call that!" another white boy calls back, as he walks over to the other end of the ping pong table.

"Matt, you know you can't play for shit!" James says back, mockingly, each trying to egg the other on.

"Okay then, put your money where your mouth is, dickhead!" Matt says, also putting a $5 dollar bill down on top of the table and looking across its surface towards James.

"It's your go, playboy," Matt says with a smirk on his face, anticipating an easy win, thinking James is just a hypeman trying to talk himself up.

As they start to play, Isabella sneaks glances around the patio, looking for Kian or Quan. After a couple of sweeps, she realizes that they either haven't arrived yet, or they aren't coming and resigns herself to watching the two white boys play beer pong while Jenna and Emily talk. "You seen Kian yet?" Jenna asks Isabella, breaking off her conversation with Emily and sliding closer to Isabella.

"No, I haven't seen either of them yet," Isabella replies nonchalantly, trying not to give Jenna a clue as to how she's really feeling about their absence.

"Oh, I'm sure they'll show," Jenna says with a grin, spreading across her face, "But for right now, just keep your pants on and try to enjoy yourself," she adds with a laugh, nudging Isabella slightly when she notices the blush spreading across her face.

"I am keeping my pants on," Isabella says, causing Jenna to laugh again.

Chapter Forty

James

As James tried to concentrate on throwing the ping pong as accurately as possible, he can't help but overhear the two girls standing next to Emily talking about the two black boys that ride in the back of his bus. The girl Jenna laughs at something her friend says before replying with "Let's see how long you keep them on after Kian gets here," which causes James to look over and miss his shot.

"Fuck!" James hisses, watching as Matt laughs at him from the other side of the table.

"You ready to admit defeat yet?" Matt asks snidely.

"You got me fucked up, dude," James replies, while Matt aims the ping pong ball, trying to line up his shot. He shoots the ball and James watches as it sails through the air before landing in the middle of James' line of cups.

"Drink up motherfucker!" Matt teases, as James plunks the ball out of the cup and tilts his head back to drink the liquor inside. After he's finished, he lowered the cup and wipes his mouth with the back of his hand, before setting the cup off to one side and picking the ball up. They continue trading shots back and forth, drinking when one of the cups get hit, and pretty soon, both James and Matt are pretty drunk.

"Are ya gon' shoot da ball, or not?" James slurs, while waiting for Matt to get himself together and finish up their game.

"I on't know..." Matt replies drunkenly, after a couple of seconds of fighting with himself, looking like he is going to puke.

"Okay then, I win," James says, reaching for the two alcohol soaked $5 dollar bills that are still laying on the table and shoving them into his pocket, Matt waving his consent drunkenly. James starts to walk away from the table to let people that had been waiting play, but as he steps away, he momentarily forgets who or what he is supposed to be looking for.

"James?" somebody calls faintly, causing him to turn slowly while he looks around for the voice that called him, fighting to keep his balance. "James, you're finally done?" a pretty blonde girl asks him as she stares at him, waiting for an answer. He tried to remember where he knows her from, and had to think hard for a second before it finally clicks that this is kind of his girlfriend; Emily, and they ride the bus together.

"Are you done or not?" Emily asks impatiently, getting a small nod in response from James, who is clearly drunk. "You're drunk as fuck," Emily says in accusation, as she takes one of his hands and leads him over to a patio chair to sit down. She sits down beside him but James had a hard time trying to stop himself from leaning over her. "Ughh, James you're squishing me," Emily whines, as she tries to hold him up and over his own side of the seat.

After a few more failed attempts she finally gives up trying to hold him up and they sit there for a while in silence, James in his drunken stupor, Emily mad and pouting at having to babysit. James leans against Emily for a little while before she finally stands up, causing him to tip over in the chair.

"I'm going to go find Jenna real quick and I'll bring you something to drink," Emily says, raising a groan out of James in response.

After a while of laying on the patio chair, James finally collects himself enough to shake back to life and function enough to sit up and move around. He sits up and stretches, as he looks around in confusion, seeing kids drinking and smoking while they chill beside the pool and look back at him with amused expressions. He stumbles off of the chair and begins to wander around the patio aimlessly looking for Emily. After searching the backyard and patio, James finds his way inside the house wandering around drunkenly.

"Emily?" James calls, lurching into the kitchen to search for her. "Emily?" he calls again, pushing past people and bumping into the counter.

"Watch what the fuck you're doing, dumbass!" a girl snaps, raising her cup above her head to protect it from James' blundering.

James leaves the kitchen and heads to the entryway of the house, where he finds Emily, Jenna, and Isabella coming down a hallway to the left. "Heeey Em," James slurs, as they approach, holding out his arms as if to hug her.

"Hi James," Emily replies reluctantly, as she allows him to hug her briefly, before stepping away to stand beside Jenna, who's trying to hold back a laugh after assessing James' present state.

"Where did you go, Em?" James asks, as he follows the girls from the hallway back into the heart of the party where the music is playing and people are dancing, mostly lewd and seductively.

"Had to use the girls room real quick," Emily answers, as they weave their way through the crowd, "Wet, wet, wet, wet, wet, wet, ohh baby..." booms from the speakers as `Pills and Automobiles` begins playing.

"Ohhh! This is my shit!" Emily squeals, looking at Jenna and Isabella before grabbing their hands and disappearing deeper into the crowd, leaving a drunken and confused James behind, as he stares after the last place he saw Emily's golden curtain of beautiful curls vanish.

Even in his discombobulated condition, James realizes that something about the way she was just acting towards him was different, as he turns around and decides to find somewhere to chill at until he can think clearly.

Chapter Forty - One

Kilo

Kilo sits in the passenger side of the Infinity, with Glizzy behind the wheel and Quan in the backseat, while Glizzy weaves through the night traffic, following the directions Quan gives him as they head to the party's address. "Turn left on Federal Highway, bruh," Quan instructs, as Glizzy makes the turn, causing Kilo to have to close his hand gently to avoid spilling the weed out of the blunt he is rolling in the process of riding over there to the house.

"It's coming up on the left in about 5 minutes," Quan calls from the backseat, as Kilo puts the finishing touches and then a twist on the blunt and puts it in a ziploc bag containing more blunts that he had pre-rolled.

"I 'ont even know why I'm even takin' y'all to this shit," Glizzy grumbles, as they begin to look for the house the party is supposed to be at.

"Cause we needed some wheels, bruh, quit cryin'," Kilo says jokingly, before spotting a big stone house with a bunch of cars parked around it. "That's got to be it," Kilo says, pointing at the house as Glizzy pulls over to the curb to let them out.

"Y'all gon' get some pussy tonight, or don't come back," Glizzy threatens playfully, as Quan and Kilo open their doors to get out of the car, causing some people chilling in the front yard to look over in their direction, admiring the Infinity.

"You already know was'sup, my Z," Kilo boasts, feeling himself for pulling up in a dope ass whip. "You ain't comin' in?" he asks Glizzy, as he checks his pockets to make sure he's got everything he is going to need tonight.

"Hell nawl, lil' bruh, fuck I look like hanging out at a high school party with high school kids for?" Glizzy asks, rhetorically, causing Kilo to smile.

"Nigga, cuz I'm here," Kilo replies, as he shuts the door and follows Quan up to the front door to knock.

Quan reaches out to knock on the door but Kilo stops him, "Fuck you knockin' for, Q? It's a party, the muthafuckin' door probably open," Kilo says, as he reaches for the handle of the door and turns it, opening the big wooden door. They walk into the house and follow the sounds of music to the back of the house where a bunch of girls are dancing in the middle of the room with spectators watching as they stand out of their way against the wall.

"Hold up, Q! Let's post up for a second and see..." Kilo says, mesmerized as he watches a Spanish girl that caught his eye while she was twerking. After watching her throw that ass for a little while, Kilo finally breaks out of his trance and he and Quan go outside onto the patio to smoke. Kilo pulls the bag of pre-rolled blunts from his pocket and fires one up, releasing a cloud of potent smoke into the screened in patio.

While Kilo and Quan smoke, Kilo notices that every couple of seconds, somebody's girl will turn around and stare in their direction, as if waiting for an invite to come and chill, so it doesn't take long for the first one to try her hand halfway through the blunt, the blonde girl from their bus is walking by when she notices them smoking and invites herself over and sits down with them.

"Don't I know you?" she asks Kilo in a friendly voice, as she sits down across from them, her knee touching Kilo's, drawing a curious look from Quan.

"Nawl shawty, I don't think so," Kilo replies shortly, as he reaches for the blunt Quan is holding hostage while he stares at the blonde girl seated across from them. "I would definitely remember being around your fine ass," Quan says, trying to shoot his shot, causing Kilo to shake his head at Quan's antics.

"I think we ride the bus together," the girl says, drawing a confused look from Quan and an exasperated sigh from Kilo.

"We do?" Quan asks stupidly, looking over at Kilo for help at identifying the pretty white girl in front of them.

"Yea bruh, she always sits with her lame ass boyfriend, James or something," Kilo clarifies, a look of understanding spreading across Quan's face while the blonde girl frowns, her eyes following the blunt.

"Umm, my name is Emily, and he's NOT my boyfriend. Thank you very much," Emily says with an attitude.

"That's cool, so why you not chillin' with him then?" Kilo asks as if she didn't just disclaim him, his patience running thin.

"Because I'm not tryna be a damn baby sitter, I'm tryna have some fun!" Emily snaps at Kilo, before rolling her eyes and turning her sights to Quan, hoping that he'll find her attractive so that she can get into his pockets, assuming that they sell drugs. "And like I said, he's not my boyfriend," Emily repeats sweetly, fluttering her eyes at Quan seductively.

"So, what you tryna say is—" Quan begins to say, staring at Emily longingly.

"Is that James is a smart muthafucka," Kilo says, interrupting Quan and earning a glare back from Emily.

"Are you always this rude?" Emily asks Kilo stiffly, as he grins and passes the blunt to Quan, deciding whether or not to answer her.

Quan hits the remainder of the blunt and looks over at Kilo to see if he wants it back before he puts it out, Kilo shaking his head 'no'. Kilo watches Quan hesitate for a second as he tried to decide what to do with the remainder of the blunt before finally deciding to put it out and save it.

"Can I hit that real quick before you put it out?" Emily asks Quan quickly, drawing a laugh from Kilo as Quan starts to hand her the blunt roach.

"Sorry shawty, we ain't friendly," Kilo says, as he intercepts the roach from Quan when he is about to hand it to Emily and drops it into an abandoned cup sitting nearby where it sizzles in the liquid inside the cup. "We only supply paying customers," Kilo says, with a grin as Emily growls and stomps away.

"What the fuck, Key?" Quan cries, turning to Kilo with a look of anger on his face at Kilo chasing Emily off.

"Trust me Q, you don't wanna fuck with a bitch like that," Kilo says, shaking his head at Quan's ignorance.

"Why not?" Quan asks, looking at Kilo for an explanation as to what he's trying to imply.

"Girls like that only want one thing, that's your money," Kilo quotes from Yo Gotti's song, 'Come Up'.

"Yea, that's all cool and shit, but there's only one problem with that Key, I'on got no money, bruh," Quan says, looking at Kilo like he's crazy for scaring away a pretty girl like that.

"It doesn't matter Q, we got drugs and to hoes, that's better than money," Kilo says, as he gets up from his seat and looks down at Quan. "Let's go find Isabella and Jenna, bruh."

They head back inside the house and go to the kitchen to get something to drink to combat the cottonmouth he is infected with. Kilo grabs a couple grape Fanta and hands one to Quan before walking out of the kitchen and back into the room where everyone is dancing at.

"Is that them?" Quan asks, pointing to two girls standing besides each other in a corner, watching Emily dance on some dude who must go to school with them. Kilo looks towards where Quan is pointing his finger and nods his head, confirming Quan's guess as to the girls' location.

They squeeze their way through the crowd towards Isabella and Jenna, who don't see them approaching until Kilo and Quan are standing right next to them. "If I didn't know better I'd think y'all was hiding from us," Kilo says smoothly, as he gently grabs Isabella by the elbow, causing her to gasp in surprise as she turns to look at him.

"Hey y'all!" Jenna says, as she turns around with a smile and hugs Quan, raising a surprised smile from him.

"What y'all been up to?" asks Kilo, as he gives Isabella a once over, admiring the outfit she's got on, which compliments her figure and skin tone.

"Not shit, we've just been chillin', ya know? Trying to find something to turn up on," Jenna says saucily, a little smirk on the corners of her pretty thin lips.

Kilo watches as Isabella turns to look at Jenna and the girls engage in a silent conversation with a lot of facial expressions. "Y'all ain't gotta do all that Morse Code shit," Kilo jokes, stopping their nonverbal communication as they both turn to look at him. "C'mon," Kilo says, letting go of Isabella's arm and turning to walk back out the room, fighting his way through the crowd, opening up a path for Quan, Jenna and Isabella to follow after him. They got to the entryway leading to the kitchen where Kilo got Quan's and his sodas from earlier, before Jenna calls his name, trying to stop him.

"We need to find our homegirl real quick," Jenna says, looking at Kilo when he turns around to ask what she wants.

"Who?" Quan asks, causing her to turn to glance over at him impatiently.

"She's talking about Emily," Isabella says, rolling her eyes at the mention of Emily, clearly not having a favorable opinion of her.

"Text her and let her know where to meet us," Kilo says, hoping that they forget about Emily and leading them upstairs where they can smoke in one of the empty or available rooms.

Kilo sits down on the bed and pulls out the bag of blunts, leaving everyone else to find their own seat. He fires up after everybody is sitting down and scrolls through some music to play, before settling on the new Kodak Black, Back for Everything album and letting that play.

They listen to Kodak Preach as they pass the blunt around and relax, trying to get to know one another a little bit better. The blunt reaches Jenna, who hits it and begins coughing almost instantly and quickly passes it to Isabella, who takes the cigar cautiously, like it might try to bite her.

"Be careful shawty, this shit some gas," Kilo advises her, a little bit too late.

"Thanks for the heads up, Kian," Jenna manages to say between coughs, as she holds her hand over her mouth.

"Here, drink some of this," Quan says, handing Jenna his soda can, which she then tips back to take a sip out of it.

They all talk and catch up on shit that has been going on with them since the last time they all saw each other at school and actually had a chance to sit down and kick it, while they smoke the blunt and vibe to South Florida's own, Kodak. After a couple songs and the second blunt about to be lit, Jenna remembers the bottle of Hypnotiq stashed in her purse. "I almost forgot about this shit!" she says excitedly, pulling the blue bottle from her purse with a flourish.

"Ohh shit, now the real party begins," Quan jokes, as Jenna opens the bottle up and looks for some cups to pour the alcohol into.

"Just use these," Kilo tells her, offering her the soda can, which she happily takes from him and begins to pour out the alcohol for them to enjoy.

"Me and Isabella don't have cups, so y'all have to share," Jenna states, looking at Kilo and Quan with a little twinkle in her eye as she scoots over, closer to Quan and drinks from his can.

Kilo shrugs as he watches Jenna chug the Hipnotiq from the grape Fanta can. "I'm from the hood shawty, I've drank from worse," he says, before taking a generous sip from his own soda can and handing it to Isabella. "Bottoms up shawty," Kilo says, looking Isabella in the eye as he wets his bottom lips with his tongue, tasting the Hypnotiq's aphrodisiac tang.

After drinking for a little bit, there is a knock on the door, causing Kilo to look over at Quan when curiosity piqued his interest. Quan sitting cuddled up with Jenna, while they take turns drinking from the soda can and smoking the blunt.

"What the fuck?" Kilo asks, as he starts to get up from his seat on the bed to go see who's on the other side of the door.

"I'on know, Key," Quan says, shaking his head, not willing to get up and risk losing the traction he seems to be making with Jenna.

"Jenna? Isabella?" a feminine voice calls from the other side of the door, causing Kilo to groan and turn to look over at Jenna, who is leaning against Quan contently, but sits up slightly with a look of abashment on her face, as the door is opened and Emily walks into the room. "So, this is where the party's at, huh?"

Chapter Forty - Two

Quan

"So, this is where the party's at, huh?" Emily asks, as she walks into the room, closing the door behind herself and strutting over to the bed, plopping down next to Isabella.

"Nawl, shawty, we just chillin'," Kian says, gritting his teeth in annoyance at being interrupted while chilling with Isabella.

"I can see that, Baby-boy," Emily replies flirtatiously, looking over at Kian before asking, "So, where's it at?"

Quan looks over at Kian, who meets his gaze with stormy clouds swirling, threatening to unleash their fury at this bitch's intrusion and nerve. "Where's what at?" Kian asks as he walks back over to the bed and sits back down next to Isabella, making sure to keep her in between himself and Emily as a safety precaution.

"The weed, nigga," Emily says, eagerly looking around the room for a hint of where it could be hiding from her at.

"We don't got no more," Kian says with a smirk on his face, obviously enjoying telling Emily she can't smoke or hang with them.

"Get the fuck out of here with that shit, Kian!" Emily snaps, rolling her eyes at him and looking over at Jenna for help. "Why can't I smoke?" Emily whines, as she glances at Jenna and trying to stir up any kind of sympathy in her, and hoping that Jenna will step up and back her play. She doesn't though.

"We don't got shit up here shawty, we drinking soda and shit!" Kian lies, trying to get the obnoxious girl out of the room so they can go back to vibing like they were before she stormed in.

"Whatever! Y'all are fucking lame..." Emily mutters before getting up from the bed and storming back out of the room, slamming the door shut.

As soon as Emily leaves, Kian gets up and rushes over to the door, locking it behind her, before heading back over to the bed where Isabella is sitting and settling back into his comfort zone with her and sighing his relief. "Thank God she's gone," Kilo says, causing Isabella to laugh at his obvious distain for Emily, which she apparently shares by her reaction to his comment.

"Y'all are so mean!" Jenna scolds, trying to contain her own laughter and failing miserably from her position, as she leans against Quan.

Kilo takes a second to scroll through his phone and Quan can already tell by his mannerisms from knowing him for all of his life that he is up to something, as a grin spreads across his face. "East Side, Bankhead, that's where I'm from, everything y'all did, it's been done, my true game and my shoe game, can't touch that shit, bitch nigga, talkin' bout fuck me, nawl, Fuck Dat Bitch!" Young Dro snaps, 'FDB' playing from Kilo's phone as he takes out the bag of blunts and lights one up while bobbing his head to the music. "Man, Fuck Dat Bitch!" Kilo says, as he takes a hit off the blunt and French inhales, trying to show out for Isabella, who Quan notices surprisingly is actually unwinding around Kilo. They all continue to vibe while they drink Hipnotiq out of the Fanta cans and smoke the weed Kilo brought along with him to the party and pretty soon, everyone is feeling the effects of the alcohol and weed.

Quan can't help but notice how Kilo and Isabella are being all touchy feely with each other, finding any reason to use as an excuse to rub up on the other as they laugh and giggle together.

"So, what y'all tryna do?" Kilo asks boldly, looking first at Isabella, then over at Jenna who has a wicked smile plastered on her face.

"I mean, I'm up for whatever," Jenna replies, looking over at Isabella first to gage her response before looking at Quan and snuggling closer to him as she runs her hand along his leg teasingly. Quan can feel his lil' soldier respond to Jenna's hand while he tries to keep his composure against her advances. Without Quan seeing, Kilo had somehow managed to include some slow songs into his play queue to be able to set the mood while chilling with Jenna and Isabella.

"Oh na-na, look what you done started, I said oh na-na, why ya gotta act so naughty," Trey Songz sings, while Quan closes his eyes and Jenna's hand continues its teasing caresses. "Here shawty, try this," Quan hears Kilo tell Isabella, as he opens his eyes to see Kilo putting the cherry of the blunt into his mouth and closing his lips around it carefully, so he doesn't burn himself, while Isabella looks at him curiously.

"It's called a 'Shotgun'," Jenna says to Isabella, who takes a second before leaning forward and wrapping her lips around the back of the blunt to inhale creating a kissing effect between her and Kilo.

"Awww! That's so cute," Jenna gushes, causing Isabella to blush and quickly pull away, Kilo throwing a glare over at Jenna.

"Sorry," Jenna mumbles, before leaning back against Quan and watching Kilo and Isabella while she strokes Quan's thigh slowly and sensually.

"Here, try this," Kilo says softly, raising the blunt to his lips and taking a deep pull off it before reaching out and gently placing his hand behind Isabella's head and drawing her forward slowly, until their lips finally touch. It seems like forever before they finally separate and Isabella expels the smoke that Kilo had blown into her mouth when their lips had met. Nobody in the room speaks for a minute as Kilo and Isabella just stare into each other's eyes for a while, comfortable in their own world, together. Oblivious to everyone and everything around them. Chirp! Isabella's phone chimes suddenly, causing her to jump out of her dream with Kilo before taking her phone out of her bag and checking her messages.

Quan watches as Kilo runs his hand over his head in annoyance while Isabella texts a reply to whoever had just texted her. Isabella looks up from her phone and over at Jenna. "My dad just texted me, he'll be home soon."

Jenna groans and looks over at Quan, who stares into her eyes, feeling like there is something deeper to these girls than just regular high school shit. He makes a mental note to bring it up to Kilo later and see what he thinks about it when they can talk freely.

"I'm sooo sorry," Isabella says, as she sets her phone down on the bed and leans forward, cupping Kilo's face with her hand.

"We don't mean to run off on you guys," Jenna adds, as she runs her hand down Quan's leg one more time before standing up too fast and stumbling, causing Quan to have to grab her waist to stabilize her. "I'm good Quan, thank you," Jenna says sweetly, before turning around to face Isabella, who is treating Kilo to the same reluctant goodbye. They exit the room and head down the hallway, back down stairs where the party is still going on, while the girls talk amongst themselves about arranging an Uber to take them back to Isabella's house to beat her dad getting home before them.

"So, when you gon' let a nigga see you again?" Quan hears Kilo whisper to Isabella, as he gently grabs her waist and pulls her closer to his side possessively.

"I don't know yet, Kian, but I'll let you know at school though, I promise," Isabella replies, as she and Jenna break away and head out of the front door of the house, leaving Kilo and Quan staring forlornly after them.

"Well, I guess we can't call Glizzy to come and get us," jokes Kilo, as they turn away from the door and head deeper into the house to go back outside to the patio to smoke. Quan watches as Kilo lights up a blunt and they walk through the party, headed outside, a trail of potent weed smoke wafting from the tip of the blunt as they walk through the crowded dance room to reach the patio door.

They got outside and looked for an empty spot to sit and relax before spotting a table over in the corner by the pool where some girls in bikinis are swimming. They walk over and sit down and begin passing the blunt back and forth between themselves while they watch the girls throw an inflatable pool ball around. "So, was it me, or did you sink into your heart a lil' bit when we was chillin' with them?" Quan asks seriously, looking over at Kilo while smoke trails from his mouth as he ponders Quan's question.

"I don't know, Q," Kilo finally says, without looking at Quan, choosing to watch the girls frolicking in the pool like beautiful teenaged mermaids instead.

While they were talking, Quan sees Emily sitting next to a drunk looking white boy, who looks vaguely familiar and who keeps looking over in their direction. "Yo, who is that?" Quan asks, nodding his head in the direction of the boy sitting next to Emily who is again, mugging them.

"That's that white boy James, that Emily deals with, Q," Kilo states matter of fact, as he briefly looks in the direction Quan indicated to see who he is talking about.

"Ohh, that's the one you were talking about earlier, huh?" Quan asks Kilo, as the blunt crackles and pops loudly in his hand when he takes a long hit from it.

"Yea, bruh," Kilo says, watching as James gets up from his seat and begins to stumble his way over to them, Emily trailing behind him with a smug expression on her face as they approach where Quan and Kilo are chilling at.

"Hey you!" the white boy James yells, as he shuffles toward Quan and Kilo. "Yo niggas!" James calls again, more obnoxiously this time, as he gets closer and Quan can see he is pretty drunk from how his movements are and from his slurred speech.

"Who the fuck is you callin' 'nigga', pussy ass cracker!" Kilo yells angrily, standing up and walking over to meet James face to face, drawing the attention of everybody within hearing range.

"I'm talking to you and your homie, who the hell else would I be callin' 'niggas' out here?" James says cockily, spreading his arms wide to indicate nobody else around. "What'chu thought? That you could just treat my girl like a whore and I wouldn't find out, you fuckin' monkey?"

"Hoe ass cracker! Who is you calling a monkey?" Kilo yells in response to James' racist remark, as he gets all up in his face and pushes him roughly, causing him to stumble back and almost fall.

"Ain't nobody said shit to that hoe!" Quan yells, coming over to stand by Kilo's side, in case James feels some type of way and tried to swing on him.

"You can't go around disrespecting my girl and slide, motherfucker!" James says, as he looks back at Emily, who is watching the confrontation going on between James and Kilo with obvious delight.

A crowd begins to gather in a circle around them, anticipating a fight, as James continues to yell at Kilo drunkenly and accuse them of disrespecting Emily.

"Fuck this shit," Kilo growls as he strips his shirt over his head and tossed it behind him when James becomes too bold from boosting himself up from his yelling and stepping aggressively forward towards Kilo. "This the only time I'ma give you a chance to back track before I fuck yo ass up, cracker!" Kilo states firmly, causing James to hesitate for a second before throwing caution to the wind and stepping into Kilo's face, Quan shaking his head at his stupidity.

Quan watches as Kilo squares up and his right jab shoots out, snapping across James' jaw and throwing his head back, knocking him onto his ass. A collective laugh rises up from the gathering crowd, as it edges forward, and Emily rushes forward to James' side, trying to help him off the floor. "I'm fine!" James screams angrily, pissed off at letting Kilo knock him down so easily, as he gathers himself and climbs to his feet.

"Arghhh!" James yells his fake war call as he is charging towards Kilo, who stands waiting across the circle of people grouped up around them, standing calm, cool, and collected with his set up, ready.

It's almost like watching in slow motion for Quan as he watches the white boy, James charge towards Kilo, who stands waiting patiently for James to attack him. Quan sees Kilo shift his fighting stance almost imperceptibly right before James gets within reach, Quan wincing, already knowing what's up his sleeve. As James crosses whatever invisible line that Quan knows Kilo has set, he watches Kilo transform into an animal as he explodes forward both fists flying rapidly, surprising James as he catches him perfectly on his chin and the side of his face, stunning him.

James stumbles sideways, as Kilo's blows connect with his face. Kilo takes advantage of this, rushing forward and unleashing a flurry of blows, destroying whatever puny attempts of defense James struggles to cobble together as he tries to protect himself. Out of the corner of his eye, Quan sees another white boy begin to try and slowly edge his way around the circle of spectators, watching Kilo beat James' ass, as he tries to get in position with Kilo's exposed back.

Quan looks around covertly for something to use and spots a beer bottle sitting nearby, which he reaches down and grabs with his right hand, before letting it hang at his side, as he slowly edges his way around the circle his eyes never leave the slowly circling shadow in the crowd. Then, he suddenly heard a loud crash.

Quan whips his head around just in time to catch James colliding into a lawn chair after taking a punch from Kilo. "Motherfucker!" a voice yells, as the other white kid rushes from the crowd, trying to jump Kilo, who spins around nimbly to face the new threat. Quan raises the beer and smashes it over the white kid's head as he rushes by in his haste to get to Kilo, glass flying everywhere as the bottle explodes against his head, dropping him instantly.

"Yo, good looks, Q!" Kilo says, coming over and dapping up Quan while everybody gathered around goes nuts from the way Kilo whooped James' ass, who is still laying on the ground on top of an overturned lawn chair, and his friend, who is knocked out face first, in the dirt after taking a blow from a beer bottle straight to the dome.

"Somebody get help! Please!" Emily cries, as she rushes over to James' unconscious form and crouches down next to him.

"Aye, Key. We needa dip fast!" Quan says, worriedly looking around at all the teenagers still crowded around them.

"Say less," Kilo says as they make their quick exit.

Chapter Forty - Three

Sin

Sin jumps into the driver's seat of his Escalade and pulls out of the parking lot of Grove Custom Auto in Delray Beach and into traffic, after concluding a business meeting with Cien Fuegos. He connects his phone to the truck Bluetooth and opens his Spotify App before scrolling down his song list, searching for the new Lil' Poppa songs to jam to. Lil' Poppa starts teaching about life in Duval County, Florida through the Memphis Audio speakers as he slides through traffic, Sin mumbling along to the music, feeling the message.

While conducting business earlier in the meeting with Cien Fuegos, Sin made a purchase of 25 bricks of pure cocaine and three kilos heroin to be able to stack up his money and bring their combined operation to a whole different level. They also discussed the recent news that Sin had received from Rampage, his spokesman inside the notorious Miami Cuban Y-lo gang that has been putting in major work in their part of the city taking over new territory now that they have a constant supply of guns and drugs, thanks to Sin. Half of the project that Sin had originally hired them to do is now nearing completion, having received news that they've managed to track down the shooter who had tried to get at Sin when he was just finished fucking two bitches in a freakfest at the telly and dropping them off.

The music stops as his phone begins to ring and he swipes the answer icon on his screen to pick up the call. "Yo," Sin says simply, waiting for whoever is on the other end to state their business for hitting him on his personal number, knowing that only a handful of people even had this direct number.

"What's good, big homie?" Rampage asks, causing a wide grin to appear on Sin's face, having been looking forward to being able to connect with the busy young killer and have a sit down to assess the full spectrum of what needs to be done to get down to the finish line of their collective issue concerning the bounty Sin had put on the head of his would-be murderer.

"Shit bruh, just got done tying up some loose ends, ya feel me?" Sin says, as he puts on his blinker to switch lanes and takes the on ramp to get on the Turnpike as he heads to his spot to post up. "I was actually heading over to the spot now, if you tryna pull up and pour me a drink," Sin adds, when there is a pause in the conversation while Rampage tries to figure out a way to ask for an audience.

"Yea, big homie, that's cool with me," Rampage replies eagerly, causing Sin to hear a female's voice in the background begin to ask questions that Rampage ignores while he is in conversation with his big homie.

"A'ight, cool. I'll hit you up when I get free, acere," Sin says before hanging up, not liking to make it a habit of talking about anything over an open phone line for too long. He re-opens his Spotify App and hits shuffle before leaning his seat back and taking a silver cigar tube out of the center console containing a genuine Cuban Cohiba stuffed with premium grade A Northern Lights Kush. He puts the cigar in his mouth and bites the end with his teeth to hold it in place as he applies a flame to its tip from a Zippo lighter he took out of the cupholder and then he inhales the rich smoke into his lungs. He holds the smoke deep inside his chest, for a count of ten, before releasing it in a steady stream which gathers into a cloud inside the truck.

Luxury at its finest, Sin thinks to himself as he looks down at the marijuana cigar clutched between his fingers with a feeling of contentment as he continues to smoke on the drive back to his trap house.

He pulls into the driveway and goes inside the house before going to his bedroom and opening the safe he had installed a couple of weeks ago. Inside rests a big velvet bag containing jewelry, watch boxes, bundles of money, three bricks of cocaine and two clean pistols sitting on top in case of an emergency. He takes a ten thousand dollar stack of money and places it on top of the safe before closing it and walking back out to the living room to chill. Sin pulls his phone out and sends Rampage a text letting him know that he's free for their sit down before sending Nikki a text asking to meet up. He presses the send on Nikki's text and a moment later his phone chimes with a reply from Rampage saying he'll be there in 15 minutes. Sin throws his phone down on the couch next to him and logs into Xbox Live to play a couple games of Call of Duty online until Rampage arrives.

It seems like time flies by as Sin focuses on chasing down his virtual enemies, wishing things were as easy in real life as they were in the game. Briiing! Briiing! Sin's phone chimes from its position on the couch and Sin feels around for it, not wanting to take his eyes from the screen and risk losing the game by letting the other team score an easy kill while his attention is diverted. He finally locates his phone and slides the unlock button on the screen to answer the call that is coming through.

"I'm pulling up now, big homie," Rampage says, when Sin answers the call.

"A'ight, I got'chu," Sin replies briefly, before hanging up and pausing the game. He gets up from the couch and walks over to the front door, momentarily brushing a hand against his hip to double check on his pistol, making sure it's still firmly in place before opening the door.

"What's good, OG?" Rampage greets, as they dap up and Sin turns around, leading him into the house as they head into the living room to sit down.

"You want anything, lil' bruh?" Sin asks, as he throws Rampage a jar of weed that was sitting on the table between them so he can roll up a blunt to smoke while they talk.

"Nawl, I'm cool with this, bruh. 'Preciate you," Rampage replies sincerely, as he splits a Swisher Sweet and begins breaking down the weed inside the blunt.

"So, was'sup?" Sin asks, sitting back against the couch while he watches Rampage roll up the two blunts out of the pack before passing one over to Sin, who nods his head in appreciation. Rampage takes a second to respond to Sin's question while he fires up his blunt and tosses the lighter to Sin, taking a couple deep pulls off of the Swisher.

"So, we got some shit goin' on with these niggas called the Zoe Mafia Affiliates and there's this bitch that everybody call Luna who runs a trap house off of Tamarind Avenue and works for them," Rampage begins, pausing briefly to hit his blunt and to make sure that Sin is following along before continuing. After receiving a nod from Sin, Rampage continues with his updates. "So, ever since we been taking over, we been on some bigger shit than just drive-bys and sticking up corner boys now, thanks to your support," Rampage says, raising two fingers to his head saluting Sin, who nods again.

"I feel you, bruh," Sin says, prompting Rampage to keep going, which he proceeds to do.

"So, anyways, there's been ongoing beef with us and Luna's squad for a while now, and we keep people posted over there just to let us know who and what's shaking, you feel me?" Rampage says, pausing for a second to puff on his Swisher again before dumping the ash onto the empty foil pack, resting on the table in front of him.

"A'ight, that's all cool and shit, bruh, but what the fuck that got to do with what we got going on, besides the fact that I'm supplying you with shit you need to get at this hoe?" Sin asks impatiently, wanting Rampage to get to the point already. Sin watches as Rampage smiles as he lets him finish speaking, showing him the respect he's worked so hard to get from the wolves still thuggin' in the trenches.

"That's what I was about to pour you a drink about, big homie," Rampage says, pausing for effect as he hits the blunt and blows a couple of smoke rings for punctuation.

"So, like I said we be having people watch the spot Luna runs and we saw a greyish or silver Infinity truck pull up there a couple months ago with two niggas inside, one of them we already know about," Rampage states, looking Sin in the eyes with confidence written all over his face. "The other nigga was a jit, probably no older than 17 or 18 at the most. But what's crazy is that he never been over there before. At all, until that day," Rampage says raising his eyebrows dramatically while raising Sin's curiosity.

"So, what the fuck's so special bout this lil' nigga that got y'all so curious," Sin asks, as he lets some smoke trail from his nostrils, making him look like he's capable of breathing fire while he waits for Rampage's response.

"That first time they went over there together was like five or six months ago, but now, he pulls up by himself every now and then in a white Nissan Sentra and everybody knows him by Kilo. Word on the street is, he's been making a name for himself inside the ZMA. Jit's been raising through the ranks like a mufucka,"

214

Rampage says in a rush, causing the information Sin just learned to swirl around in his head.

"That's a lot to know about some unimportant lil' nigga," Sin says, leaning forward and snuffing out the rest of the blunt on the foil pack sitting on the coffee table while Rampage looks at Sin evenly.

"I ain't bringing this lil' nigga, Kilo up just because we both got beef with them ZMA niggas, big homie, you already know that me and the gang got mad love for you for pulling us out the mud and giving us the opportunity to elevate ourselves," Rampage says passionately, looking at Sin with a serious expression on his face, telling him. "We're pretty sure that Kilo's the one who shot up ya whip, bruh. I had somebody follow him a couple of days ago and he pulled up to that same house that you said you dropped that bitch off at and he gave a lil' boy some money. Now, you tell me, where's the connection in that, OG?" Rampage asks, an ominous feeling rising up inside of Sin.

"Is there anything else that I need to know?" Sin hears himself ask as if speaking from a distance, as goosebumps spread across his skin, his nerves on edge, anxious to hear the rest of Rampage's report.

"Nawl, that ain't all, big homie," Rampage says seriously, looking into Sin's eyes and taking a deep breath before continuing. "This nigga Kilo's been fuckin' with ZMA hard, ya feel me? But besides hearing that he's started making a name for himself, we also found out that he's Maniac's oldest son."

At hearing this, Sin roars in anger and punches a hole in the 70 inch flat screen TV on the wall, cutting his hand. "Argghh! Fuck!" he yells in frustration and anger while clutching his bleeding hand to his chest.

He turns and storms into his bedroom and snatches the stack of money off of the top of the safe where he left it at and heads back into the living room where he left a surprised Rampage. "Go and find this hoe ass nigga! I want him dead, and I want his ass dead now!" Sin growls, tossing the money to Rampage, who snatches it out of the air and counts through it quickly as a malicious grin slowly spreads across his face.

"Say less, big homie, there's a big football game tonight between John I. Leonard and Lake Worth High, so I'm sure it won't be too hard to find him, especially if he heads over to the house afterwards, ya feel me?" Rampage says, already heading to the front door.

Sin sits down on the couch and looks down at the drops of blood that are falling from his wounded hand and onto the floor with a wet plopping sound and thinks back to the day he killed Maniac, trying to remember if he ever noticed anything out of the ordinary that day that would lead his son to have the ability to know who it was that killed his dad, then after a while of turning it over in his mind with no results, he begins to speculate that ZMA might have something to do with having him shot at. He remembers that Maniac was one of the founding members of the ruthless street gang with his ties to Haitian Sensations and Zoe Mafia Family being so tight, but he can't decide if the shots in the dark that night would come from ZMA, or this lil' nigga Kilo, that Rampage laced him up about.

"It doesn't even matter at this point, he's ZMA to the death now, so I'm gon' make sho he has a spot right next to his soft ass daddy, in the same graveyard," Sin says out loud, talking to himself.

He looks down and notices that the flow of blood has slowed down a little bit and gently reaches over with his good hand for his phone still lying on the couch nearby. He checks his text messages and sees that Nikki texted back letting him know that she is currently at work right now, but she will let him know as soon as she is free, which brings a smile to his face, as he remembers that it all had started with her.

He decides to take a nap now because he already knows that when he links up with Nikki later tonight, her sexual appetite will drain the life out of him, so he wanted to be prepared.

He heads back into his bedroom and strips off his shirt, which he then wraps around his hand so no blood stains the thousand thread count sheets, and climbs into bed.

"I'll make sure to knock that lil' nigga off the map," Sin mumbles to himself sleepily, before he starts to drift off to sleep.

Chapter Forty - Four

Kian

Kilo puts on his football jersey in the locker room of John I. Leonard High School next to his best friend and day one homie, Joquan Adams. As he prepares himself for the football game about to begin within the next ten minutes, his mind races through all of the possible maneuvers he has been working on lately when he stays after school for practice. He turns to Quan, who is sitting on the bench, next to him, tying his cleats, "Game time, bruh," Kilo says, giving Quan a confident grin.

"Stay on point, Key," Quan says, reminding him that when he usually gets the ball, he doesn't remember to focus on his flanks.

"A'ight," Kilo replies, putting one foot up on the locker room bench and finishes tying his cleats up tight, as he waits for Quan to finish getting ready.

Once all the players in the locker room are ready to line up in front of the doors of the gymnasium leading out to the football field to face their opponents, The Lake Worth High School Trojans. As they race through the doors, the football players yell, then they jog out to the field in a tide of orange and black, their school mascot, a horse of some type, running beside them. As Kilo and Quan jog out onto their side of the football field where their hometeam stands are, Kilo scans the crowded bleachers for Dice and Glizzy.

He finally spots them and raises his helmet as he grins, waving his arm through the air to get their attention. Dice looks over at the players flooding into the field and spots Kilo waving his arm wildly, standing next to Quan and raises his arms in acknowledgement, nudging Glizzy who is sitting next to him looking down at his phone. Kilo nods his head at Glizzy when he looks up from his screen before following Quan over to the team benches where the rest of the football team is crowded around their coach, waiting to hear what he's about to say.

"Adams! Hayworth! You're starting," Coach Garrett yells over the noise, as he looks up from his clipboard, searching for Kilo and Quan amongst the other players clustered around.

Kilo locks eyes with Coach Garrett and nods his head in understanding, before putting his mouth guard into his mouth and placing his helmet on his head, trotting out onto the field beside Quan. "Good luck, Q," Kilo says, looking over at Quan, who nods his head before they separate, taking their positions on the field.

The Trojans kick the ball off and Kilo watches as it tumbles through the air, end over end, as it seems to float slowly over to their side of the field before starting its descent back down to Earth , straight into Kilo's waiting hands. He takes off down the field, charging towards their opponents' end zone 90 yards away, running slightly behind and to the right of one of his teammates, number 57, for a little bit of cover. Kilo trots behind number 57 and lets his eyes scan the field in front of him, taking in the players on the other team charging towards him while he takes his time picking out their weak points.

As the two teams meet up in the center of the field in a clash of padded bodies, Kilo shoots out from behind the player he was using to shield him and charges down the field, stiff arming a Lake Worth High School Trojan man who manages to get too close to him. From within the confines of his helmet, Kilo's eyes scan the left and sprints towards it, spinning to avoid another defender who dives at his ankles, trying to take him down, as he crosses the white paint marking the 50 yard line. Kilo pumps his legs faster, feeling the plastic spikes sinking into the turf and tearing free with every powerful stride.

He manages to juke out another defender who comes barreling towards him as he charges towards their end zone, but all of a sudden feels like he's been hit by a semi truck from the left, sending them to the ground in a tangle of arms and legs.

"Ughh," Kilo groans, fighting to get the weight of the other players off of him, as he picks himself off of the ground.

He looks down to see who tackled him before heading over to his side of the line of scrimmage and he sees number 25 grins at him while wagging his index finger back and forth, in a 'no-no' gesture, taunting Kilo.

They both head back to their respective sides to line up, 25 whooping at being the first to get a tackle in the beginning of the game. Kilo ignored him, while he was trying to pinpoint a way to break through their defenses. The players line back up and Kilo bends down, placing his hand on the ground to balance himself while he waits for the snap, counting down silently in his head, knowing how Quan likes to play.

Once his mental countdown reaches 5 Mississippi he hears Quan yell, "Hike!" and he races forward as the ball is snapped back to Quan. Kilo shoots down the field and breaks to the left heading as deep as possible while his internal countdown continues to tick while he waits on Quan to pick him out. He suddenly cuts to the right and accelerates, trying to lose the Trojan who was trying to stick with him.

He spins around and watches as Quan hesitates for a second before deciding to trust his gut and launching the football deep into enemy territory, aiming for Kilo before he is swarmed by defenders. The ball sails true through the air, Kilo tracking its trajectory as he races over to where his instincts are telling him that the ball is headed.

Out of his peripheral vision, he spots a flash of Maroon colored movement, alerting movement, alerting him that his adversaries are closing in. He returns his full attention to the tumbling pig skin and flexes his fingers inside his gloves as he prepares to make the catch. Kilo jumps up and snatches the ball out of the air before landing and jetting across the turf chased by three Trojan defenders dressed in Maroon and silver and white, as he crosses the 20 yard line.

He lowers his head and pumps his legs, striving to achieve maximum speed and shake the players on the rival team howling at his back like blood thirsty wolves while they try to run him down. As Kilo leaps over the boundary line of his opponents' end zone, bringing the score clock up to 6 points for the home team, he can hear cheering from his team's side of the bleachers.

He drops the ball and jogs over to where Quan is standing with bright green stains on his jersey from getting tackled. "Good shit, Key!" Quan shouts, slapping Kilo on his helmet as they line up and resume play.

Over the course of the next hour, Kilo and Quan teach the Lake Worth High Trojans not to show up on their field ever again with anything less then their A-game. They sprint off the field after crushing them 48 to 36 with the sounds of cheers still ringing in their ears from their friends and families sitting in the bleachers, cheering their victory. They enter the locker room and everybody starts to head to the showers so they can hurry up and get back to their waiting supporters, ready to start turning up to celebrate.

"Adams! Hayworth! Let me see you guys for a minute," Coach Garrett hollers into the noisy locker room, ushering Quan and Kilo into his office when they come. He sits on his desk and smiles at them.

"What's up coach?" Kilo asks, when him and Quan settle into the office and face Coach Garrett to see what he wants.

"Good play out there tonight, you guys," Coach Garrett says, now openly grinning broadly and placing a hand on both of their shoulders, causing them to smile even bigger than they already are, happy to get approval from their coach.

"Adams, I just wanted to say that I liked how even though you two have history and know how the other plays, you still managed to spread the glory around to everyone," Coach Garrett compliments, looking Quan in the eyes.

"Thank you Coach," Quan says with a smile, ecstatic after the 12 point lead they managed to rack up tonight against the Trojans, which they never were able to recover from.

"You know what that does for a team, Adams?" Coach Garrett asks, still talking to Quan, as he sits on the ledge of his desk and looks at the Dynamic Duo.

"Makes for a great quarterback?" Quan guesses, glancing over at Kilo for help answering Coach Garrett's trick question.

"What it does, Adams, Hayworth, is create trust within the team, and as the players learn to trust their QB, the whole team grows stronger," Coach Garrett explains patiently. "When you spread the butter around on the toast evenly, you get one even, flavorful piece of bread," Coach Garrett says, confusing the boys for a second, before he continues with his explanation. "Instead of globing it all in one spot, making it taste gross, you spread it all out evenly, so you can enjoy it to the fullest, as it was meant to be enjoyed," Coach Garrett says, finally finishing his strange analogy.

"Okay Coach, I feel you," Quan says, still a little bit confused by Coach Garrett's explanation of team bonding while for some strange reasons, using a buttered bread for an example.

"Hayworth," Coach Garrett barks, making Kilo snap his eyes back to Coach Garrett's face from where they were wandering across the wall looking at old team photos.

"Yes sir?" Kilo answers, waiting for Coach to point out any strengths or weaknesses he saw tonight when Kilo was playing out on the field.

"Your yardage is phenomenal, as well as your ability to penetrate the defense line, but what I need you to work on more, is your ability to pass up an opportunity, even if you think you can score, I need you to be able to trust your teammates more," Coach Garrett says truthfully, looking at Kilo fondly, like an uncle would when delivering a tough love speech to a troubled nephew.

"Coach, I..." Kilo begins, before Coach Garrett stops him by raising his hand, asking for Kilo to give him a chance to continue to speak.

"I'm not knocking anything you're doing or anything like that, Starboy," Coach Garrett says, referring to The Weeknd's new song, which had been played to death lately on the radio. "I'm only giving you a little constructive criticism," Coach Garrett adds, receiving a nod from Kilo, before shooing them out of the office. "Okay, now get the hell out of here and go celebrate your victory, guys!" Coach Garrett yells, loud enough for the whole team to hear him inside the locker room, raising a chorus of shouts in agreement.

Kilo and Quan walk through the door, out into the parking lot, where Dice and Glizzy stand waiting beside the Infinity with YFN Lucci flowing out of the Bose speakers. The song rings out with knowledge as the students mingle in the parking lot before heading off to celebrate tonight's victory.

"Y'all niggas was the truth out there tonight! Real talk!" Dice yells, when Kilo and Quan walk over to where he is standing by the truck and dap him and Glizzy up.

"Yea, that was dope!" Glizzy compliments, taking a Black & Mild from behind his ear, 'freaking' it before lighting up.

While they stand around the Infinity and chill, Kilo looks around the parking lot for Isabella and Jenna, who he saw in the stands earlier while he was on the field. Ever since the party where he beat up the white boy James, things have gotten even better between him and Isabella. They've become a lot closer than Kilo thought he could ever get to somebody besides Dice or Glizzy, even Quan.

"Kian!" Kilo looks around the crowded parking lot, trying to see who called him by his government name.

Ever since he started working for Dice and became a member of ZMA, nobody calls him by his government name anymore, save Isabella, who stubbornly refuses to call him Kilo. "Kian!" the voice calls again, much closer this time. Kilo turns in a circle, trying to spot the light-skinned beauty he now knows is calling his name from the inflection in her voice.

He spots the top of Isabella's head bobbing through the crowd toward him, and as she breaks free and runs toward him, he can't help but be mesmerized by her Divine beauty. Isabella jumps up into his arms, wrapping her legs around his waist, before kissing him, causing Glizzy to snicker in the background, while Quan wraps Jenna up in his arms as well, after she comes to stand next to him. The world seems to disappear as Kilo focuses on the feel of

Isabella in his arms, the smell of lavender on her skin and in her hair, the taste of cherries on her lips as she kisses him.

"I'm so proud of you, Key!" Isabella whispers excitedly against his mouth, softly as he gently lowers her feet back to the ground, and the parking lot becomes back into focus.

"Hi Jenna," Kilo says, waving at Jenna, who smiles brightly and waves back, leaning comfortably against Quan.

"You played great tonight, guys," Isabella says, looking first at Kilo, then over at Quan, who nods his head in appreciation, before winking at her.

"A'ight! Enough of this parking lot smooch fest, let's head to the spot," Dice says loudly, before jumping into the driver's seat of the Infinity and starting the truck.

Everybody piles in and Kilo settles into the backseat with Isabella sitting on his lap while Dice steers the truck toward his crib, where they plan to chill and turn up tonight, as they celebrate the win against their most hated enemies, Lake Worth High.

While they ride in the backseat, Kilo enjoys the feel of Isabella's ass settled in his lap. Every now and then he squeezes her thighs, causing her to look back over her shoulder at him as she squirms in his lap, teasing him and making him brick up, something he knows that she is well aware of from the wicked little smile of her angelic face.

It has been 5 months since he, Quan, Isabella and Jenna all chilled together at the party and even though they've grown a lot more comfortable around each other, even kiss and make out, she hasn't allowed him to get to any of the bases past First Base yet, a privilege he is determined to obtain soon. He squeezes her thigh again before leaning forward and nuzzling against her shoulder and neck, whispering in her ear.

"So, wus'sup? You finally gon' unlock that Pandora's box for me tonight, baby girl?"

She looks back over her shoulder at him with a smirk on her face, "All good things come to those who wait, Kian. Besides, patience is a virtue," Isabella says, causing Quan, Jenna, and Glizzy, who are all obviously eavesdropping to burst out into laughter, which made Kilo growl at them.

"Y'all mind your own damn business, what are you messing with my protege for, when he tryna focus on him and his lovely lady?" Dice asks, standing behind Kilo, everybody easily enjoying the energy of the night flowing around them, as they pull into the driveway of Dice's house and he parks the truck. "A'ight everybody! Out!" Dice yells, ushering them into the house, to get the party started.

As Kilo goes to pass by him, Dice stops him by laying a hand on his shoulder. "I just want you to know that your pops would be hella proud of you, kid," Dice says honestly, looking at Kilo with nothing but love and respect in his eyes for the young hustler after having been getting to know him over the last 6 months of him joining their family and living under his roof.

Kilo is silent for a minute while him and Dice stare at each other and he can't help but feel overwhelmed by the respect that he feels for Dice and Glizzy and basically the whole Zoe Mafia Affiliates family for taking him in when he was at his lowest.

"Yo, for reals Big Homie, I appreciate everything y'all have done for me. You took me in when I ain't have shit and gave me a chance to be somebody. To provide for myself and my lil' brother and sister, and I don't got nothing but the ultimate respect and love for you and the whole ZMA family," Kilo says quietly, reaching out and engaging Dice in the complicated ZMA handshake that his own father, Maniac had helped to create.

"Your pops was a legend out here in these streets, Kian," Dice says, calling him by his government name to let him know how important the rest of what he is about to say is, "But he was an even bigger influence in the Zoe Mafia Affiliates than anyone ever knew," Dice continues, while they walk up the driveway and to the front door of his house and stop right outside the door.

"I'm already hip, Big Homie," Kilo says, before quieting himself to allow Dice to finish his thought that he was still in the process of putting into words for him.

"But you? You're going to make a bigger mark on both, than he ever did. I can see it written on the wall and in your destiny," Dice finishes saying, before turning the handle of the door, walking inside, leaving Kilo still standing on the threshold, stunned by the prophesy Dice just gave to him about his life.

Several minutes passed by with Kilo still standing outside before Isabella comes looking for him. "Bae, why you still standing out here? Bring your cute lil' ass inside and relax! Y'all played hard tonight, and I already know you're tired," she says sweetly, coaxing Kilo out of his thoughts and leading him into the living room, where everybody is chilling at, drinking and smoking, while music videos play on the big flat screen TV mounted on the wall in front of Dice's personal leather chair.

Kilo goes into the kitchen and grabs a couple drinks for himself and Isabella before walking back into the living room and sitting down on the couch beside Quan, who is currently in the process of rolling up a gang of blunts out of some new type of strand of weed that Dice says he ordered through a sponsor from a dispensary.

Kilo takes one of the finished blunts off of the table and fires it up, while Isabella sits on his lap and they pass the blunt back and forth between themselves, enjoying each other's company, already knowing that the girls can't stay the night due to Isabella's dad's work schedule. So, in the meantime they're just content to live in the moment and let life take them on its roller coaster ride...

Chapter Forty - Five

Skyla

Skyla sits in her dirty bedroom counting out change from a jar as she continuously scratches and picks at her arms and leg, the monkey on her back raging savagely. Over the last couple of months, her addiction has taken her to the lowest she has ever been in her entire life and has made her do things she never thought in a million years that she would ever do just to get a fix.

About two weeks after she kicked Kian out, she found herself pawning all of her expensive designer clothes and her jewelry that Maniac had bought her, including her engagement and wedding rings. A month after that it was her kids' nice school clothes, shoes, and game stations along with their TV that she had sold in order to get a couple of grams of coke for her habit. Once that ran out, she decided that powdered cocaine was too expensive and she then settled for crack, which is where her decline really started to accelerate like there was no bottoming out at all, she had found the glass floor. She began walking the streets in the most obscene clothing that she could find in order to earn enough money to combat her cravings long enough to feel like a human being again, instead of a bottomless pit of despair and sorrow.

Thoughts of her two youngest children stuck in the house starving never even crossed her mind, while she was on the streets sucking dick in alleys or getting trains ran on her by dirty strangers who stained her clothes with their semen and laughed at her afterwards when they would give her a couple of dollars while she would beg for more until they beat her senseless. There were multiple nights where she woke up in some dark alleyway, covered in blood and semen, but never noticed how far she had fallen from grace as long as she had a few of those precious white rocks clutched in her hands so she could smoke to take the pain away.

She began to notice that even though there was never any food in the house, for some reason Jermaine and Imani never turned to skin and bones, and that Kian must be finding a way to supply them with money. That night she searched their rooms and didn't find any money, but she did find Jermaine's new football jersey. She still had enough sense left to know that it wasn't from back when Maniac used to always take them to football practice and could afford to buy new team jerseys for them to play in every year. That was also the first night that she beat her kids.

To give him credit where credit is due, Jermaine never once begged her to stop or cried out loud while she whipped him with one of Maniac's old leather belts, he didn't even fight back or try to put his hands on her while she beat him mercilessly and asked where he got the money to pay for the brand new jersey. He also didn't fold and never told her where he got it from either. But then, when she went and tried to pry the information she wanted out of Imani, he turned into a demon and fought her tooth and nail to protect his baby sister. He even took every lash for her while he shielded her with his body while she wailed until Skyla was too weak and tired to continue and finally collapsed in a heap on the floor, spent from all of the exertion.

Skyla's count reaches $10 dollars and a ghoulish smile spreads across her once beautiful face as she gathers all the dirty grungy coins together and puts them into a bag she has on the bed. She gets up and walks down the hall to Jermaine's room before opening up the door and sticking her head inside the room, not even bothering to knock. "I'm going out, watch your sister," Skyla tells him, receiving a blank look in response, which she chooses to ignore and not let him ruin her mood or get on her nerves.

She closes the door and heads back down the hallway and out the front door before walking down the block carrying her bag of change along with her, as she heads down to where she knows she can find the best bang for her buck and get the biggest crack rock she can find.

As Skyla approaches her local pit stop where she knows her favorite crack dealer, Yank, is most likely posted up with his two homeboys, Iceberg and Sike. She can't help but notice all the traffic that is flowing up and down the block tonight. She spots Yank chilling on his usual corner, in between Iceberg and Sike, and starts to walk over, the bag of coins swinging in her hand with every step.

"Was'sup shawty," Yank says in greeting trying to sound like a down south player, after spotting Skyla approaching them from down the street.

"Hey Yank, let me get a dime," Skyla says, holding out the bag of coins to him, while Iceberg shakes his head and Sike laughs at her.

"You know I don't take that shit, it's got to be bills, shorty," Yank says, losing his fake southern drawl and getting his New York accent back, shaking his head and making no move to take the bag from her hand.

"Please Yank! I need it!" Skyla begs, then starts to scratch her arms and fidget, as her craving grows worse.

Yank just shakes his head again, saying, "I been told yo' ass before that I ain't no fuckin' laundry mat, I don't take no fuckin' coins. So, if you tryna shop with me then take yo ass down the block to the corner store and get them to give you bills for that shit," Yank advises, as he waves a hand at the bag of coins jingling in her hands.

Skyla becomes desperate and is about to start begging, when Sike grabs her arm roughly and leers at her, "Or, you could show me what them niggas be talkin' bout and put that mouth to work and I'll just give you the money right now," he tells her, causing Iceberg to shake his head in disgust.

"Sike, man you foul as fuck, son," Iceberg says, which just makes Sike laugh and shrug his shoulders.

Skyla begins to lead Sike over to the alley on the side of the corner when a white Nissan starts to pass by. She hears Yank and Iceberg begin to yell at the driver, causing them to pull over at the corner.

"Hold up," Sike commands her, tugging on her arm, stopping her in place, as she turns to see who just pulls up.

From where she's standing in the mouth of the alley behind Sike, Skyla can't see the driver as he gets out of the car and walks over to Yank and Iceberg to dap them up, but she can see a gorgeous light-skinned girl sitting in the passenger seat and a pretty white girl in the back seat.

"It be wilder than a Mardi Gras, where them pit bull dogs get fought until they jaws rip off, and er'body on 8-balls, not 8-balls the quarts, 8-balls of soft, they call dis da Raw! This is where I come from, this where I get my game from, now tell me where you come from, y'all know where I came from...." The rapper Triple J's iconic hit from the early 2000's was beatin' down in the trunk, as they were starting to bring retro Palm Beach County music back in style.

"Yo, was good, Kilo?" Sike hollers, as he walks over to where Iceberg and Yank are standing in front of the driver of the white Nissan and holds out his hand to dap the man Kilo up.

"What's good, y'all? What the fuck y'all niggas up to over here?" Kilo asks in answer, his voice sounding strangely familiar, which draws her out of the alley and over to where the four men are gathered.

"Not shit, bruh. Nigga was just bout'a handle up, ya feel me?" Sike cuts in, trying to jump into the conversation taking place without him.

As Kilo turns to look at him, Skyla gasps, recognizing her son, Kian standing in the middle of Iceberg, Yank, and Sike and tried to hide behind them in embarrassment. Her startled gasp draws Kian's attention, and he looks over in her direction in annoyance to see who else is standing there.

As their eyes meet, Skyla can see all the hurt and resentment flash across her son's face at seeing her again before he realizes why she is there and his mind registers seeing her and Sike just come out from of the alley.

"Yo Sike, what you just handling up, bruh?" Kian asks with an edge in his voice that makes Skyla tremble in fear, reminding her of Maniac's anger when he was about to fly off the handle. But it clearly goes over Sike's head as he is still smiling.

Skyla tries to move forward to stop Kian before he flies into a rage, but her feet are frozen in a place, as Sike starts to reply to Kian's question.

"I was just bout'a take this bitch into the alleyway and get my dick su—"

Smack!

The sound of Kian smacking Sike with a pistol sounds off, before Yank and Iceberg start yelling.

"Yo! What the fuck, bruh? Chill out!" Yank hollers, trying to get in between Sike and Kian, as Kian begins pistol-whipping Sike while he lays on the ground, helpless.

Smack! Smack! Smack!

The sounds of metal hitting flesh and bone, plus the yelling, brings the other occupants running over from the car to try to help stop Kian, as he continues to beat Sike damn near to death.

"Pussy! Ass! Nigga!" Kian yells in a rage, while he fights against the multiple arms trying to pull him away from Sike's balled up body before he kills him.

"Kian STOP!" the gorgeous light-skinned girl screams, as she gets in Kian's space and grabs both sides of his face in her hands, finally bringing him back to reality, while Skyla stood frozen in a place, staring at the scene in front of her in shame and horror.

"Fuck is wrong with you, bruh!" Yank yells, pushing Kian away from Sike's still body roughly and reaching towards his waist for his gun.

"I wouldn't do that if I was you, bruh," Kian says, emotionlessly, as he aims his blood splattered pistol at Yank's head, stopping him in place before he slowly raises his hands above his head in compliance.

Kian turns and stares at Skyla for a second, and the fury she sees in his eyes makes her catch her breath in fear, and it makes her begin to shiver.

The girl looks at Kian first, before turning to look at Skyla, taking in her disheveled and grungy appearance, before Skyla sees understanding appear in her beautiful hazel eyes, and she turns to look at Kian gently and places a hand on his shoulder.

Quan suddenly appears on the other side of Kian and takes in the scene before his eyes sweep across Skyla's face and he steps forward, trying to de-escalate the situation before it becomes worse. "Yo Key, chill the fuck out, bruh! They ain't know," Quan pleads with Kian while he still holds Yank at gunpoint.

Iceberg steps up and Kian instantly points his gun at him, causing him to raise his hands to show he's not a threat.

"Yo, what the fuck is going on? Will somebody please lace a nigga up, please!" Iceberg asks, as he stares in confusion at Kian, who is breathing heavily while he tries to control his fury.

"That's my Old Girl..." Kian says, trailing off, obviously still on the edge and trying to decide what to do about finding Skyla here, about to trade sexual favors for drugs.

Iceberg and Yank stare at Kian in disbelief and astonishment for a second, as what he just told them sinks in and they process the whole situation.

"Fuck, bruh..." Yank says, swiping a hand across his face before looking down at Sike, who is squirming around the cement and groaning in pain.

"My bad, Kilo. I didn't know this was your moms," Iceberg says, as a wave of embarrassment floods through Skyla again and she begins to cry, which brings the pretty light-skinned girl over to her, putting her arm around her and leading her back over to the car, helping her into the backseat.

While Skyla cries, she hears Kian tell Yank that nobody better serve her anything else, or the next time this happens, bodies are going to start dropping, to which Yank agrees, before Kian, Quan, and the two girls climb back into the car and pull away from the curb, where Yank and Iceberg watch over Sike, as he begins to wake back up.

Chapter Forty - Six

Isabella

The inside of the crowded car is dead silent as Kian pulls away from the curb, leaving the two men standing over their unconscious homeboy that Isabella saw Kian beat senseless with his gun. They bend a couple of corners before Kian pulls into the driveway of a small house with overgrown grass that looks like it has seen its better days behind it.

Isabella watches from the passenger seat, while Kian stares at the house for a second before opening his door and getting out. He walks to the back driver's side door where his moms is sitting, still sniffling, and he opens the door.

"Get out, ma," Kian says, emotionlessly, before turning around and heading towards the front door of the house, where Isabella sees a little boy of about 11 or 12, standing in the open doorway, staring at them as they walk towards him.

Isabella watches as a smile appears on the boy's face as he starts to run towards Kian, but then the sound of a revving engine and some tires skirting round the corner, suddenly pierces the quietness of the evening.

Kian whips around, pushing his little brother down behind him and startling his mother as a powder blue Honda with three men inside comes flying down the road, gun barrels sticking out of the passenger side windows of the car.

"Y-Lo Bitch!" Isabella hears a voice scream, a second before they start firing while Isabella, Jenna, and Quan duck down inside Kian's Nissan and scream at the top of their lungs in fright.

Even though Isabella is cowering inside the car, she retains enough of her senses to hear a third gun sounding off as the men in the Honda spray bullets in their direction, pretty much missing everything, as if not even aiming their ridiculous automatics, spraying everything like spray paint and missing most of everything.

Tatatatatatatatatatatat! Tatatatatatatat! Tatatatatatatatatatatata!

The sounds of gunfire fills every available coherent space in Isabella's mind as she cowers on the floor board of the car before silence finally takes over, leaving her shell shocked.

Isabella hears Kian's voice yelling something, as if from far away, and it takes a second, but she can make out what he's saying.

"Ma! Are you alright? Ma! Get up!" Kian screams, the fear in his voice brings Isabella's head up, to cautiously peek out the windows, seeing Kian crouching down on the ground next to his mother with his gun and empty shell casings strewn around them.

Isabella opens her door and runs over to where Kian's crouching next to his mother, seeing him rip a long strip off his shirt and tie it around her arm to stop the bleeding from a bullet wound.

"Are you okay?" Kian asks, turning to look at her as he hears her footsteps approaching.

Isabella still too scared to speak, so instead she nods 'yes' in answer to his question.

"We can't stay here," Kian says softly, looking around fearfully, hearing the police sirens approaching from the distance.

"We can't leave, Kian, they'll think we're suspects!" Isabella replies, finally finding her voice as Kian looks down at his gun and up towards where the sound of the sirens sounds closest.

"Jermaine!" Kian yells, calling to the little boy who's laying down in front of the car, still too scared to come out, even after the shooting has stopped.

At the sound of Kian's voice, he pokes his little head up and looks over towards them, before climbing up to his feet and creeping over slowly. Kian hands him the gun and points to the couple scattered shell casings lying on the ground nearby, "Pick these up for me and then go hide all this shit in the safest place you can find," Kian instructs, getting a nod in reply before Jermaine begins picking up all the spent brass and carefully grabbing the heavy gun before running into the house to do as Kian asked.

Isabella chooses not to argue with Kian's decision to trust a little kid with a gun, figuring he knows what he's doing and instead scoots closer to his wounded mother, untying the makeshift bandage from around her arm to check on the injury. She notices that the bullet went straight through and decides to wait for the EMS before she does anything else as she spots the first of the police cars beginning to arrive.

"Isabella," Kian says quietly, looking over at her intensely, once he's sure he has her full attention he instructs her not to say anything about him having a gun or shooting back at the men in the blue Honda.

"I didn't even see anything from where I was, and I doubt that Jenna and Quan did either, Kian. Besides why the hell would I even do that in the first place?" Isabella replies, earning a shrug in response.

A handsome black man wearing a collared shirt, obviously a detective, approaching them while they still sit beside Kian's mother on the ground. "Well, isn't this a not-so pleasant surprise?" he says to Kian, before turning his gaze to Isabella and introducing himself. "I'm Detective Jones."

Over the course of the next couple of hours, Detective Jones asked each one of them for their version of what happened and pretty much got the same story every single time. After securing the scene and having EMS load Kian's mom into the ambulance, Detective Jones hands Isabella, Jenna, Kian and Quan his card; each of them got one and tells them not to hesitate to call if they can remember anything else that could prove to be helpful to the investigation, before allowing Kian to load his little brother and sister into the car and pull away from the crime scene, telling them that it could be a couple days before his mother is released from the hospital and they finish gathering all of the evidence from the house.

Once Kian judges them safely far away enough from Detective Jones, Isabella sits quietly in the passenger seat with Kian's little sister, Imani, sitting on her lap, while he makes a phone call. She watches Kian's facial expressions while he waits for the person on the other end to answer their phone and when they finally pick up, she can tell that the next phase of what just took place back at his house rests on Kian's mind heavily, as he fills Dice in on what just happened.

After he hangs up, Kian is silent for a long time while he follows the directions she gives him to take her and Jenna back to her house to drop them off before her dad comes home from work. After about 20 minutes inside the tense atmosphere of the car, they finally pull in to the driveway of Isabella's house and she and Jenna climb out of the car after they each kiss their respective boyfriend goodnight.

Jenna heads inside while Isabella trails behind her, but after a second thought turns back around and races back down the driveway to catch up with Kian before he could pull off. She reaches the car just as he's starting to back out of the driveway, causing him to pump the brakes and roll down his window to see what she wants as she walks over to the driver's side window of his white Nissan.

Isabella's heart is hammering wildly inside of her chest as she bends down to look into Kian's tormented eyes, wondering what possessed her to race back down the driveway and stop him. She cups his face gently in her hand and looks deep into his eyes for a second, "Whatever happens next, I just want you to know that I'm here with you every step of the way," she tells him before he pulls away, knowing he had a real rider on his side. One day she will be his wife, he thinks to himself.

Chapter Forty - Seven

OG Dice- ZMA

Dice sits in his leather chair while Kilo recounts the shooting that just took place, filling him in on the details, while his little brother and sister sit on the couch playing Grand Theft Auto 5 on the Xbox 360.

"There were three niggas in a blue Honda who pulled up and just started bussin' at us," Kilo says from his seat in front of Dice, where he is rolling up a blunt of loud to try and calm his nerves.

"Did you see what they looked like or remember anything specific, lil' bruh?" Dice asks Kilo, trying to refresh his memory and get details they can use to their benefit.

Dice watches as Kilo takes a second to think while putting the finishing touches on the blunt he is in the process of rolling. "Yea. Just before they started shooting, they yelled out something about Y-Lo or some shit like that?" Kilo explains to Dice.

Dice turns the details Kilo just poured him the drink about over in his mind and watches as he puts the flame to the tip of the blunt, inhaling deeply.

"Do you know what that is, big bruh?" Quan asks Dice while he waits for Kilo to pass him the blunt.

"It's them lil' niggas 'round the way from Luna's that's always beefin' wit her people," Glizzy says from the kitchen, where he's heating up left over pizza in the microwave.

"I'm already hip to that nephew, what I'm tryna figure out is why the fuck they all the way over here shootin' at Kilo," Dice replies, as Quan hands him the blunt and he hits it a couple times while he thinks. He turns the cigar over in his hand a couple times before hitting it again and passing it back to Kilo. Dice looks over at his protege for a moment trying to figure out why he would be a target for these Cuban Y-Lo niggas. "You rolled this mufucka, lil' bruh," Dice says, complimenting Kilo on his blunt rolling skills.

"Thanks, Big Homie," Kilo replies absentmindedly, smoke billowing from his mouth. "Oh, I also need'a lace you up about some shit that happened before we got shot at," Kilo says to Dice, looking him right in the eye.

"Was'sup?" asks Dice, already having a feeling that something triggered him to start acting withdrawn, the way he is now. "So, when we left here to drop the girls off, I passed by Yank and dem, posted up in their usual spot on the block, and they flagged a nigga down," Kilo says, unable to continue to maintain direct eye contact with Dice while he recounts what happened. "I jumped out to say what's up to them and Sike was walking out of the alley with...with..." Kilo says, freezing up, unable to finish what he is saying, as his emotions flare up again.

"Go on, lil' bruh," Dice says gently, trying to help Kilo push forward and get out whatever it is that he is trying to say. "He walked out of the alleyway, with...my moms," Kilo says finally, owning the fact that his mother is full blown out there, tearing up slightly at the embarrassment and anger Dice knows that he is feeling from seeing his own mother at her lowest point.

"Are you serious?" Glizzy asks in anger and disbelief, walking into the living room from the kitchen with his plate of warm pizza.

"Yea, Z. I snapped and beat the fuck out of that nigga with my pistol, and when Yank and Iceberg tried to intervene, I upped on them and held them at gunpoint," Kilo says honestly, looking around with fury blazing in his eyes, daring them to tell him that he is in the wrong.

"I would'a killed that bitch ass nigga where he stand!" Glizzy growls, before taking a big bite out off his pizza and chewing hungrily.

"I almost did..." Kilo says quietly, as his emotions flash across his face, making Dice's heart hurt for his little hustler.

"Where's your fire at now?" Dice asks Kilo, looking at his hip and noticing that he doesn't have it on him like he usually does, knowing that Kilo wouldn't be caught dead without his fire on him.

"I had lil' bruh hide it for me, right after those Y-Lo niggas lit up the block," Kilo tells Dice, his hand drifting to his empty hip, feeling vulnerable at the absence of his gun and not looking very happy about it.

"Don't trip, lil' homie, I got a replacement for you," Glizzy interjects, before setting down his empty plate, and heading over to a bookshelf which he proceeds to manhandle away from the wall.

Dice watches Kilo and Quan's eyes grow big like saucers as Glizzy pulls two MAC 10 machine pistols from the stash spot behind the bookshelf and sets them on the kitchen counter before reaching back into the stash spot, withdrawing a few boxes of ammunition along with the extra magazines, which he passes over to Kilo and Quan, who sat with looks of excitement on their faces.

"We'll go get your other heat later, lil' bruh," Dice says to Kilo. "But when going to war against an unknown enemy, I always like to hit hard and fast, ya feel me?" Dice finishes, watching as the two boys turn the vicious weapons over in their hands, examining their new toys.

"You sure you ready for this type of pressure, lil' bruh?" Glizzy asks, walking over and sitting down next to Dice after pushing the bookshelf back into its normal place to conceal the stash spot cut into the floor.

"You already know I'm wit it, Big Homie!" Kilo replies eagerly, a wicked smile spreading across his face, as Dice watches him slap one of the pre-loaded magazines into the machine pistol, Quan following Kilo's lead.

Dice can see the cold look of hunger swimming in his protege's eyes, eager to unleash his wrath on the man who murdered his father in cold blood, setting the world and the hood right again.

"Then we're in agreement, family," Dice says solemnly, as he slowly looks around the room, staring into each and every pair of eyes, seeing the hunger reflected within their pupils. Then, once Dice has finished his visual sweep around the room, he turns and locks onto his nephew with his dark, steely gaze.

"Get Champ and Haze on the line and tell them niggas to put the word out that everybody needs to strap up and prepare for war," Dice instructs Glizzy, who reaches into his pocket for his phone and proceeds to follow his uncle's orders to alert the family and get them all war-ready.

A heavy silence settles in the room around them while Glizzy instructs the lieutenants to prepare themselves and their crews for the storm to come behind Dice's decision to move against the attacks that have been costing his operation valuable resources, and to avenge the attempt on Kilo's life.

Dice can feel a chill creeping into his bones as he silently wonders if he's made the right decision. We've lost too many good soldiers already, Dice thinks to himself, taking a puff off of one of the forgotten blunts that are still smoldering in the ashtray on the coffee table, as a foreboding feeling travels slowly throughout the living room.

"There's something else that I need'a put you up on game about, OG," Kilo says, breaking the previous eye contact that he had held as well as the silence in the room. Dice trained his gaze on the young hustler, a spitting image of his father, Maniac. He was like the younger version.

"Shit, just keep it a hunnid wit' me, lil' bruh," Dice says honestly, leaning forward in his chair to give the young hitta seated before him his undivided attention.

Dice watches as Kilo takes a moment to collect his thoughts before taking a deep breath, as the words fight to be released from within and set his mind at ease.

"I'm the one that first clapped at that pussy nigga Sin," Kilo says aggressively, staring deeply into Dice's eyes, daring him to judge him and find him in violation.

"What?" Glizzy asks in surprise, turning to look over at where Kilo and Quan are sitting, with shock plastered across his face, momentarily forgetting the phone in his hand with an ongoing call taking place to one of the prominent members of the Zoe Mafia Affiliates family, as he lets them know about Dice's order.

Dice calmly waves his hand in the air, signaling his nephew to return to what he's taking care of without breaking eye contact with Kilo, who is sitting across from him on the couch with Quan sitting tensely next to him, unable to meet Dice's gaze.

"I'm already aware of this, lil' homie," Dice says, nonchalantly, fighting the smile that is threatening to break free from his carefully maintained facade at the astonishment he sees flashing across Kilo's face at Dice's revelation, and the guilty look Quan is having difficulty hiding.

"But, how the fuck...?" Kilo stutters, looking confused, as Dice watches the two boys glance at each other, trying to understand how Dice could know that Kilo had shot at Sin without one of them putting him on point.

"It don't take a rocket scientist to figure that much out, lil' bruh," Dice says with a chuckle, before continuing his explanation. "You're Maniac's son, plus Sin has been operating smoothly for a whole two years unopposed until now, when suddenly he's attacked down the street from where he smoked your pops, and if that ain't poetic justice, I don't know what it is," Dice says calmly.

"You don't need to trip though, lil' bruh. Your pops was my day one, and I'll ride for my family any day of the week!" Dice adds forcefully, leaning forward to stare deeply into Kilo's wide eyes. Everything in the house fades into silence as Dice watches the raw emotion swim in Kilo's dark gaze, before he breaks the silence between them with a single question.

"Are you sure you're ready for this?"

"I been waiting for this for the last two years, Big Homie, I'm hungry for revenge," Kilo replies heatedly, unwavering in his determination to avenge his father's death.

"So be it, lil' bruh. Prepare yourself for war," Dice answers with a cold smile of his own, as he leans back in his seat.

Chapter Forty - Eight

Sin

Sin sits at the kitchen table in his Greenacres trap-house feeding stacks of various denominations of bills into three separate money counting machines while smoking a thickly rolled Cuban cigar stuffed with premium marijuana supplied by his connect, Cien Fuegos.

He's just finished neatly stacking a counted bundle of money together and securing it with a rubber band from the pile on the table when he is interrupted by the ringtone of his personal cellphone lying within easy reach.

Sin takes a moment to set the money down with the rest of the finished stacks lying in an organized pyramid in the center of the table, before picking up his phone and pressing the green answer button on his screen, trying to catch it before his voicemail kicks in, not bothering to check to see who it is on the other end calling.

"Speak," Sin orders calmly, before placing his phone back down on the table and pressing the speaker option displayed on the screen as he reaches for another handful of money from one of the numerous plastic grocery bags lying on the floor at his feet and loading the bills into the empty machine to begin another load of currency.

"Yo Big Homie, I'm on the way over to ya spot right now to lace you up," Rampage pants into the speaker of his phone, causing his voice to sound slightly distorted.

"I'm in the middle of some shit right now, Acere," Sin says with an edge to his voice, aggravated at the thought that Rampage would have the nerve to show up at his trap before receiving permission or a summon from Sin himself, first.

"I already know, Big Homie," Rampage says quickly in an apologetic voice, before pressing forward quickly with his explanation. "I don't mean any disrespect, but we just took care of that job for you and some shit happened, and there's news I think you'll definitely appreciate hearing, ya feel me?" he finishes saying, as the other two money machines beep, and Sin rubber bands the two stacks of money that he pulls out of the trays, which he quickly places with the rest of the growing pile at the center of the table while his mind swirls with possibilities of the importance of the meeting Rampage is requesting right now.

"A'ight, bruh. Pull up then," Sin finally says, relenting as he writes down the total number of the counted money sitting before him, after letting the three money machines finish their current loads and wrapping up the plastic grocery bags lying on the floor before hiding them under the kitchen sink, planning to finish the count right after Rampage leaves his trap once he receives the debrief from the young killer, concerning the job Sin had hired him and his camp to take care of for him.

"Say less, Big Homie. I'm ten minutes away," Rampage replies quickly, before hanging up the phone on his end.

Sin checks the time on his screen and figures he has enough time to put the medium-sized pile of money away in his safe while he waits for Rampage to arrive and deliver the news that is apparently considered important enough to risk invoking Sin's rage over showing up unannounced and without permission at his main spot of operations.

He begins placing the bundles into a couple of empty bags until they're full and carries them into his bedroom, before dropping them on the floor in front of the safe hidden in the closet. He types the code into the keypad and waits briefly for the beep and green light to flash, signaling the entry of the correct code before pulling the door open and beginning the tedious process of cramming stacks of money into the already crammed safe.

After about ten minutes of fussing with the interior contents and trying to fit the last bit inside, which he visually counts at around 25 bands, he hears a car pull into the driveway and stuffs the bags containing the rest of the money that won't fit into the safe into the back of the closet, before forcing the door of the safe closed with a heavy shove and heading out of the bedroom as his phone begins to ring on the table where he left it.

"Yo," Sin says as he answers the call while heading to the front door of the house quickly making sure to peek out the blinds to see who it is, while he clutches his Israeli made .50 caliber Desert Eagle hand cannon tightly.

"It's me Big Homie," Rampage replies from his end of the phone, "I'm outside."

"A'ight bruh, I see you," Sin responds before hanging up and sliding his phone into his back pocket as he unlocks the door for Rampage and one of his homies that Sin doesn't know; a tall, light-skinned skinny Cuban looking dude with a black bandana on his neck who saunters into Sin's trap behind Rampage.

"What's good, Big Bruh?" Rampage asks Sin in greeting, reaching over to dap him up before turning around to introduce his homie to Sin.

"OG, this is Flaco," Rampage says, nodding his head at the tall Cuban who extends his hand to Sin to dap him up as well.

Sin nods his head in greeting as he accepts dap from Flaco silently, before leading the two men over to the living room and sitting down around the coffee table waiting for Rampage to lace him up.

Sin waits while Rampage and his homie, Flaco get settled on the couch and he begins to split a couple blunts to roll up from the jar of weed sitting on the coffee table in between them.

Rampage waits patiently while Sin puts the finishing touches on the blunt before passing one across to them to smoke.

Sin applies the flame to the tip of his blunt and exhales the rich, potent smoke while Rampage takes a couple deep puffs and passes it over to Flaco.

"Okay, so I got two of my homies to spin with me and we pulled up on that jit, Kilo, you sent us after," Rampage begins, catching Sin's attention and causing him to lean forward intently waiting for Rampage to continue.

"There was a couple hoes with him along with some lame-ass lookin' nigga, and an older bitch dressed like a street walker when we started bussin' at him," Rampage says, as he receives the blunt back from Flaco, pulling deeply and holding the smoke in his lungs for a count of ten, before releasing it in a voluminous cloud, as Sin waits anxiously for the rest of the story.

"We really wasn't aiming for anybody other than Kilo, but I'm pretty sure we got a bonus and hit the streetwalker bitch before he started clappin' back at us," Rampage says, a wicked smirk appearing on his face.

"A'ight, so the bitch you think is a prostitute is actually his moms, Skyla, and even though she has some amazing pussy, she's strung out on that girl and that hard," Sin says, referring to powdered cocaine and crack cocaine, as surprise takes over the prominent position on Rampage's face.

"None of that shit matters though, tell me what happened after he started shooting back," Sin says, excusing his own interruption of Rampage's story and gesturing him to proceed.

"So, we had the drop on them until he started clapping back, and we had to pull off, because he hit my driver in the shoulder and killed the passenger, our homie, Flip," Rampage spits venomously, as he crosses himself in respect to his dead homie, killed in action while putting in work on a mission for their cause.

"So, what you tryna tell me is, some young green-ass nigga, still with Similac on his breath, kill one of ya homies, and run you off, without completing the assignment y'all was given and paid to do?" Sin asks explosively, raising from his seat with his humongous gun appearing in his hand like a flash before their eyes, causing both Rampage and Flaco to cower under Sin's penetrating gaze.

"Nah, Big Homie, it ain't even much like that," Rampage tried to explain, as he and Flaco raise their empty hands in the air in compliance, hoping Sin will chill the fuck out and let off the gas, so they can finish with the debriefing.

"So, what the fuck else you got to say, lil' nigga?" Sin snarls, looming over the two frightened men seated before him, hoping for mercy concerning the fuck up their gang just had let happen under his watch while on assignment.

Sin watches as Rampage shoots a quick glance over at Flaco, before returning his frightened gaze to the huge pistol clutched tightly in Sin's fist, aimed in the general direction of his head.

"We're pretty sure that his moms got hit, if you say that streetwalker bitch was her, OG, because she's currently at the hospital, and we got some soldiers waiting on orders to finish her after we get the green light from you to take the hoe out," Flaco says thickly with a Spanish accent that Sin has to strain to decipher.

"Okay, so the fuck what?" Sin asks, annoyed at the stupidity of the two seated in front of him, as Flaco waits for Sin to look back down at him.

"So, we got good news, Big Homie, you know I wouldn't come with anything but the best when it comes to wiping your opponents off the board," says Rampage eagerly, trying to get back in Sin's good graces and avoid becoming a target for the big gun still leveled at his noggin.

"So, we've been keeping Kilo under watch and we know where the general area of one of the ZMA's main house is located at, along with some other crucial information I'm sure you'll love to hear," Rampage says with a smile on his face, as Sin sits back down in his seat and lays the Desert Eagle softly in his lap, eager to hear the rest of their news.

"We got an informant that hit us up the other day, who is tryna get into contact with somebody who can pay his price for the information he's willing to provide, as long as it ends with Kilo's head ending up with three holes in it, like a bowling ball," Rampage adds, as Sin takes in the news he's just heard that could help him and his connect, Cien Fuegos, win the war with ZMA before it even pops off, once they figure out who's been lighting their ass up, if they don't already know.

"I just got off the phone with him, and all I'm waiting on now, is the go ahead from you to give him your number, so he can talk to you directly, ya feel me?" Rampage says, as Sin turns over his phone to Rampage, who types the number into it, before handing it back."

Ring! Ring! Ring! Ring!

Chapter Forty - Nine

Sike

The traffic is heavy with 'buddies' coming to cop the Haitian Brown heroin and Sike is posted on the corner of C Terrance and 12th Avenue South as per usual, catching a sale, while Iceberg and Yank loiter around, waiting on their next play to come through when his phone starts to ring.

Brrriiiiinnnggg! Brrriiiiinnnggg! Brrriiiiinnnggg!

Sike takes his iPhone 14 pro out of his pocket and checks the caller ID, not recognizing the number, but deciding to answer anyways.

"This Sike," he says, after pressing the green answer button on the phone and holding it up to his ear, fighting to hear the caller on the other end of the line over the noise and commotion of the evening block activity.

"I heard you was tryna holla at somebody who could put some money in your pocket, homie," a man's deep baritone voice replies arrogantly from the other end, putting a smirk on Sike's face.

He looks over to where Yank and Iceberg stand, leaning against the side of a building scrolling through their phones distractedly, before he quickly darts into the same alley that he had planned to fuck Kilo's mom in, before Kilo had beat him senseless with his pistol, the irony leaving a sour taste in his mouth that quickly dissipates with the next couple words the caller utters from their side of the line.

"If you're serious about getting on the winning team, then we should set up a situation ASAP, if that's cool with you, of course," the voice says, causing Sike to anticipate the riches he feels are being withheld from him, along with a promotion to a more prominent position within an organization that truly appreciates him and what he brings to the table.

"I hear you, big dawg, but what's the benefit to me? and how do I know that I'm not being set up?" Sike asks cautiously, peeking around the corner to make sure that Iceberg and Yank don't wander into the alleyway and discover him conversing with an enemy over the phone.

"Shit, what type of guarantee are you lookin' for, homie? You hit my people up askin' to talk, sayin' you could provide valuable information. To me that's worth ten racks, upon the guarantee that it's official, of course," the voice tells Sike, easily causing the greed to rise within his heart like yeast in baking bread at the thought of turning on his homies for a mere $10,000.

"Where you tryna meet up at?" Sike asks eagerly, his fingers already anticipating the feeling of counting through the money he's selling out his brothers for.

"We can meet tomorrow at Grove Custom Auto in Delray Beach at one o'clock, if that's straight with you," the voice proposes, Sike nodding his head in agreement quickly before realizing that they can't actually see his nonverbal response from where he's hiding at in the dirty alleyway.

"Yea, that's cool with me, bruh," Sike stutters in excitement, kicking a broken quart bottle with the toe of his '95 Airmax sending it tumbling into the darkness further back into the alley, where he hears it shatter.

"A'ight, acere, one p.m. then, don't be late," the voice says briefly, to seal the deal between them before hanging up, leaving Sike standing in the middle of the grungy alley alone with just the desires of his treachery and greed.

"Punk ass niggas, I'ma show y'all that y'all picked the wrong nigga to fuck with," Sike mumbles under his breath as he walks out of the alley, back on to the block where Yank and Iceberg stand looking around for him in confusion by his sudden disappearance.

"Yo Sike! You good, bruh?" Yank asks, reaching out to hand him the blunt they had rolled up and started smoking without him when he had stepped into the alley.

"Yea bruh, I just had to tie up some loose ends with this punk ass bitch, ya dig?" Sike says, with a disarming grin as he takes a puff off of the blunt Yank handed him.

"You took care of what you needed to take care of, dawgs?" Iceberg asks, as the blunt get passed his way.

"You already know how I get down, bruh, I play all my cards close to the vest until it's time to unleash the fury," Sike replies with a sinister smirk that seemingly goes unnoticed by either Yank or Iceberg as Sike plots the fall of Kilo, uncaring about collateral damage to the members of the Zoe Mafia Affiliates that he once called family until he decided to take a bite out of the forbidden fruit and cast his lot with the enemy as his desire for revenge and greed grew within his heart while he stood on the block and pushed their product. All the while scheming to dismember the entire operation over some petty rivalry that could've been avoided, or at least, dealt with in a better way. But it is just too late now, the die has been cast and he would have to face the consequences, whatever they might be.

Chapter Fifty

Glizzy

Glizzy hangs up his phone with a look of incredulity on his young face, as he couldn't believe the information he just received. All of it from Dopefiend Willy, at that! Dopefiend Willy had been Basshead Porky's best friend, but then, during one of the 'Basser Wars', which is like "Bum Fights" in Lake Worth City, Glizzy had him fight Bastos in front of Porky and Dopefiend Willy had refused to share in his rocks with Porky after Porky hadn't helped him, when Bastos had gotten the best of him. Bastos and Porky had been a tag team smoke house sensation since then, leaving Willy on his own. Willy had lived in a dumpster in the alleyway behind the 12th Avenue South store, and that was good luck for the ZMA team. Well, that and the fact that corner store still had an antique pay phone in front of it, and it actually worked. Glizzy could see now how Dopefiend Willy had been keeping up with his habit, he had all of the hood gossip on smash.

"What's up, bruh?" asked Kilo from the backseat.

"Unc, turn the truck around, we don't move 'til tomorrow at one p.m. We will catch 'em all in one good sweep, and guess what else?"

"What's good?" asked Dice from the driver's seat, as he maneuvered the Infinity truck in a U-turn, heading back to their spot.

"Dopefiend Willy was sleeping in his dumpster and overheard a ZMA member making plans to sell us out tomorrow at one or more accurately, sell Kilo out, since his deal was dependent upon Kilo's downfall and—" started Glizzy.

"Fucking Sike! I should'a seen this one coming," Kilo interrupted.

"Exactly," said Glizzy.

"A'ight, lil' homie. Y'all don't even need to stress shit, don't say nothing to Iceberg or Yank, an dem. We finna hit 'em Y-Lo niggas with everything we got. I'ma drop y'all off, so get ready and I'm gonna meet up with da Big Homie, Gunz an dem, and we'll all be ready to be on and poppin'," said Dice, as he wheeled the truck to drop the boys off.

§§§§

Glizzy decided to give Iceberg a call, just to check the temperature and verify what he already suspected; that Iceberg and Yank were in the dark about the moves Sike was making behind their backs, selling his soul for revenge.

"Speak on it," said Iceberg, answering on the second ring.

"Yo, what's good, my Z?" asked Glizzy, nonchalant as ever.

"Same ole thang, tryna get to da bag, ya know already..."

"Well, look here, I'm bout to holla at this lil baby tonight, so I wanted to make sure y'all straight so I don't be MIA if y'all finna be hustlin' all night, so y'all good 'til tomorrow? Let me know now, ya dig?" Glizzy checks the temperature with his story.

"Yo, Yank! You need to holla at Glizzy? Where Sike at?" Glizzy could hear Iceberg speaking as he held the phone down so as not to scream in Glizzy's ear.

All Glizzy could think, was that Berg sounded as normal as could be, up until he was asking where Sike was at. That right there reinforced in Glizzy's mind, that Berg and Yank were unaware of any ill intent from slimy ass Sike.

"Dawgs, we good and I'm sure that nigga, Sike good too, cuz he too busy talkin' on his phone to even answer a nigga, so you good bruh, I'll see ya tomorrow! Give her ass a good smack for me, thug!" laughed Berg as he hung up his end of the phone, back to his block hustle of hand to hand transactions.

Glizzy felt a whole lot better now, as there was no way that he was hearing an Academy Award winning performance from his homie, they were truly unaware of Sike's evil intent for tomorrow.

Glizzy thought back to the 'Gangstas & Thugs' DVDs from the beginning of the 2000's, and what they did on those DVDs; fights, shootings, murders, and laughed to himself. He was going to make those DVDs look like kiddie shit compared to what he and his Zoe Mafia Affiliates were going to do to Sike, as well as his new chosen family, the Cuban Y-Lo's gang and their friends. It is time for a reckoning. Glizzy can't wait.

Epilogue

Kilo

It's D-Day at 12:45 in the afternoon. Dice and his group are facing the front of Grove Custom Auto, a machine shop in Delray Beach. They've been sitting in stolen cars, parked across the street in the post office employee parking lot since 9 a.m., trying to get a feel of the scene and have the ups when their targets showed their faces. Kilo was sweating a little bit in anticipation and trying to will Sin and Sike to show themselves so he can send them back to their maker just as quickly.

Kilo knew that Big Homie Gunz and his soldiers are out back in between the garage bays and small businesses trying to blend in. They would catch any of these cockroaches when they scurry out the back, trying to escape the overwhelming warfare that ZMA are waging in the front of the mechanic's building.

Luna and her team from Tamarind Ave, Downtown, were split between the south and north sides of the building, in case any roaches were able to escape out of the barred up windows. Although such would be highly unlikely, Gunz had placed them there out of an abundance of caution. Since once the shooting was starting, all the teams would converge on the building in full force, Gunz having given the order to leave nothing in their place breathing, there would be no chance for anyone to get away anyways, plus Kilo was out for blood and wouldn't stop until they payed for crossing him.

As all teams were linked by the Bluetooth earpiece tethered to their disposable burner phones, which are linked to a merge call between Gunz, Luna, and Dice, all of them cocked and loaded, ready for action. Quan sat next to Kilo in the back of the Ford

Explorer that Glizzy had stolen from the longterm parking lot at Palm Beach International Airport earlier in the morning. This would be Quan's first time putting in work, yet he seemed uncharacteristically calm and focused. He is comfortable.

It was at that moment that a Cadillac Escalade, pearl on white, had pulled up with Sin driving and two of his shooters in shotgun, and back passenger seat positions, getting out of the truck together.

Kilo started, but Dice grabbed his leg, staying him. "Everyone hold positions, we waiting on the birthday boy to show to his party, and yep, that's him pulling up now, a'ight y'all, let's go get these hoe ass paintchos!"

As the nigga, Sike, got out of the 1985 box Chevy Caprice, he looked around nervously, before continuing inside the opened garage bay door. As soon as his back was to them, all of the ZMA soldiers rushed towards the building after him, right on his heels.

Grove Custom Auto machine shop is a huge red brick building made in the late 1940's with a lot of burglar bars added to all the windows and doors, as Delray Beach is a ghetto, where anything not tied down is subject to be stolen by the smokers. The big bay doors leading to the spacious mechanic's shop and an office beyond all of the machines and tools were perfect for a group entrance.

Kilo's anticipation, and Quan's loyalty to Kilo, had put them in front of the rest of the older gangstas, as their athleticism had taken over, their highly conditioned football player legs running faster than anyone else. As they ran, Kilo lifted his machine pistol at the first target he should have already killed, yet had let make it. His mistake had brought them all here.

Sike turned just in time to lock eyes with his killer, as Kilo lifted his MAC-10 and opened fire, turning Sike's white Tee into a tie dye shirt, as about 10 holes appeared on it, turning it different shades of red. He was dead before he hit the dirty shop floor, already a memory.

As Kilo slowed down, reveling in his sweet revenge, another short burst of rounds exploded right next to him. Quan.

Tatatatatatatat! Tat! Tat! Tatatatat!

A skinny Cuban had popped up to his left from nearby the cash register, just lifting his big chrome Barretta 9mm when Quan had saved Kilo, opening fire on him, and ending his life with a vertical line of shots from his chest, going through his neck and finally, a head shot.

Time seemed to stop as shots were ringing out all over and the rest of the ZMA from all sides had entered the building, engaging with Y-Lo's all around the garage. There really wasn't anywhere for them to hide as the shop was a big open space, only rows of different machines and tools separated them from being wide open.

Kilo took it upon himself to start duck-walking towards the office. Shots came within inches of his head and one even hit his left shoulder. He saw the big Cuban with face tats coming out of the office door in slow motion and a smoking gun dropping its magazine out of the handle, his intention to replace it with a new magazine. Kilo raised his MAC and only unloaded with about 15 of his remaining rounds, ending him. Repaying the big Cuban for shooting him in the shoulder. Kilo ejected his empty mag and slid in his only spare, ready again.

Shots continued to ring out as Kilo creeped into the office hallway separating the front desk from the manager's office, from where the big Cuban had popped out of. A flash of a face with braids on his head popped back behind the door, thinking Kilo didn't see him.

Kilo approached the already ajar door cautiously. He couldn't hold back any more, thinking the best way to flush a rat is with brute force, not cheese. He kicked the open door as hard as he could, hearing a grunt and low crunch in the same split second before he let a spray of rounds loose, pointing downwards, intending to maim, not kill. When Kilo took Sin's life, he wanted to do so while looking in his eyes. Wanted to tell him why he was dying and who was killing him. Nothing short of which would honor Maniac.

"Arg-ahh! Mothafucka!" shouted Sin's voice.

Kilo bent around the broken office door that Sin had been trying to use to catch Kilo slipping in an attempt to hide behind it and catch him off guard. He was able to smile at the sight before him: Sin on the dirty floor, knees both shattered by his busted knee caps, from the damage of Kilo's bullets, and his broken nose gushing from the hit from Kilo kicking the door into his face.

"You got away the first time bitch-ass nigga, but I knew you would fall into my hands eventually! Karma's a bitch, ain't she, Sin?" Kilo asks quietly and reserved, as if he was born to do this.

"Lil' fucking Maniac, huh?" asks Sin, smiling an evil and resigned smile through the pain, playing it down some, so as not to appear weak.

"—the fuck you smiling at, fool? I'm bout to send you to hell—" started Kilo.

"I'm laughing cuz you ain't even know what really brought us here to this moment! How you think I even met Maniac? I'm from out West! I knew I should'a searched that house that day! She ain't tell me y'all was home, that's how you knew it was me—"

"She? She-who, nigga? You're a fucking liar!" screamed Kilo as he shoots Sin in his knee cap again, splattering blood everywhere, along with some of his bone fragments and ligaments, Kilo was amazed that he was still conscious through this type of pain.

The shooting had all but stopped. Glizzy and Quan came in, standing behind Kilo. Seeing this, Sin started to laugh at them, he knew it was all over for him.

"Nah, not your moms, Jit. Your 'Aunt Nikki'! She's who even introduced me to your pops! And I fucked them all!" Sin started laughing again. "I killed your dad, fucked your moms, and even put 'Aunt Nikki' in your—"

Tat! Tatat! Tatatatatata! Tat! Tat!

"Die, mother fucker!" screamed Kilo, squeezing his trigger finger again and again, the firing pin landing on an empty chamber.

Click! Click! Click! Click! Click! Click!

"It's okay, Key. I got ya, homie," says Quan, reaching for his machine gun with one hand, while wrapping his other arm around Kilo's shoulders and slowly taking his gun, trying to gently guide him away from the grisly scene that Kilo had made, with his arm around his shoulders. "C'mon, Key, we gotta go..."

Kilo took one last look at the work he had just put in, the head resembling a smashed Jack-O-Lantern with flaps of skin hanging from the scalp, only the braids keeping it all attached. The legs were mangled and full of holes with chunks of bone and muscle detached and splattered all over from the automatic gunfire. The work that Kilo had put in made Freddy Kruger or Chucky look like...well, Child's Play.

As they started walking out of the office, they saw Luna's killers coming out of a storage room, each of them had their hands full of bricks of white and some of brown color as well. It seemed as though they had lucked up on their plug's storage room. As they passed, walking out, Kilo caught view of the 'storage room'. Its walls were lined with bookshelves filled to the top with all kinds of kilogram bricks, and full bags of different types of pills.

There were Hispanic bodies lying everywhere in the shop. Kilo didn't care about that, though. He hesitated, his body stiffened. He knew that everything had happened very fast, but a lot was starting to register.

"Come on, Key! It's over man, you got him..."

Kilo looked into Quan's eyes, then Glizzy's, who had been following behind them, a gleam in Kilo's eyes told them both what he didn't have to say, but did anyway.

"It's not over, bruh," said Kilo.

He ran back and grabbed Sin's phone.

"It's definitely not over. It's just beginning..."

Soon to Come: The Second Installment of

"A Razor's Edge of Revenge", entitled:

"A Double Edge of Revenge"

www.freetaboopublishing.com

Free Taboo Publishing, LLC. presents

A VICTIM *of* JUSTICE

BOOK CLUB QUESTIONS

TABOO

About the Author

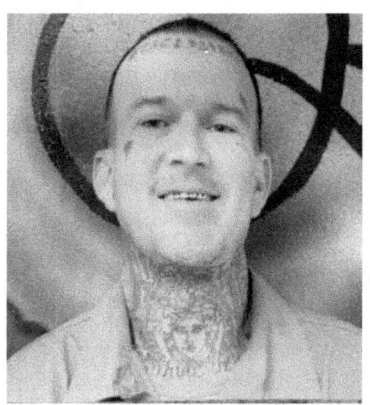

Taboo, or Brian Micko Yeary, is a Federal Prisoner who has been sentenced to die in prison for non-violent, victimless gun and drug possessions charges. Being an advocate for Criminal Justice Reform and while waiting for retroactivity to apply the First Step Act to his stacked 924(c) sentences, Taboo started FREE TABOO PUBLISHING, LLC to bring attention not only to his own situation, but to also help to publish other talented authors and poets who are also Victims of Justice incarcerated in this criminal INjustice system.

Sentenced to 91 years for a draconian 924(c) sentencing enhancement that has since been corrected by Congress, Taboo still sits under this unfair and ridiculous sentence. Convinced by Tom Cotton of Arkansas, Congress decided that the 924(c) law is only unfair to those who were sentenced AFTER 2018 and not those who are actually still suffering right now from the unfairness of it, so they withheld retroactivity from older cases sentenced before the First Step Act.

Most convicts in Taboo's position would become a product of

their environment in a Maximum Security Penitentiary overrun by gangs and violence, but this author instead persevered and established FREE TABOO PUBLISHING in April 2022 and introduced his debut novel, "A Victim of Justice" shortly thereafter. He has two new authors to introduce and a trilogy of his own coming out soon. He lives in Lee County US Penitentiary with no cats, dogs, yet a lot of hope in Congress to pass legislation for retroactivity and equality in sentencing reform.